JOHN W. WELLS III

The Last Angel Warrior

The Kalib Andrews Chronicles Book #1

LOUD FRIDGE

First edition

ISBN: 978-1-7354313-0-7

Editing by Erin Young
Editing by Connor Welter
Cover art by Hampton Lamoureux
Proofreading by Casey Fenich
Proofreading by Blazing Butterfly Edits
Advisor: Douglas Griffin

This book was professionally typeset on Reedsy.
Find out more at reedsy.com

To Samarra and Jacob
You were my very first readers. Thank you for giving me the
courage to keep writing. This book is for you.

Contents

Acknowledgement

"You forget this from time to time ... you are not alone. I am here. Your family is here."
— **Shane Arbuthnott, Terra Nova**

There is absolutely no way I could have written this book on my own. From the very beginning, my motivation came from those who believed in me along the way. My family and friends. Those willing to brave the dark crevices of my mind and report to me, honestly, what they thought of my ideas. Without these raw and vulnerable conversations, I would have never had the strength to keep running toward the finish line.

To my parents: Thank you, Mom and Dad, for always supporting my creativity. There may have been times that you didn't understand me, or wondered how you ended up with such an eccentric child, but you never tried to stifle my creativity. You always supported my artistic expression, and you have been my biggest cheerleaders since the day I was born. If it wasn't for you, who always gave me the freedom to be me, and who taught me to never give up, (because Wells' are not quitters!), I never would have had the natural drive and tenacity to fuel me toward the finish line.

To my sister: Jontrice, I know I was always your weird little brother, and there were many times throughout our lives that you wondered, "how are we related?" But you have never passed up on an opportunity to tell me how proud you are of me. Thank you for always supporting me.

To my niece: Samarra, if there was ever anyone that made me feel special, it is you, Chipmunk. Thank you for making me feel like a rockstar.

To Ryan: I would be remiss if I didn't acknowledge you, my childhood best friend. I remember when we were kids, making up stories and pretending to be superheroes. You taught me what comic books and fantasy stories were. If it wasn't for your influence, I never would have discovered my love for the supernatural. Thank you for giving me the courage to explore new worlds.

To Eddie: If there is an example of blind faith it would be you. You have supported my dream ever since I met you. Thank you for putting up with all my revisions and ramblings. Thank you for all the time and the energy that you invested into my brand. I couldn't ask for a better advocate.

To Felicia: My best friend. My ride or die. My confidant. Your support and kind words have meant more to me than you could ever imagine. You have always believed in my dream and have done everything possible to encourage me to keep dreaming. You believed my dreams would materialize before I did, and I owe you the world for that.

To Josh: You have been there since the beginning. Twelve years of encouragement and inspiration. Thank you for being the first person to take my characters from concept to realization. It is because of your amazing drawings that I was able to visualize my characters and meet them first hand.

To Hannah: Thank you for putting up with all my revisions and delays. You have been so patient with me. Thank you for believing in this project, and doing all you can to get the word out about my book.

To Douglas: My coach, my mentor, my guide. You were the final piece to this puzzle. And without your wise words and determination to see the best from me, this story would not be the story it is today. Thank you for helping me focus my story and tell it the best way I can. I look forward to working on many more stories with you. I still have more to learn.

To my student test readers: I am grateful to the classes at Harvest Hill Steam Academy and Leonardo Da Vinci Charter School. Thank you for allowing me into your classrooms to read. Your feedback was invaluable and crucial to the development of the story.

And to my Beta Readers: There is nothing as important as a beta reader to the development of a story. I am so grateful for the honest and transparent words from all of you who took the time to read. Without your wise and insightful words this story would not be what it is today. I am forever grateful for your support.

If I have forgotten any person from the above list of acknowledgments, this was unintentional. It is a very long list and I am only human. However, you should know that your contribution and your support is valued. Thank you.

1

A Blind Date With The Shadow Man

The first time I saw him was on the last day of summer at The Georgia Peach Diner, where I worked. It was a relatively slow shift, mostly moms dragging their kids off to the mall for last-minute back-to-school shopping. I was putting in yet another order for a hamburger with ketchup when my best friend, Triston, beelined toward me, bumping into tables and knocking over condiments as he ran. "Kalib, that's him," he said, his mouth to my ear as his hand clasped my shoulder. "That's the man who moved into the Old Vic this summer." Triston's red hair and pale face matched the red and white uniform we were forced to wear at work.

The man was sitting three booths back on the other side of the diner—my section.

It was rare for someone new to come here unnoticed. Hainesville wasn't a particularly large place. The only new people that turned up were usually here to visit RavenTech Labs, the large prosthetics company at the edge of town. Whenever someone new moved in, people talked.

Triston took gossiping about newcomers to a whole new

1

level. He was a class A nutcase. He always babbled on about conspiracy theories and our imminent doom. The week before, he'd convinced himself the government was tracking everyone through their smartphones. The week before that, it was something about TV and autosuggestions brainwashing us to think what *they* wanted us to think. This was just the latest in a long list of conspiracies. Apparently, the man *looked* at Triston funny on the street earlier that day as he'd walked into work. Now, he'd be convinced the man was following him.

"I'm telling you, Kalib, there's something weird about that guy," Triston said, followed by a quick and painless jab from his elbow. "Quit staring! He'll see you."

"Relax," I sighed, rolling my eyes and reaching for the next order. "I've got to give the guy his pie." I was running a little late that day, and someone else had already given the man his coffee. I grabbed a slice of pie from the counter and pushed past my friend, humored by his overreaction.

Up until that point, the day had gone as normally as any. The diner was dotted with the same faces having the same conversations. Damien Daslic was slumped over his grilled cheese sandwich at the end of the bar, *don't bother me* practically written across his face.

Sarah Withers, from school, beckoned one of my coworkers to her table with her newly remodeled prosthetic arm. Courtesy of RavenTech.

Mr. and Mrs. Abernathy sat at a booth in the back corner by the window, looking out and bickering about the weather as usual.

Mr. Jones, the CEO of RavenTech, sat opposite the Abernathys with his daughter Caliyah on their weekly family outing.

And then there was the stranger. I suddenly realized he'd had his eyes glued on me as I made my way across the diner.

"Your pie, sir," I said, presenting the plate. That's when things got weird.

"Thank you, Kalib," he replied as the edges of his lips curled. His smile was forced and unnatural. I looked down at my chest to see if I was wearing a name tag. I wasn't.

"H-how'd you know my name?"

"You're Mayor Donovan's kid." He feigned nonchalance as he pried the plate from my hands. I heard the slightest hint of an accent. Not too strong, but enough to notice it was there.

I squinted. *What is that, Irish?*

"I've seen you in pictures. You don't move into a new town without doing your research." He picked up his fork, cutting into the flaky crust of the peach pie.

"Oh, uh … yeah," I muttered, ignoring the growing knot in my stomach.

"Kalib Donovan, right?" The stranger spoke as if he'd just remembered my name, but even this sounded well-rehearsed. The fork scraped across the plate en route to his mouth.

"Andrews, actually," I corrected. "I go by Kalib Andrews."

"Oh." The man bobbed his head up and down. "That's right. You're adopted. I think I read that somewhere. Well, it's very nice to meet you, Kalib."

I tried to swallow, but my mouth was too dry to allow it. *Research,* he said. *More like stalking. Who is this man?*

I mean, sure, a person would have to be blind not to know I didn't look like Donald and Susan Donovan. Anyone with eyes could see I was adopted. It wasn't just my appearance, either. Aside from the contrast of my bright blue eyes, curly

3

brown hair, and mocha-colored skin, with their straight hair and slightly pink complexion, I had simply never felt like their son. I suppose that's why I never called them Mom or Dad. It had never felt right.

The Donovans, both of them, were about politics and appearance. I, on the other hand, never fit that mold. I learned young that I didn't care for politicians. They always seemed to be talking in circles, never saying what they meant. I preferred honesty. I could always tell when someone was hiding something, and it seemed my family was hiding a lot.

"Now, that's an interesting necklace," the stranger said, dabbing the sides of his mouth with his napkin. I reached for the pendant that hung from my neck, passing it between my fingers. I was used to people asking about the necklace; it was a unique piece of jewelry. Three arrows welded together to make a silver triangle, and at the center of it was a blue stone. I wasn't sure what kind of stone it was, but I assumed it was valuable. But what most people were curious about were the strange silver symbols engraved onto the stone. The symbols wrapped around the pendant, so every angle revealed a different mysterious image when you looked at it.

"What are those inscriptions?" the man asked. "Those symbols, they look foreign. Do you know what they mean?"

"Oh. No, I don't," I admitted. "It's a family heirloom, I think. I've always had it."

The man's eyes locked on the pendant for a moment. Then meeting my confused gaze, he asked, "A family heirloom from Andrews, you mean?"

Maybe it was the way he said it or the way he leaned forward on his elbows, eyes fixed on mine. His foot tapped anxiously beneath the table. Something about this man didn't sit well with me. A voice inside of me said *get out!*

"Yeah," I whispered, so intimidated I could barely push the word out.

"Have you met him?" His voice seemed to drop in volume as if telling a secret.

"No," I admitted, "all I have is his picture and his name."

The stranger considered me for a moment. "Blue's a good color on you," he said, clearing his throat. "It matches the color of your eyes."

"Well, I … I should be … getting back to work."

"It was a pleasure to meet you, Kalib." The man extended his hand towards me.

"Thank you. Uh, you too."

I reached out, and the moment my hand touched his, I felt something, as if a thousand insects scuttled up my arm. Voices—whispering voices—filled my head. Thousands of them. My legs turned to putty, and I fell.

I fell through a dark, endless void as the whispers erupted into a singular chorus. A deep rumbling laugh. And a voice, rising from deep within my mind, said:

> *Though death, magic, and fire rehashed,*
> *The blood of the Angel Warrior shall be paid at last.*

The pounding words seared across my mind. "*Soon,*"it said with a final boom, and a bright white light burst through my head, blinding my senses, drowning out the noise. I closed my eyes, overwhelmed.

And then I was back at the diner.

I stared up at the stranger who had caught me from tumbling to the ground. The light fixture above the table flickered, but no one else seemed to have heard the voice.

Damien Daslic slid cash across the bar, hopping off his barstool and starting toward the door.

Mr. and Mrs. Abernathy, meanwhile, were in a heated discussion about hurricanes.

For the briefest moment, as I steadied myself against the table, the stranger looked at me with terror in his eyes. "You alright?"

"Yeah. Just feeling a little lightheaded." I caught sight of Triston peeking at me over the vinyl seat of the table he was pretending to bus. I tried not to make eye contact.

"You should sit down." The stranger gestured toward the booth. "Please."

"Actually, no. I—I have to go," I muttered, my feet moving before the words even left my mouth. I turned and ran toward the back, nearly colliding with Mr. Jones as I did so.

"Where's the fire?" he said as I rushed past him.

Okay, I know what you're thinking. A stranger comes into town, does some weird ritual, and a hero is born. But let me set something straight. Full disclosure, I'm not going to be the good guy in this story. You should know that before you get the wrong idea. You're probably expecting that I'm some kind of hero, warrior, or chosen one. Yeah, I've heard it all before. But I'm not. I'm just a normal kid. Some would even argue that I'm evil, and I guess … I am. It's complicated; you'll see.

At the end of my shift, I rushed home. I'd walked that route a million times before, but for some reason, it was creepier than usual. I found myself jumping at every sound and shadow.

I couldn't explain what happened at the diner; that voice and the light. Maybe it was exhaustion? I'd been putting in late hours at work. Was it all catching up with me?

When I finally made it to my usual shortcut, the alleyway between Georgia and North Carolina, I froze. It was a creepy back alley at the best of times, but today? It was somehow darker and even more menacing than usual. I couldn't shake the feeling danger was nearby.

No. I stopped before stepping into the alley. *I'll stick to the main streets.*

It would add ten minutes to my walk home, but at least I would be around people. I'd seen enough scary movies to know how this could go down.

Strangely, no one was out that night. No one at all. The main drag down the middle of Hainesville was completely empty. The shops had closed up early. Café and convenient store workers had all gone home. It was like everyone had the same feeling I did—only they were smart enough to stay off the street. All I needed was to get past St. John's Lutheran Church at the end of the street, and I would be as good as home. My neighborhood was the next block.

I made it halfway down the road before I heard the sound of footsteps, as if someone were walking behind me. I looked around, but there was no one there. *I'm hearing things*, I convinced myself. *I'm jumpy from earlier.* I resumed my journey, walking faster down the street.

Where is everyone?

I heard the footsteps again. The sound bounced off the stone walls and echoed down the street. Someone was there, but I couldn't see them. I stopped, afraid to move, afraid to turn around, and listened for the source of the steps. I heard nothing but my own erratic breathing and my heart pounding in my chest. There was no one there, nothing but an empty street stretching out as far as I could see. I scanned the lifeless

7

storefronts, wondering what could be lurking beyond those doors, waiting for me in the darkness just beyond the shadows. Peering at me. Watching me sweat. Spying me jump at every sound. But it felt like the person—whoever it was—was behind me. I stared into the darkness, but no one was there. *Am I imagining things?*

"Who are you?" I shouted. *Why are you messin' with me?*

"Akaaaaakkkkiiiiooossss," a cold chilling voice echoed along the row of houses. It was barely human.

"Akaaaaakkkkiiiiooossss." At the end of the street, a winged figure shrouded in darkness extended a cloaked arm in my direction.

"Akaaaaakkkkiiiiooossss," it chanted a third time. A shiver ran down my spine. I wanted to run, to get the heck out of there, but my feet were bolted to the ground.

In a flash, the figure appeared halfway down the street, and then right in front of me. The smell of rotten eggs and burned hamburger meat filled my nostrils. If I hadn't been so scared, I might have vomited. The figure extended its talon like hands toward my throat. Its ragged cloak was made of swirling ethereal shadow. The claws at the end of its spindly fingers, dug into my neck as it lifted me from the ground. Its hands were like ice against my skin, and I couldn't see its face. There was nothing there but blackness.

I thrashed in the air, trying to break free from its grasp. My fingers were useless against its grip. It tightened, trapping terrified screams in my throat, suffocating me. I kicked and thrashed but hit nothing. I tore at its fingers, but its grip only tightened further. My insides burned, and my head began to spin.

Darkness crept into my vision as the figure stretched its

other hand toward my throat. This was it. I was about to die. In the fading corner of my vision, an object shimmered in the darkness, but I couldn't make out what it was. Just as everything faded to black, something inside me exploded. A white light burst from me and, just like that, the figure was gone.

2

Taking A Ride In The Phantom

I blinked. A car's horn blared, headlights blinding me as they sped in my direction. "Get out of the road!" an old man shouted, poking his head out the window and shaking his fist as the car swerved around me and screeched down the street.

"Sorry, Mr. Abernathy," I shouted, realizing I was standing in the middle of the street.

It was the same street, but no longer empty. Now, men and women bustled in and out of the previously deserted shops and cafés. I looked around before rushing to the sidewalk. *What just happened?* I gingerly touched my neck, remembering the talon-like fingers squeezing the life out of me. I had no bruises.

Am I going crazy?

I shook my head and hurried toward the direction of my home, searching the sidewalk for answers. I probably should have been paying more attention because a few steps in, I ran directly into Patrick Jones. You remember, the tech CEO I nearly collided with earlier at the diner.

"Whoa there!" Mr. Jones said.

"Sorry," I stammered, "sorry."

"Kalib?" Mr. Jones beamed down at me, his teeth luminescent in contrast to his onyx skin. "We've gotta stop meeting like this. That's twice today."

"I-I'm really sorry. I should have been paying attention."

"Are you alright?" he asked, "You seem out of sorts."

"Yeah. I'm fine." I took a deep breath and forced a smile.

Mr. Jones studied me for a moment. "Caliyah and I were school shopping. I just dropped her off to her mother at home and was headed to the office to pick something up. I could give you a ride."

"Oh, I'm really not that far from home," I said, shoving my hands into my pockets.

"Nonsense," he insisted. "My car's right over there. I'll have my driver drop you off on the way." Mr. Jones ushered me across the street where his—you're not going to believe this—Rolls Royce Phantom was parked. "Besides, it'll give me a chance to get to know you a little better."

He opened the door, allowing me to slide into the white leather seats before he did the same. Mr. Jones was a giant of a man; his shoulders were about the width of an NFL linebacker's with football pads on. I wondered how he ever made it through standard sized doors, let alone fit in his car.

"Drink?" He offered, pointing to the champagne bar at the other end. "I've got some soda on ice if you'd like."

"No, thank you," I said as politely as I could muster. I glanced cautiously out the window, still shaken from whatever the heck had just happened.

"Suit yourself," he replied, signaling the driver. He pushed a button, and the partition between us and the driver began to rise.

"You know, I'm a huge fan of your father. I think he's done a fantastic job. I was one of the first local businessmen to endorse his campaign."

"I know," I answered. "I think you were his biggest endorsement. He probably wouldn't have won without it."

"That's very kind of you to say, Kalib." Mr. Jones tilted his head. "Thank you."

I nodded, glancing around the spacious cabin. The hand-crafted wooden interior was lined with strategically placed ambient lighting, that only added to the lavish interior.

"You know, your parents mentioned that you were looking for a new job?"

"Did they?" I asked. That was the first I had heard of it.

"I've been looking for an intern to serve as my personal assistant at RavenTech Labs," he explained. "Now, I don't normally extend this offer to high school students, but I hold your parents in high regard. It's the least I can do to repay their support. I'd like to offer you the internship at RavenTech. How would you like that?"

My mouth fell open. An internship at RavenTech? That was the last thing I expected him to say. And the last thing I wanted. It was bad enough that all the kids at school thought I got a free ride just because I was the mayor's son. The last thing I wanted was for my co-workers to think that too; another thing handed to me just because of who my parents were.

Unlike most kids my age, I didn't work at the diner because I needed to. I chose to work there because I actually liked it. It was a place I could go after school where I could hang out with my best friend, and not feel like the mayor's privileged son. Working at RavenTech would be the opposite. Everyone would know that I was there because of who my parents were, not because of my hard work.

"I …" I didn't know what to say.

"Why not take some time to think about it?" Mr. Jones grinned. "I'm sure we'll have plenty of time to talk about it soon." The Phantom came to a stop in front of my house, and Mr. Jones opened the door. "I believe this is your stop?"

"Thank you for the ride, Mr. Jones." I slid out of the car and closed the door behind me.

"Until next time, Kalib," he said through the lowered window of the car. I watched, not really knowing how to feel, as the black vehicle drove away and disappeared at the end of the street.

* * *

"I'm home!" I shouted as I opened the door. Nobody acknowledged my announcement. I assumed Donald and Susan must have already gone to bed. The floorboards creaked as I made my way up the stairs. I'd never be able to sleep that night, not with the day I'd had. Between the weird vision at the diner, Mr. Jones's internship offer, and … whatever that thing was on the street, I was having trouble deciphering what was real.

I flipped the lights on in my bedroom, tossed my bookbag against the dresser, and plopped onto my bed on the other side of the room. *Hearing voices* and *seeing things?* I stared up at the glow-in-the-dark stars that Donald had bought me for my tenth birthday. *I must be going crazy.*

It was like I had crawled into a crazy plot from *Goosebumps*, except *Goosebumps* was more believable. *What was that shadowy figure on the street?*

I grabbed my laptop from the floor, popped open the browser, and typed *'shadowy figure'* in the search bar. The only results were pictures from comic books and Disney movies. What did I really expect? There was nothing like the figure that I saw ... or didn't see? I was still trying to decide which one it was.

I started scrolling through the next few pages of results, but my search was cut short when I heard a scraping from the window. I snapped my eyes toward it, expecting to see the shadowy figure again. To my relief, it was an eagle that I knew, Hunter, scratching at the window with his talons.

Now, you might be thinking, c'mon Kalib, a pet eagle? You've gotta be kidding me. That is so unrealistic. The stranger in the diner, the weird voices in your head, the creepy shadow man, sure. But a pet eagle? That's just too unbelievable. Yeah, most people feel the same way, but it's true. Hunter was a golden eagle, and he frequently visited me. Mostly at night, even though eagles aren't nocturnal. And to be clear, he wasn't really my pet. He'd probably snap at your fingers in retaliation if you called him that to his face. Hunter was a wild bird who, from time to time, *allowed* me to feed him and stroke his golden-brown feathers while he ate. I had rescued him from a bird trap a few years earlier, and ever since then, he kept coming around. He was my friend.

I walked groggily toward the window, undoing the latch and lifting it, allowing Hunter to hop inside.

"You must be hungry. Slim pickings in the wild tonight?" I asked, sitting on the sill and stroking the feathers atop his head. "You're in luck!"

I rushed to my dresser—dodging a minefield of video games

14

scattered on the floor and nearly tripping over a pile of dirty clothes, which had ironically been left directly beside the hamper—and grabbed my bookbag. I pulled out a bag of beef jerky and crossed back to Hunter.

"I brought a treat home for you," I said, holding out a piece of dried meat for the bird. "It isn't much, but it's something." Hunter snapped the jerky from my hand and ate while I watched. When he finished, he leaped off the ledge and soared back into the sky. His feathers glowed in the moonlight as he disappeared over the woods across the street from my house. I smiled and moved to close the window.

That's when I saw it again. On the street, standing in front of our house and lingering on the lawn below my bedroom window—there was a man. He was wearing a gray hoodie, and his hands were in his pockets. A pair of yellow eyes stared back at me.

I slammed the window shut and ducked behind the sill. Had he seen me? My heart rattled in my chest as I tried to regain my nerve. I didn't get a good look at him, but the man was familiar. I slowly peeked over the windowsill to get a better look, but he was gone. Vanished.

3

That's A Historic Discovery!

I splashed water on my face the next morning as I got ready for the first day of school. I tried not to think about what happened the night before—that figure on the street and the man beneath my window. But I couldn't get the image of those glowing yellow eyes out of my mind. I'd told my parents about it but when they investigated, they found no trace of the man I'd seen. They later resolved that I'd been dreaming. By the next morning, I wasn't so sure either way.

I took a deep breath and splashed more water onto my face, groaning as I caught a glimpse of my reflection in the mirror. I hadn't slept a wink that night. Even with my brown skin, my face looked pale and clammy. My blue eyes were bloodshot with bags under them, and my curly hair had twisted itself into an unkempt mess.

Perfect. First day of school, and I look like a sick, homeless kid.

I showered, pulled on my clothes, and hurried down the stairs. "I'm leaving!" I yelled, picking up an apple from the fruit bowl on the dining room table and holding it in my mouth while stuffing a textbook into my book bag.

"Make sure you grab something for breakfast!" Susan shouted from the kitchen as I headed out the door.

Now, don't let Susan's facade of maternal nurturing fool you. Neither Susan nor her husband, Donald, cared whether I ate breakfast or not. They simply didn't want the school calling and asking if I was being properly fed at home. Donald and Susan didn't really care what I did as long as I didn't make them look bad. Donald's running for Congress next year. For the most part, I stayed out of their way, and they stayed out of mine, and that was the way I liked it.

I met Triston at the end of the street. His house was just a block over, and he always waited for me at the corner so we could walk together. He normally rambled on about current events that he'd inevitably connected to his latest conspiracy theory. I'd nod every few seconds, pretending to be engaged in the conversation, and that morning was no different. Triston buzzed excitedly about something he saw on the news—I think he said explosions—but I wasn't really listening. I was too preoccupied with what had happened the night before and wondered if it had all been in my head.

"Kalib, are you even listening to me?" Triston chided.

"Of course, I am," I lied, almost too naturally.

Triston looked at me skeptically. "What's gotten into you? You've been acting weird all morning."

I didn't know how to even begin to explain what had *gotten into me*. What could I say? That I was afraid the *shadow man* had attacked me the night before? Yeah, I could see exactly how that conversation would go. What did it look like? I don't know. Did it have scales? I don't know. Did it have teeth? I don't know. Are you going crazy? Probably.

To be honest, Triston was probably the one person that I

could've told about this. He loved the supernatural, and he ate the whole unexplained mystery thing right up. Time lapses, blackouts, men with yellow eyes, it was all right up his alley, but I was still trying to wrap *my* head around what had happened. I wasn't ready to get on Triston's level just yet.

"I'm just a little nervous about the first day of school," I said, plodding through the imposing ironclad doors of Woodcreek Academy.

Our school looked like a prison, probably because it was designed by the same architect who built the state penitentiary back in the year nineteen-something-something. Despite the cheerful "Welcome Back!" banners and the black-and-green cougar signs plastered all over the walls—undoubtedly the school's shameless attempt to make the bleak halls feel more welcoming—Woodcreek Academy still felt as cold and life-sucking as a jail cell. And yeah, the doors were literally ironclad. There was no escaping this place.

"Watch it!" a gruff voice said as I ran right into Damien Daslic, knocking his textbooks to the ground. "What are you blind or something?" His icy blue eyes glared at me as I scrambled to collect his books.

"I-I'm sorry," I stammered. "I wasn't—"

"Watch where you're going next time, priv!" Damien snatched his textbooks from my hands and stormed down the hall. I watched as Damien's platinum blonde hair, so bright it was almost white, disappeared around the corner at the other end.

"Geesh," Triston said, "Someone's not a morning person."

"I don't think Damien is an 'any-time-of-the-day' person," I admitted. "That guy hates me."

"Why does he call you 'priv'?" Triston asked. "What does

that even mean?"

I shrugged. 'Priv' was short for privileged. Damien had taken to calling me names, years ago when we first met. He was a foster kid himself and had been in and out of group homes for as long as I'd known him. I guess he figured I was a sell-out for being adopted, and by the mayor no less. I don't know how that would even be my fault, but ever since Damien had found out about it, he'd seemed determined that we would never be friends. I shook my head and walked toward my locker a little ways down the hall.

"Junior year, huh?" Triston beamed, leaning against the cougar statue that stood in the hallway next to my locker. "We did it! We're finally upperclassmen. This is the year I rebrand myself."

I laughed, entering the combination and opening the door. Triston had said the same thing every year since the sixth grade. "This year, I'm not just going to be Kalib's geeky friend. I'm going to be *Triston—geeky all by myself.*" Personally, I didn't think Triston needed rebranding. I didn't see him as geeky or dorky. I had only ever seen him as my best friend.

"Hey, Kalib," a voice said from the locker next to mine. I didn't have to look to know who it was. Caliyah Jones, the daughter of Patrick Jones, and my locker neighbor for two years in a row now. Whenever she was around, the smell of lilacs intoxicated anyone within a two-hundred-foot radius. And trust me, there wasn't a guy in school who hadn't been intoxicated by Caliyah Jones.

"Happy first day of school!" she exclaimed happily, holding her tan book bag, with brown lining, on one shoulder as she keyed in her locker combination. "I saw you at The Peach yesterday, but I was busy presenting my case to Mom and Dad

19

on why they should let me try out for the cheerleading squad this year."

"Really?" I asked, stunned.

"Yeah, why?"

"You just don't strike me as the cheerleading type."

Okay, let's point out a few high school clichés. Naturally, you would think that the most popular girl in school would be the head of the cheerleading squad, dating the captain of the football team, and generally, not very interested in school at all. But those criteria did not describe Caliyah Jones. Sure, she was the richest kid in school, but she was also a straight-A student, at the top of our class, and was the nicest person you'd ever meet.

"Why's that, Kalib?" Caliyah's lips curled into a mischievous grin that told me I had walked right into a trap. "Because only ditzy barbies can join the cheerleading squad? Cheerleaders can't be smart?"

"No, I was just—"

Caliyah's chestnut-colored eyes wrinkled with smile lines. Her laugh rang like music, and her smile could light up a street in the dead of night. It was the kind of perfect laugh and beautiful smile only an angel could have. "Don't be a tool of the patriarchy, Kalib. Cheerleaders become business owners."

I chuckled a goofy laugh and quickly changed the subject. "Any luck with your parents?"

"They said the same thing they always do." She shrugged. "'You'll never own a Fortune 500 company from the top of a pyramid. So non-progressive of them."

Caliyah's parents were old-school. They kept a *work hard, play never* mentality. Caliyah wasn't allowed to bring home any grade lower than an A++, and the only extra-curricular activities she was allowed to do were the ones college admissions drooled over.

"Anyway, see you in class!" she said, prancing off toward a group of girls down the hall.

"Wait, what?"

Her tight curls bounced as she turned. Her lips pursed in a way that twisted my stomach into a pretzel. "Kalib, you haven't looked at your schedule!" she tsked. "We have a class together. History."

Woodcreek had a funny habit of posting the class roster online during the summer. The hope was that students would pair up and "get ahead" during summer break so that the school year would be easier. Of course, no one did, and I had no intention of laying an eye on anything school-related during my summer break. Hence, the reason I had no idea Caliyah and I had history together this year.

"I guess, we're two for two then," I joked.

Caliyah squinted her eyes, "What do you mean?"

"Classes," I clarified, "you know, since we had a class together this summer."

"What are you talking about, Kalib?" she said, "We've never had a class together?"

"Oh, my bad," I apologized, a little embarrassed. It was surprising that she didn't remember, we'd definitely had a class together. I sat behind her the entire time. But I'm sure there were plenty of people in that class who were more interesting than me. "Well, see you there."

Caliyah smiled, twirled back and disappeared into the group of girls who squealed upon her arrival.

"Wow," Triston sighed, stepping out from behind a nearby trash can. Like every guy in school, Triston also had a crush on

Caliyah. His bloomed in the fourth grade when she'd loaned him a pencil. He kept it for three months, refusing to sharpen it, preserving the teeth marks where she must've nervously nibbled during a test. Now, whenever she came around, he froze or made an excuse to go somewhere. Or just flat out hid. Like now, behind a trash can.

"If you like her so much, why don't you just talk to her?" I nudged him a little with my elbow.

"It's not that easy," he whined, his face growing redder by the second. "It's obvious she likes *you*, Kalib."

I looked at him nervously. "What are you talking about? No, she doesn't. Caliyah's just being cordial. Her dad probably told her to be nice to me or something."

"Why would he do that?"

"It's nothing." I shrugged. "C'mon, let's get to class." I brushed past Triston and started down the hall to our first class.

History. I hated history, but this year we were supposed to explore Greek and Roman mythology. I guess I was excited about that—a little.

Towards the front of the classroom, a group of girls were chattering about the new teacher, who still hadn't shown up. "Christie Smythe says he has an accent," someone said. Most everyone else was using the opportunity to catch up with their friends, telling stories about their summer vacations.

Triston leaned over his desk to continue rambling to me about the explosion at the First Savings Bank he had heard about on the news. He believed it was all a coverup so we wouldn't notice an alien invasion. "I mean, a guy walks into a bank and blows it up? That doesn't even make sense!" he muttered. "If you're gonna rob a bank, you're not going to destroy the money you're trying to steal." I pretended to listen, silently hoping the new teacher wouldn't show up at all.

As soon as I dared to hope, however, a man rushed through the door, papers cradled in one hand, and a brown leather messenger bag tucked under the other. And I felt like the floor had dropped out from under me.

I sat glued to my seat. It was the man from the diner! The man who knew way too much about me. I glanced at Triston, watching the color draining from his face. His eyes were frozen on the new teacher.

"Sorry, I'm late," the man fretted breathlessly, "Forgive me. I got a little lost. First day of school."

"Triston—" I whispered.

But Triston didn't say anything. He swallowed hard and nodded, staring wide-eyed at our new teacher. When Triston had warned me that there was something off about the town's new resident, I'd thought he was exaggerating as usual. Now I wasn't so sure. How much more would Triston freak out if he knew this was also the man I saw beneath my window? I was trapped in a classroom with the man who was stalking me.

The stranger set his brown messenger bag on his desk and immediately began speaking. The night before, I had thought I recognized the man beneath my window, but I hadn't been sure. But now that he was right in front of me, I was positive.

"My name is Mr. Macelton," he said, spelling it out on the whiteboard behind him. "As in Mac-Elton. And, as you really ought to have guessed by now, I am your new history teacher."

He stared at the class for a moment, a blank expression painted on his face. And then, with sudden humor, he burst into laughter, inviting the class to laugh with him. The other students seemed to lighten up as he talked about his expectations and how much fun we were going to have, but I wasn't buying Mr. Macelton's *nice-guy* act. Had he known yesterday he was going to be my history teacher? *Research*, he had said.

Is that how he knew my name? Is that why he was beneath my window? Research?

I didn't know what Mr. Macelton was up to, but something was going on beyond a new and overzealous teacher in town. I glared at him, but he wouldn't meet my eye.

Are you avoiding me?

He looked different in his work clothes, all dressed up and polished, but somehow younger. Twenty-seven or twenty-eight years old maybe. His brown hair was neatly combed, a tie was pulled snug around his neck, and his sleeves were rolled up just enough to reveal a hint of a tattoo on his bicep. It was only a matter of seconds before the entire class decided that Mr. Macelton was the cool new teacher from out of town. Even Caliyah sat there, all doe-eyed and fawning. He'd won her over. He'd won them all over except Triston and me.

I tried to get Triston's attention again. *"Triston,"* I whispered. Nothing. *"Triston!"* I said a little louder. Too loud. Mr. Macelton looked up from his papers and turned his attention to me for the first time since he had entered the room.

"Is there something you'd like to share with the class?" he asked, taking a moment to glance at the class roster. "Mr...."

Is he pretending not to know my name?

"Kalib Donovan, isn't it?"

I wanted to wipe that smug smile off of his face. He knew what he was doing. "Andrews," I said, parroting our conversation at the diner. "I go by Kalib Andrews."

"Right," he said, writing a note on the paper as if he had no recollection of our previous conversation. Then, a flash of silver caught my eye. It was a ring, a signet ring, or the kind of ring you would see in medieval movies. He wasn't wearing it at the diner—or at least I didn't notice it. I squinted, trying to make out the design. On the top of the ring was a silver triangle, just like my necklace, but instead of three arrows, there were metal swirls circling inward from each corner. At the center, a blue stone. It was the stone that caught my attention. The blue stone with silver symbols carved into it was identical to the stone in my necklace. The one Macelton had been asking about the night before. *Why would he question me about the stone if he had one of his own? Why wouldn't he have pointed it out?*

There was something else too, but I couldn't figure out what. Something tugged at the back of my mind. Like there was something I should be remembering but couldn't.

For the briefest moment, Macelton and I locked eyes. *Had he seen me staring?* He looked away and addressed the class. "You know, I'm really looking forward to teaching you this year," he said, sliding his hands into the pockets of his blue slacks. "I know we'll have a wonderful time getting to know each other *much* better."

Was he talking to me?

A while later, I scanned the cafeteria for Triston. Lunchtime was the most important part of the first day of school. It was during lunch when all the cliques claimed their territory for the rest of the year. The student government kids grabbed the table closest to the food. That way, they could regulate food portions. The jocks kicked the chess club out of the back table in the corner of the cafeteria, where they would host chugging competitions and talk about upcoming parties. The cheerleaders took the table opposite theirs. The drama geeks were near the stage; the band nerds next to them. The skaters? They were in the middle of the room. And the math club sat near the door, ready to escape should the football team get bored.

"Kalib!" I made out a streak of red hair amongst the crowd. Triston had found an empty table and staked his claim.

"Scored us a table," he said proudly. "We don't have to eat next to the trash this year."

"Good work, Tris!" I placed my book bag on the table next to his before making my way to the line of students waiting for food.

I glimpsed Mr. Macelton walking with a few other teachers down the hall toward the teachers' lounge. I glanced at his hand, hoping to get another look at the ring, but it wasn't there. He must have removed it sometime after class. *Why is his ring so similar to my necklace?* I thought. *Could it just be a coincidence?* I felt like there was something I was missing. Something I'd forgotten. But I couldn't figure out what it was. Mr. Macelton must have noticed me staring at the ring earlier, but why had he taken it off? *What are you hiding, Mr. Macelton?*

Whatever he was saying must have been hilarious because the other teachers wouldn't stop giggling. Mrs. Chaney blushed and covered her face every time he looked in her direction. First day of school and even the faculty members were eating out of his hands.

I mean, I suppose he was handsome, I guess. He looked like a swimmer or gym rat. His tailored and pressed clothes were too perfect. I guess the accent added to his charm, but I still didn't see what everyone was infatuated with.

Our eyes met as he passed. He tilted his head in a friendly

greeting, then continued on his way, and that's when it happened. For a brief second—so quick, I almost missed it—his almond-colored eyes flashed yellow.

I blinked. *Did I just see that?* Before I could get a second look, he disappeared into the teachers' lounge with his gaggle of groupies.

"Move it, priv!" Damien shouted from behind, shoving me so that I almost went face-first into the mashed potatoes. A gap had formed in the line between me and the person ahead, who was already grabbing her tray and selecting a chocolate pudding from the desserts.

Triston nudged me. "Kalib, the line's moving."

I took a giant step, picked up a tray, and scooped a spoonful of runny mashed potatoes on my plate.

"Are you sure you're okay?" Triston asked. "You've been acting weird all day, and you completely skipped over the desserts."

"I'm fine," I said. "I'm just not that hungry."

"Okay, now I know something's wrong." Triston finished loading up his tray with chocolate pudding. "You? Not hungry? That's like saying a fish isn't wet. Is this about the new teacher? Because I told you there was something weird about him from day one."

I didn't say anything as I walked toward our table. I knew I could tell Triston anything, but I didn't know how to begin. "Something weird happened last night," I murmured as I slid into my seat at our table.

Triston looked at me cautiously, hesitating before putting his tray down. "What kind of weird?"

I poked at my food with a plastic fork. I really wasn't hungry. "I think someone attacked me."

"Like, mugged you?" Triston's eyes were the size of hockey pucks. "Did they take anything?"

"No, not mugged," I clarified, there weren't words to even begin to explain. "Like … I think he tried to kill me."

I told Triston everything that happened after I'd left the diner, how I was attacked by a shadowy figure that I could barely see. He stared at me, goggle-eyed, as I recounted the events.

"And then everything just went back to normal?" he asked once I had finished.

"It was like it never happened!" I explained, "Like the people had been there all along."

"Wow," Triston said softly.

"That's not all."

"There's more?"

"Last night, after I got home, I saw Mr. Macelton standing beneath my window."

"What?" Triston's eyes bugged out of his head. "Are you sure?"

"No. I didn't get a good look at him." I shook my head. "But I just know it was him. I got this weird feeling. And then just now—"

"Hey, guys!"

Caliyah set her lunch tray next to Triston and slid into the seat across from mine, cutting our conversation short.

Triston, whose face turned three shades of red, seemed to be regretting not having found a table near the trash. He had nowhere to hide.

"So, Dad tells me you're taking a job at RavenTech," she said sweetly. "Looks like I'll be seeing more of you."

Triston almost spat his creamed corn clear across the

cafeteria.

"What?" he squeaked, pushing past his fear of talking to girls. "You're taking a job at RavenTech? And you didn't tell me?"

"It just happened yesterday—and no I'm not," I clarified, looking back and forth between Triston and Caliyah. "He offered me an internship yesterday when he dropped me off at home after the—anyway, I'm not sure I want to take it."

Triston and Caliyah spoke simultaneously.

"Why wouldn't you take it?"

"That's too bad."

"RavenTech is the biggest company in Hainesville," Triston continued around a mouthful of corn. "Why would you turn that down?"

"Because I didn't earn it," I said. "It's just something that Mr. Jones offered me because he feels he owes Donald and Susan something. I don't want to get a job riding on my parents' coattails."

"Kalib, my dad offered you the job because I told him you were smart," Caliyah replied matter-of-factly as she organized her eating utensils into a neat row on her napkin. "He said he was looking for a new intern and told me your parents suggested you. I thought you'd be a good match, so I said so. Besides, he's making me work there too. He thinks it'll get me into Yale or something. I thought it would be nice to have someone cool around that place to talk to."

She thinks I'm cool? I was shocked to hear Caliyah even noticed me. I loved working at the diner with my best friend, but the idea of spending more time with Caliyah wasn't such a bad thought either.

"Hey, what happened to your necklace, Kalib?" Something in Caliyah's tone pulled me back.

"Huh?"

"Your necklace," she repeated, gesturing to it. "I've never seen you without it. Did it break or something?"

I jerked my hand to my chest, but all I felt was the fabric of my shirt. My necklace. It was gone. How had I not noticed?

"That's an interesting necklace."

The memory of Mr. Macelton in the diner flashed through my mind. He had pretended that he didn't know what the symbols on the stone in my necklace meant, but the symbols on the stone in the ring, that he was wearing during class, were identical to the ones on the necklace. That couldn't have been a coincidence. But there was something else, too. Something that had been scratching on the door of my consciousness all morning, demanding to be recalled.

On the street that night, I saw an object from the corner of my eye. It shimmered in my face, but I couldn't make it out before that flash of light, and everything went back to normal. All day that day, I had been trying to figure out what my subconscious was trying to remind me, but it wasn't until Caliyah mentioned my necklace that I knew. I had seen the ring before. The night I was attacked. The image was clear now. The shimmering object I saw on the hand that was choking me was the ring Mr. Macelton was wearing in class.

"I have to go." I jumped up, rushing out of the cafeteria without looking back, my mind whirling as I struggled to put the pieces together.

"Kalib, wait!" Triston raced after me. "Where are you going?"

"I know who tried to kill me!"

"You do?!" Triston said breathlessly, trying to catch up. "But you said that you weren't even sure it actually happened."

"I'm sure now," I said, "and I think I have proof." I rushed down the hallway toward Mr. Macelton's class.

"Kalib, slow down! Kalib! What proof?" But I was already gone.

Lunch was almost over. I only had a few minutes to get into his classroom and out again before he came back for his next class. I rounded the corner. I needed to be discreet. I tried the door handle and, thankfully, it was unlocked. I nudged it open and crept into the dark classroom, careful not to be seen through the large windows that ran across the wall on either side of the door.

Triston burst through the door seconds later, doubling over and panting for breath. "Why are we here, Kalib?" he said a little too loudly between gasps.

"Keep your voice down!" I hushed, shoving a finger to my lips. "*We* aren't here." I gestured between the two of us. "*I* just want to check something out." I answered, tiptoeing toward Mr. Macelton's desk at the front of the classroom. "You should go. I'll catch up with you later."

"This is about Mr. Macelton, isn't it?" Triston asked, ignoring my previous request for him to leave. I rolled my eyes.

"No, Triston," I said sarcastically, "This is about Mrs. Chaney's home economics class. That's why I'm in *Mr. Macelton's* history class right now."

"You think Mr. Macelton stole your necklace, don't you?" Another astute observation from the peanut gallery.

"In class, Macelton was wearing a ring that was almost identical to my necklace." I wiggled the top right drawer open and began rummaging through it. "When he noticed I was looking at it, he slid his hands in his pockets so that I couldn't see the ring anymore. And then at lunch, I noticed he had taken it off. He obviously doesn't want me seeing the ring. I don't think it's a coincidence that my necklace is missing. I just don't know why."

There was nothing in the top drawer but a few markers and old papers left behind from the previous history teacher, so I moved on to the next one. His desk was old and creaky, and it seemed like every drawer was swollen shut.

"Makes sense." Triston nodded, leaning back on one of the desks and tapping his watch. "But you probably should hurry. Lunch is almost over."

"Then why don't you make yourself useful and keep watch at the door?" I pulled at the next drawer and continued my investigation. Triston hurried to the large window and looked out in both directions, occasionally ducking as people walked by in the hallway outside the room.

"You know, I do have a theory about the attack," Triston noted. "What if you were attacked by a werewolf?"

"A werewolf?" I looked up from the drawer and raised an eyebrow. "You think Mr. Macelton is a werewolf?"

"It makes sense."

Triston dared a glance at me from the window. "Some creepy stranger with an unplaceable accent comes into town and exchanges words with you. And then that same night, you're attacked by a creature with yellow, glowing eyes."

"I wasn't attacked by a werewolf."

"Just hear me out," Triston said quickly, holding both of his hands in the air, telling me to pump the brakes. "Wolves have this special layer behind their retinas called the tapetum lucidum. It's a retroreflector that makes their eyes glow yellow—"

"I know what wolves look like," I said while yanking the top left drawer open.

"You know what *wolves* look like," Triston emphasized, "but have you ever seen a werewolf?"

The top left drawer was filled with paperclips, broken pencils, and a bag of Whoppers.

"*No*, because *werewolves* don't exist." I thought about taking the Whoppers. I've always liked those. Can't get distracted.

"Shh," Triston hissed, putting his finger to his mouth and gesturing toward the window. We froze as someone walked by the room.

"It could be an alien," Triston muttered after a brief moment. "We both know they're invading."

I rolled my eyes and jerked the middle drawer open. Pens rolled forward to the edge of the drawer. There were papers, markers, a few erasers, but no ring. Maybe I really was going crazy, but I just knew that something was going on.

I started to shove the drawer closed when something silver and shiny rolled out from the back. It was the ring. The blue stone shimmered as I examined the symbols. This was all the proof I needed. Mr. Macelton *was* the one who had tried to kill me last night.

Had I been paying closer attention, I might've noticed that something in the room changed. Triston had stopped talking.

"*Ahem.*"

A man cleared his throat. I looked up to see Triston ducking behind a chair, and Mr. Macelton standing at the door with Principal Jenkins at his side. "Mr. Andrews. Mr. McLain," Principal Jenkins began. "Fancy meeting you here."

4

I Won A Trip To The Principal's Office

The clock's second hand pounded like a war drum as Triston and I waited outside Principal Jenkins's office. On the other side of the door, our parents were discussing the consequences of breaking into a classroom with Principal Jenkins and Mr. Macelton. I was sure if Jenkins had his way, Triston and I would be expelled. I shifted in my seat; my eyes fixed on the wooden door with "Principal" engraved on it. Principal Jenkins had always had it out for me. I don't know if it was because I was the mayor's son or if he just didn't like me, but it always seemed he went out of his way to "keep me in line" as he put it.

He found a way to pin anything that went wrong at the school on me, like that time in freshman P.E. when the fire alarm went off unexpectedly and flooded the entire gym. Jenkins had suspended me for a week, claiming he had a witness who saw me pull the fire alarm. But I hadn't been anywhere near it. Or that time in sophomore computer science when every computer in the lab exploded except mine.

34

That time Principal Jenkins said that I was on the dark web, which caused the other computers to short-circuit. Whenever Principal Jenkins had the opportunity to suspend me, he did, and I was sure this time wasn't going to be any different.

Triston tapped his fingers nervously. There was no one in Hainesville more suited to solve a conspiracy than Triston. Unfortunately, his father, Sheriff McLain, didn't appreciate his propensity for mysteries. He'd even told Triston that if last year's shenanigans were any indication of the trouble we would get in this year, Triston should expect to be grounded until he was thirty-five. McLain was a tough man on the best of days, but when it came to Triston, well, let's just say he put the *"over"* in *"over-protective parent."*

"What do you think they're talking about?" I whispered to Triston, only to be shushed immediately by Mrs. Mulberry, the school's receptionist, who couldn't have been younger than one hundred two years old. Mulberry peered at us over her large coke-bottle glasses, which made her look like a fish. She put her bony finger to her lips, and Triston shot me a warning look. Between Triston's hyperactive imagination and my inability to hold my tongue, we always seemed to be in trouble. And normally, it was my fault.

The door to the principal's office swung open. Without saying a word, Principal Jenkins gestured for us to enter. We squeezed into the already overcrowded office and sat beside our parents—well, beside Triston's father and my adopted father, Donald. Susan was busy wringing campaign donations out of the little old ladies of the garden club and couldn't be bothered to show up. Triston's mom had a much better excuse. She'd passed away when Triston was eight. Ever since, Triston's dad, the Sheriff, had been trying to pull himself together long enough to raise his stepson alone.

Anyway, I sat next to Donald, who was leaning back in his chair, hands clasped across his stomach and legs spread as far as they could go. Donald wasn't a particularly large man, but he seemed to take up space wherever he went. Triston sat next to his dad. It wasn't easy on Triston having the town's Sheriff for a father. To the Sheriff, nothing was ever just a conversation. Even the simplest of things turned into an investigation followed by a full jury trial, and finally, a severe judgment. The Sheriff clasped Triston around the shoulder and drew him in tight.

Principal Jenkins sat in his high-backed, leather rolling chair and folded his hands on his desk. "Breaking into a teacher's desk is a serious offense, gentlemen," he began. "If it were up to me, you would both be expelled."

I could have sworn everyone in the room was glaring right at me as if they'd already decided it was my fault we were there.

"Nonetheless," the principal continued, "Mr. Macelton has graciously asked me to let you go with a warning, which is a lot more than you deserve if you ask me." His eyes narrowed on me. "You better feel lucky. You're off the hook—for now."

My stomach tied itself into knots of fury. *Off the hook?* If anyone should be letting anyone *"off the hook,"* it should be me. And I had no intention to.

Principal Jenkins adjusted the name plaque on his desk and then looked at Triston and me expectantly. "Well," he asked eventually, "don't you boys have something to say to Mr. Macelton?"

Sure. I had a lot of things to say to Mr. Macelton. How about, *you're going to jail once I'm through with you.* I glared at

Macelton. His eyes met mine, but it wasn't a threatening look. It was a dog pleading with his master. Macelton was *begging* me to stay quiet.

Triston, meanwhile, stared at his shoes and muttered an apology, something about being sorry for not respecting boundaries and property. Then, to my disbelief, he thanked Macelton! Triston thanked him for letting us go with a warning. Anger rose inside of me.

"You're a murderer and a thief."

I felt the heat of every person in the room on me, but I kept my eyes glued on Mr. Macelton.

"What did you just say?" Donald asked.

"Mr. Macelton isn't who he says he is," I announced. "He's stalking me, and yesterday, he tried to kill me."

The room fell silent. Donald, Jenkins, and McLain exchanged glances as if mutually deciding who should take the lead. Sheriff McLain won.

"These are serious accusations, Kalib," he finally said, flipping open his notebook and diving into investigation mode. "I would think long and hard before you continue. We can't take any of this lightly, so if what you're saying isn't true, you could get into very serious trouble." All the eyes on the room were on me, including Mr. Macelton's, who'd returned to the same calm and collected expression as when we'd first entered.

"We all understand—you're just a kid," the Sheriff continued. "Sometimes, kids say things to get out of trouble. Stupid things. It's okay. We can just stop and walk away now—"

"I'm not," I interrupted as a flash of anger rushed into my body.

Just a kid?! I'm almost sixteen! I took a deep breath. *Pick your battles, Kalib.*

"I'm not making this up."

"Then why don't you tell us everything?" Sheriff McLain said calmly. "Why do you believe Mr. Macelton tried to kill you?"

I shot a glance at Triston, who wriggled, avoiding eye contact with everyone in the room.

"Yesterday at the diner, Mr. Macelton approached me," I explained. "He talked to me. He knew things about me, things a stranger shouldn't know about someone he'd just met. He kept saying he was doing 'research.'"

"Well, that's not too hard to believe. You're the son of the mayor!" Donald said, somehow taking up even more of the cramped office space than before. "When you're attached to someone as important as myself, people want to know who you are. You'd better get used to it kid because it's only going to get worse once I get a seat in Congress."

"Go on, Kalib," Sheriff McLain encouraged, waving aside the commentary in the room.

I looked at Mr. Macelton, half expecting to meet an infuriated glare, but he appeared perfectly calm. In fact, if it wasn't for a slight glint in his eyes, I would have wondered if Mr. Macelton had even heard what I was accusing him of. But it was there, faint and subtle, but unmistakable—that look of pleading. His eyes said, "Stop now, Kalib. There is no way this is going to end well for you."

My throat dried up like I hadn't tasted water in years. My tongue was thick and leaden. For a moment, it refused to form words, but there was no turning back.

I told them everything. Starting from the moment I left the diner. I told them about the eerie walk home—how there was no one else on the street that night. I told them about the weird voice whispering from the darkness and how I was attacked by the shadow figure that had tried to kill me. When I finished, the entire room sat in silence. I did it. I'd rendered a room full of professional speakers, speechless.

Donald spoke first. "Now hold on, kid." I could tell that he was trying to speak delicately.

"I want to believe you; honestly, I do. But didn't you tell Susan and me that you got a ride home from Mr. Jones last night?"

"Yes." I nodded. "I ran into Mr. Jones after the attack, and he gave me a ride. He said I looked flustered."

"And you didn't tell him what happened?" the Sheriff asked.

"N-no sir," I admitted. "At that point, I wasn't sure it had actually happened." McLain tilted his head to the side questioningly. "I-it seemed surreal. And afterward, everything had gone back to normal, like the street was never empty at all. But then later, I noticed my necklace was gone."

"So, you think Mr. Macelton stole your necklace?" Principal Jenkins asked skeptically.

"He seemed really interested in it at the diner," I noted, "and then an hour and a half later, I was attacked, and almost killed, and my necklace was taken."

Sheriff McLain studied me for an eternity. I saw the wheels in his head turning. What would he say to a story as unbelievable as mine? How would he proceed with his investigation? He looked me up and down, jotted something quick in his notepad, and then turned to Mr. Macelton.

"Mr. Macelton," Sheriff McLain asked, "do you have anything to say regarding these accusations?"

Mr. Macelton took a deep breath, his face steely calm. Didn't he care that everyone knew? If he did, nothing showed on his face. Instead, he sat poised and tranquil. "I can confirm I was at the diner yesterday evening, and I did, indeed, speak with Kalib. I heard Mama's Peach Pie was to die for, and being new to town, I needed to try it. Kalib served my pie, and I had recognized him from a newspaper article I read earlier that day," he said. "That's why I knew who he was. You can't be the son of the mayor in a small town without being recognized. Especially a mayor who has done as much for this town as Mayor Donovan has."

I almost laughed. So that was his tactic? Flattery? My amusement was short-lived when Donald chimed in.

"Wait a minute! I do recognize you," Donald said. "You were at the town meeting last week. You proposed the raffle for the Hainesville annual Peach Festival as a way to raise funds for charity. I've been taking your suggestion into consideration. You are a welcome addition to our community!" I couldn't believe it, Donald was buying Macelton's story.

"I appreciate it, Mayor Donovan," replied Macelton impassively, "and I assure you, you can count on my vote for Congress."

I was sick to my stomach. After everything I told them, all Mr. Macelton had to do was say a few quick compliments, and Donald was on his side.

"Did you know at that time Kalib would be your student?" the Sheriff pressed further.

"No. It wasn't until later that evening," Mr. Macelton continued. "During our faculty meeting at seven. You remember, Principal Jenkins."

Principal Jenkins faltered, trying to remember the faculty meeting.

"Principal Jenkins," Sheriff McLain asked. "Can you confirm

this faculty meeting took place?"

"Yes," said Jenkins slowly.

"And can you confirm—Emmanuel—was it?"

Mr. Macelton nodded.

"Can you confirm Emmanuel's attendance at this faculty meeting?"

Principal Jenkins hesitated, struggling to remember for a moment before becoming suddenly confident. "Yes. I absolutely can," he said, jumping out of his seat and rushing over to a filing cabinet, scooting Triston out of the way so he could pull out a drawer. "I have the sign-in sheet around here somewhere!"

"Emmanuel, what time would you say the faculty meeting was over?" the Sheriff asked.

"I think it ended around ten o'clock," said Mr. Macelton.

"Seven to ten," he repeated, jotting it down on his notepad. "And Kalib, this attack occurred after you left work? Around what time was that?"

"Yes, sir," I replied. "My shift ended around eight o'clock."

"Here it is!" Principal Jenkins called from the filing cabinet, pulling out a lined piece of paper with names written and signed on it. "The sign-in sheet for last night. We use these papers to confirm attendance and as a reference for payroll." Principal Jenkins held up the paper for all to see. There it was, on the third line, written in bold black ink: Emmanuel Macelton.

My heart dropped. *How could that be?* It had to have been Mr. Macelton who attacked me. I knew it was him.

"Well, Kalib," Principal Jenkins said, leaning back in his desk chair, "it looks like Mr. Macelton's alibi checks out."

"I'm telling you it was him that attacked me," I said desperately. I looked around the room for any sign someone believed me, but no one was interested. Principal Jenkins was content with his disbelief. He was more than happy to see me make a fool of myself in front of the Sheriff. Donald studied me cautiously, but I could tell he didn't believe a word of what I was saying.

But Sheriff McLain? He seemed … compassionate. I was pretty sure he didn't believe me, but if anyone was going to be on my side, it was him. He wanted to give me the benefit of the doubt.

"Sheriff, you have to believe me," I pleaded. "I know it was him."

"Kalib, sometimes we believe things so strongly that—"

"I *saw* him!" I interrupted. Everyone in the room halted. "Last night. He was outside my bedroom window."

"Kalib—" Donald began.

"I'm telling the truth!" I snapped, "After I got home, I was looking out my window, and Mr. Macelton was standing right there on the road."

"And you are sure it was Mr. Macelton?" The Sheriff leaned in.

"Yes." I was trembling.

"How do you know?" The Sheriff glanced at Mr. Macelton and then back to me.

"Because … because …" I knew I needed to say something. They had to believe me! Then it came out. The words practically fell out of my mouth before I could catch them. "Because his eyes glowed yellow."

I knew immediately I couldn't take it back. Every adult looked at me like I had lost my mind. Sheriff McLain sighed, closed his notepad, and leaned forward on his knees, eye level with me.

"Kalib, when we go through a traumatic experience, those things sometimes resurface as dreams. Those dreams can seem so real we can't tell the difference." There was true compassion in the Sheriff's eyes. "Sometimes adopted children have rep—"

"This isn't about me being adopted!" I fumed. "This isn't some repressed fever dream. I know what I saw."

"But Kalib," Donald interjected, "you're the only one who saw these things. When Susan and I investigated, there was nothing there. I'm not saying that you didn't experience something real, but could it be that whatever you did experience, was ... in your head?"

"No," I repeated. "I know what I saw. A man with yellow eyes attacked me on the street last night, and Mr. Macelton's eyes flashed yellow this afternoon during lunch."

"I see." Sheriff McLain leaned back.

"Look, I know you don't believe me, but—"

"I believe that *you* believe you." The lines around Sheriff McLain's eyes wrinkled gently. Compassionate, sure, but he wasn't buying a word of this. I realized then he had experienced this sort of thing with his wife, Triston's mom, before she died. Triston didn't talk about it often, but she was schizophrenic. Hearing voices and all of that. And I guess, toward the end, she was also a little paranoid. Well, a lot paranoid. She was convinced she was being followed. Sound familiar?

But this wasn't like that. I knew what I saw. I wasn't just paranoid. I glared at Mr. Macelton, who looked back at me, expressionless. *You're up to something. And I'm going to figure out what it is.*

5

It All Happened In The Woods

After my conversation with Sheriff McLain—more of an interrogation than a discussion—Principal Jenkins dismissed Triston and his dad but kept me behind. Mr. Macelton assured Jenkins that it was all a misunderstanding and that he was confident it wouldn't be a problem in the future. Principal Jenkins still lectured me for an hour more about his expectations for the school year. He also assigned me an essay about the criminal justice system, to be on his desk by Friday morning.

Donald didn't say much during the meeting. In fact, he looked more uninterested in what Principal Jenkins was saying than I was. When the meeting was over, Principal Jenkins escorted the two of us out of his office. Donald put his hand on my shoulder and muttered, "Wait till Susan hears about this," before leaving me to return to class.

Susan had one rule: don't make her look bad. As long as I abided by her one rule, she and I were okay. But getting suspended from school? That would make her look bad, and when I made Susan look bad … let's just say, no one was happy.

It was no surprise to me that Susan picked me up from school that day. Most days, I walked from school to The Georgia Peach for the early dinner shift. Susan knew this, but that day, she insisted on driving me the two blocks from school to work. I knew this couldn't be good. We sat awkwardly in silence the entire ride to the diner. I caught her glimpse over at me a few times, but still, she remained stoic. Her driving me, of course, meant I would be at work a little early. When we got there, I slid out the car and started for the door.

"Hold on, Kalib," Susan called behind me. She held her hand out toward me. "Not so fast. I thought I'd get some pie and ice cream. Join me, won't you?"

In our house, pie and ice cream was code for, *Lucy, you've got some 'splainin' to do!* And I knew this was no exception. Ten minutes later, I was in a booth across from Susan, who silently picked at her pie.

"Kalib," she finally said after a long period of silence. Susan wasn't silent because she didn't know what to say. I think Susan had learned a long time ago that silence can be tremendously more intimidating than yelling, and she had learned how to use that to her advantage. "All of this is very concerning to us."

She dipped a small piece of pie into her ice cream and brought it to her mouth. I hated the way she picked at her food. She ate in small pecks like a bird. "Landing yourself in the principal's office on the first day of school? I thought we talked about this. With Donald's campaign coming up, we really can't afford for you to behave in a manner that is less than ... ideal."

There it was. I knew it was only a matter of time before this was turned into a campaign issue. It hadn't even been two hours since the meeting in Principal Jenkins's office, and she was already worried about Donald's "public image." Donald and Susan never really cared what I did or where I went, as long as it didn't affect their image. Me being expelled from school like Principal Jenkins was itching to do? That would definitely affect their image. Me having a psychotic breakdown, like Donald feared I was? Well, that wouldn't look good for their image either. I picked at my apple pie, pushing the slices around my plate as they floated in the melted soup that was once a scoop of ice cream.

"If there is an issue," she said, "it is important that we deal with it at home. Family matters remain family matters, so if you *are* seeing things or having … episodes, it's important that you let us know immediately. I'm sure we can find the best professionals to deal with it."

"Yes, ma'am." I nodded.

"You know I just want what's best for you, right?" she said gently. I didn't look up. "I know we've had our differences, but all Donald and I want is for you to have the finest things in life."

I poked at my soggy pie soup. I didn't believe it at all. *Donald and Susan* wanted to have the finest things in life. I couldn't have grown up in the Donovan house and *not* understand that I was only an accessory to the fine life they wanted so desperately.

"And that's why, Kalib," she continued, tapping her fork against her plate to get my attention. "This will be your last shift here at The Georgia Peach."

"What?" I snapped my eyes up from my plate. "Why?"

"I've spoken to Patrick Jones," she said, adjusting the sleeves of her blouse and grabbing her handbag. "He's informed me that he's taken up my offer to allow you to intern as his personal assistant at RavenTech. This is a real opportunity for you, Kalib, and will only lead to greatness in your future. And since you seem inclined to constantly find yourself in trouble at school, I hope that a little more responsibility will curb this childish behavior."

"But I don't want to work at RavenTech," I protested. "I like my job here."

The light above our table flickered. Susan glanced at the hanging lamp and frowned before returning her gaze to me. "This is a done deal, Kalib," she replied sternly. "I've already spoken to the owner, and she's agreed to allow you to return to this job when your internship at RavenTech is complete, assuming that Mr. Jones doesn't offer you a permanent position after your internship."

"So, you just went behind my back and forced my boss to fire me?"

For a split second, the entire diner went dark. Susan glared disapprovingly.

"Not fire, Kalib," she said, "You will be on temporary leave."

"But I don't—"

"Kalib!" she interrupted. "This is not up for discussion. RavenTech is what's best for the future. Not some diner that can't even afford to pay their electric bill. I will hear no more about it."

I tightened my jaw. *Best for the future? Best for who's future?*

"I've gotta get to work," I huffed, sliding out of the booth and storming into the back.

The next several hours of work seemed to fly by. It was difficult to enjoy my last day at the diner when it came so suddenly. Under any other circumstances, working at

RavenTech would have been a dream. I would get to work with cool technology, and I'd be spending more time with Caliyah, and what red-blooded teenage boy didn't want that? But I wanted to earn it. I hated being forced to do it.

"Hi, Kalib." Speaking of the devil, Caliyah pulled me back to reality.

"Caliyah? What are you doing here?"

Caliyah tapped her fingers on the counter. "My dad placed an order for a pie he wanted me to pick up. Is it ready?" I scanned the order sheets at the pick-up window until I found hers.

"One cherry pie coming right up," I said, pulling a pie from the display and prepping a box for her.

"So, Dad tells me you're going to take the internship."

"Not like I really had a choice," I huffed, sounding more bitter than intended. I looked up from the box and smiled clumsily in attempt to lighten the blow.

"Look, Kalib. I know that you want to feel like you earned the position at RavenTech," she said gently. "Trust me, I get it. People like us practically get things handed to us. You want to feel like you did something on your own, accomplished something because *you* were good at it. I just wanted to tell you that you'll still have the chance to prove that there. I promise you this isn't going to be an easy job. Dad says that you'll be working closely with me. It's mostly data entry and organizing, but I think we're gonna have a lot of fun." She smiled in a way that turned the already existing butterflies in my stomach into fully grown fruit bats. I grinned sheepishly at her in return, sliding her pie box across the counter.

"I guess that's the—" I started to say, but before I could finish my sentence, Triston burst through the front door. "What happened after I left?" he asked, rushing the counter from the door where he stood. "Did you get expelled?"

Caliyah raised a questioning eyebrow at me. "Why would you be expelled?"

"Would you keep your voice down?" I hissed at them both.

"I can't believe you *made* me break into Mr. Macelton's classroom with you," Triston continued.

"I didn't *make* you break into Macelton's classroom," I defended. "I very clearly told you to go."

"Wait." Caliyah almost dropped her pie. "You *broke into* Mr. Macelton's classroom? Is that where you rushed off to at lunch? Why?"

"It's a long story," I groaned.

"My dad's pie can wait."

"All you need to know is that I'm not expelled," I said. "Mr. Macelton seems to think that I'm not a threat, so it won't interfere with my eligibility for the internship or anything like that."

"Mr. Macelton vouched for you?" Triston asked. "Go figure. Maybe it wasn't him who attacked you."

Caliyah perked up, tilting her head in my direction. "Is that what this is about?" she asked. "You think Mr. Macelton *attacked* you?"

I let out an exasperated breath. The more I told the story, the crazier I felt. Still, I had to tell Caliyah.

"Really?" Caliyah said excitedly when I'd finished relaying the whole story. She leaned in with both of her elbows on the counter. She was more interested in my story than I had expected. "And that's why you broke into his classroom?"

"It wasn't until you pointed out that my necklace was missing that I remembered how interested in it he had been,"

I explained. "When I realized it was gone, I thought it had to have been him who took it."

"But you were wrong." Triston slapped his hand on the white surface of the counter. "You didn't find anything."

"That's not entirely true," I admitted, pulling out the ring that I had taken from Macelton's desk.

Triston's eyes widened. "You stole from Macelton?"

"Triston, this is proof that Macelton tried to kill me," I replied, holding the ring out between us. "I knew I recognized the ring from somewhere. And look, the stone in the ring is identical to my necklace. Proof that he knew more than he was letting on. What if all this time, I was wearing a million-dollar piece of jewelry around my neck, and I never even knew it."

"But I don't understand," Caliyah interrupted. "If you already had the ring, why didn't you tell anyone?"

"They never would have believed me. You should have seen them. They had their minds made up about me before I even came into the room."

I glanced at Triston, who nodded in agreement. Caliyah was still deep in thought. "But if Macelton stole the necklace, why would he vouch for you? Wouldn't he want to have you expelled to get you out of the picture? It would seem to me that he would want to invalidate your confession. If you were expelled, no one would believe he did anything at all."

I hadn't thought about that.

"She's right." Triston blushed, his hair flopping over his eyes.

"Macelton must be up to something else then," I reasoned. "Something bigger."

"Like what?" Before I was able to answer, Richard Marsden, a shift lead at work, interrupted our conversation.

"Sorry to interrupt … whatever this is, but do I pay you

to talk to your friends, or do I pay you to work?" Richard, or Rich, as he liked to be called, was the town's biggest suck-up. Ever since he'd been promoted to shift lead at the diner, he was known to bark orders to anyone he considered to be his subordinate. The only problem was he didn't *have* subordinates. He was only in charge of scheduling shifts, but that didn't stop him from getting drunk off of his non-existent power any chance he got.

"*You* don't pay me at all, Richie," I said grabbing my apron from beneath the counter and tying it around my waist. "You don't pay anyone."

"Whatever," Richard huffed. "Mamma wants you to take out the trash."

Mamma owned the diner. No one knew her real name; it was just Mamma and had been for as long as anyone could remember.

"And don't call me Richie!" Richard yelled at my back. I chuckled as I made my way through the kitchen toward the dumpster. Nothing brought me more joy than knocking Richie down a few pegs. I pushed the back door open with my shoulder, two black garbage bags dripping at my feet. *Gross,* I thought, making my way to the dumpster against the brick wall on the other side of the narrow alley. I dropped the bags at my feet, lifted the lid, and tossed the first one in. It made a thud as it hit the bottom of the empty dumpster.

That's when I felt it again. Goosebumps rose on my skin, and the hair on the back of my neck stood straight up. It was the same feeling I felt when—

Rattle.

Someone's here. I swallowed hard, remembering what happened the last time I felt this way.

Rattle.

My eyes snapped to the dark corner where the sound was coming from.

Rattle.

I took a step toward it, straining my eyes to see if there was something there. All I could see were a couple of wooden crates and two tin trash cans. The rattling was coming from a particularly dark area of the alley. I took two steps toward the trash can, and my pants pocket suddenly felt heavy. I slipped my hand in and felt the round shape of the ring graze against my fingertips.

I pulled the ring out and held it in front of me, taking another step toward the sound. My heart was pounding, and the ring was getting warmer the closer I got to the tin cans. In fact, it looked like the symbols on the ring were glowing. Getting brighter. With the ring still extended in front of me, I reached out to open the lid.

BANG!

A car backfired on the street. The lid burst off the trashcan, and two raccoons jumped out, chattering angrily as they landed on their feet and scurried down the alley. I took a moment to catch my breath, laughing at my own stupidity. *What did you expect to see, Kalib? A monster?* I looked at the ring, there were no glowing symbols. It was just a normal ring. *My eyes must be playing games on me.* I shook my head, turning back toward the dumpster. *It must've been a trick of the light.* I tossed the second bag into the dumpster and turned to go back into the diner.

Just as I reached for the door, I saw Damien Daslic out on the street. There was something suspicious about the way he kept glancing left to right as if making sure he wasn't being followed. He walked a few more steps, stopping outside of the gap between two buildings on the opposite side of the road. Damien looked both ways, checked his phone, and then shoved his hands into his pockets and disappeared into the darkness of the gap.

What are you up to, Damien?

Curiosity got the best of me, and before I knew it, I had stepped out from my hiding place and followed Damien's moonlit silhouette down the dark path into the woods, occasionally hiding behind a tree to keep out of sight. He finally arrived at a large white oak that stood at the center of a clearing. I ducked behind a bush, using the shadows of the trees to get as close as possible.

"I'm here," he said. At first, I thought he was talking to the tree, but then a man jumped down from the top of the tree, landing right in front of Damien. When the man stood up, my heart leaped into my throat. It was Mr. Macelton.

6

Advice From An Expert

I knew Mr. Macelton was up to something, but why on earth would he be meeting with Damien Daslic in the woods? Something wasn't right about this. I wasn't close enough to make out what they were saying, so I crept quietly to a thicket of bushes within earshot of the meeting. In darkness, I could barely make out a handshake exchanged between the two.

"Did you bring it?"

"Swiped it from him this morning."

I was able to get close enough to see Damien hold something up between them. I strained my eyes to make out the object. It took everything inside of me not to shout in anger. Damien was holding *my* necklace. How did *he* get it? The memory of colliding with Damien in the hallway that morning at school flashed through my head. That clever thief, he stole it from me then and still managed to blame me for it.

"Why did the priv have the stone, anyway?" Damien examined the pendant that dangled from his hand. "And why was it so important that you have it right now? Why not let him keep it?"

"All you need to know is that it *is* important," Macelton said, taking the necklace from Damien.

Damien rolled his eyes and puffed out a breath of air. "So, what next?" He sounded a bit irritated, but whether that was a result of Macelton's evasion or his normal level of irritation, I wasn't sure. "I just gave you the necklace. You have everything that is needed to make the payment."

"Not everything." Macelton shook his head. "Kalib took the Halfling Ring."

Damien puffed out another breath of air. "So it was all useless, like I said it would be. You have the necklace, Kalib has the ring, and we're back to where we started. What now?"

"If the prophecy is to be fulfilled," Macelton said matter-offactly. "Kalib's blood will be spilled by the night of his sixteenth sun."

My heart pounded at the sound of my own name. *My blood would be spilled by my sixteenth sun? What does that mean?* I needed to get out of there. Whatever they were planning didn't sound like it would be good for me. I shuffled backward on my hands and feet slowly, trying not to make a sound, but my arms were shaking, and it was difficult to hold myself up.

Snap.

I looked down. I had snapped a twig beneath my right hand.

In an instant, Macelton jerked his head in my direction. I froze, covering my mouth, forcing back a gasp. His eyes had changed. They were glowing yellow.

Macelton walked slowly toward the thicket of bushes where I was hiding. I didn't know what to do, if I ran now, they would certainly see me, but all Macelton had to do was walk a few more steps and he'd be right in front of me. I looked around and found a rock about the size of my hand sticking out of the grass. I reached for it. If I was going down, I wasn't going down without a fight. As Macelton edged closer, I tightened my grip and prepared for a fight.

There was a ruffling of feathers somewhere above me. That's when I noticed Hunter, perched on a low-hanging branch. Hunter looked at me in a way that made me wonder if he understood the situation, and then, like a transaction made between the two of us, he leaped off of the branch swooped down, flapping his wings in Macelton's face before flying right over his head. Macelton shielded his face and then turned to watch Hunter disappear over the trees. He stared for a moment in silence.

"It was just a bird," he said, looking into the horizon where Hunter had just flown, then addressed Damien. "Keep a watchful eye. Something tells me others have learned of Kalib's return. Our time is running out."

Macelton tilted his head and then disappeared into the trees, leaving Damien in the clearing alone.

* * *

I told Triston everything I'd seen once I had gotten back to the diner that night. Naturally, it was all he could talk about the next day at school, making guesses about what it all meant. Most were off the wall theories involving time loops and multi-dimensional paradoxes.

"More have learned of Kalib's return?" Triston repeated. "I still can't get over it. It's like you're in the middle of a mystery."

"Yeah, but it doesn't make sense," I said, shouldering my book bag and pushing through the school doors. "Kalib's return? I never went anywhere."

"Maybe you're an alien sent here from a dying planet to

repopulate your species." Triston gasped, "Oh my god, you're superman!"

"I'm not superman, Triston." I rolled my eyes. "I just don't understand what they want with me. They said my blood will be spilled by the night of my sixteenth sun. What does that even mean?"

Triston scrunched his face, "Well if SciFi has taught me anything, I'd say by sun they mean 'Earth sun.' It takes a year to rotate Earth's sun, which means ... your sixteenth Earth sun would be ..."

"My sixteenth birthday," I noted. "That's next week."

"Are you sure they were talking about you?"

"They said my name so—yeah, I'm pretty sure."

"Well, you gotta call the cops," Triston said, bending down to tie his shoe.

"And tell them what? Your dad already thinks I'm disturbed after I accused Macelton of trying to kill me. They'll never believe me."

"But, you've got proof, right?" Triston replied hopefully. "You've got the ring, and you know Macelton has the necklace. You could just show it to them."

"All that would prove is that I stole Macelton's ring. Besides, technically, Macelton didn't steal my necklace. Damien did."

"We'll figure something out," Triston huffed. "No way I'm letting some deranged history teacher '*off*' my best friend."

If there was one thing I liked about Triston, it was his loyalty. He was always there when I needed him, even if it meant facing imminent doom, which in his mind was every day. He had a way of seeing the bright side. As if to prove my point, Triston changed the subject entirely.

"Today's your first day at RavenTech, isn't it?"

I shrugged, shoving my hands into my pockets. "Yeah. I'm actually supposed to be heading there right now."

"Wow," Triston said dreamily, "One-on-one time with Caliyah Jones every day. What I would give to be in your shoes."

"Yeah," I laughed, "one-on-one time with Caliyah … and her dad. I'm sure it's going to be super romantic."

"It doesn't matter, bro! You get to spend every day with the prettiest girl in town. Every guy in Hainesville is going to be jealous of you."

"If you say so," I said. "Well, I better get over there. I wouldn't want to be late on my first day. Susan and Donald would have a cow."

"Call me later. I want to know everything."

Triston and I fist-bumped before heading in opposite directions.

RavenTech was at the edge of town, so it would take me a bit longer to get there than it did to get to the diner. Luckily, Hainesville wasn't a very large town, so the difference would only be a few minutes. It would have been even faster in a car—if I had a car, which was a present I had hoped to buy myself for my birthday. I'd been saving up for months. But now, I may not even make it to my birthday, considering the circumstances.

The long driveway leading to the RavenTech building was surrounded by trees. RavenTech was so secluded from the rest of Hainesville, that if it hadn't been the most successful business in town, no one would've even known it was there.

I opened the large glass doors and stepped onto the marble floors of the circular lobby and glanced around the domed room.

"Can I help you?" a voice said. I noticed a receptionist's desk at the opposite end of the lobby.

"Oh!" I said, "I'm Kalib. The new intern."

"You're the new intern?" The receptionist looked about as uninterested in me as a dog is a veterinarian.

"Y-yeah," I stammered, "I'm supposed to start—"

"Kalib! You made it," Caliyah's voice echoed around the room. I looked around to spot her head peeking out from behind the large double doors on the right side of the room. "I'm glad you're here. Come on in. Daddy's waiting on you."

I glanced back at the receptionist, who glared at me expressionlessly. I gave her a thankful nod and wave and rushed toward the doors.

"Don't worry about Judy," Caliyah said once we made it beyond the wooden doors. "She's got resting witch face. It isn't you."

The room beyond the double doors was not at all what I expected. I expected to walk into a chaos-filled room, with geniuses creating humanoid robot arms and biosynthetic legs. Instead, we were in a large warehouse with several employees wearing jeans and t-shirts who were all either glued to their computer screens or tinkering on smartphones.

"I know," Caliyah said, noting the disappointment on my face. "It's a little underwhelming, isn't it? The Hainesville facility dedicates most of its attention to schematics."

"C'mon, Dad's office is on the top floor." I followed Caliyah to the elevator. She punched the Level 15 button and waited for the doors to close. We sat in awkward silence for a few moments. This was the most alone time I'd spent with Caliyah since ... well, since ever.

"So," she said, searching for something to fill the silence.

"So," I repeated, instantly hating myself for it.

"Any more leads on that ring you showed me yesterday?"

"Oh, no. I haven't really thought about it much," I lied. In fact, it was all I *could* think about. Even now, the ring was heavy in my pocket, just itching for me to pull it out. But I didn't know what I would do with it once I had. A part of me wanted to march right up to Mr. Macelton, throw the ring in his face, and tell him if he wanted me, come and get me. The other part of me—the more sane part that wanted to live—wanted to keep my mouth shut and hide under a rock for a few years.

When the elevator reached the top floor, I followed Caliyah into a large corner office. Mr. Jones sat in a high-backed leather office chair, peering over paperwork scattered across his mahogany desk. Framed degrees and certificates dotted the walls, and to his right was a floor to ceiling window overlooking the surrounding woods.

"Kalib." Mr. Jones stood up extending his rather large hand in my direction. "Welcome to RavenTech! Please, have a seat."

Caliyah and I both sat across from Mr. Jones at his desk. I didn't realize, until I sat, just how massive the desk was. I guess it had to be to accommodate someone as humongous as him. I felt like a kid in comparison.

"I am glad to have you here, Kalib. Caliyah informed me that you have concerns about getting this job as a perk of your parentage. That's an admirable trait, son. You want to work for what you have."

"Yes, sir."

"Well, I assure you, this isn't going to be an easy job." Mr. Jones leaned forward in his chair. "RavenTech Labs is the world's leader in prosthesis, so things move at a pretty fast pace here. We cover all facets of the industry, from innovation, conceptualization, schematics and design. You will serve as my personal assistant, so you will be expected to keep up. And since you're only here four hours a day, you'll spend most of your time organizing my schedule, running errands, and of course, filing. Do you think you can handle that?"

"Yes, sir."

"Good." Mr. Jones smiled, leaning back in his chair. "In that case, why not put your badge on?"

I hadn't noticed before, but sitting in front of me on the desk was a blue RavenTech badge with my name on it.

"Thank you, sir." I reached for it, proudly clipping it onto my left shirt pocket.

"Caliyah, why don't you give Kalib a tour of the building." Caliyah's nose wrinkled as her sweet smile spread across her face.

"Yes, daddy," she said, sliding out of her chair and gesturing for me to follow her.

Four hours flew by. The building was more impressive than I had initially thought. On the second floor, they had computers and 3D printers that did things I never could have dreamed of. After the tour, we returned to Mr. Jones's office to organize his filing cabinet. Between filing, organizing, and trying not to get caught staring at Caliyah, the time sped by. But even amazing technology and working alongside the prettiest girl in school couldn't keep my mind off of what I had seen in the woods.

What did Macelton mean by my 'blood will be spilled on the night of my sixteenth sun'? Triston seemed to think that meant my sixteenth birthday. But there was nothing I could do about it. I couldn't go to the police. Sherriff McLain already thought

I was crazy. There was no way he was going to believe me now. He'd probably suggest that I be institutionalized, and knowing my parents, they'd send me away to the furthest psych ward if it meant protecting their image.

"Something bothering you, son?" Mr. Jones asked at the end of the day when I was handing him a newly organized file. "You seem distracted."

"Oh, I'm sorry," I stammered. "I'm not. I just have—"

"It's okay, Kalib." Mr. Jones said, "You're allowed to be distracted. Got a lot on your mind?"

"No, I just—" I started, but something told me that there wasn't much I could say that Mr. Jones wouldn't see right through. He looked at me knowingly, folding his hands on his desk.

"Come, have a seat." He gestured to the chairs in front of him. "Problems at school?"

"Something like that."

"Well, you're a smart guy. I'm sure you'll be able to get to the bottom of it."

"Yeah." I looked out the window. I didn't even know where to begin.

"It's just…" I couldn't tell him the truth. The truth was just too crazy. "Okay, I have this friend, and, my friend … he was attacked a few days ago."

"Oh my. Is your friend okay?" Mr. Jones asked.

"Yeah, yeah, he's fine," I continued. "But he—my friend— thinks he knows who attacked him. He told the principal. He even told the sheriff, but he didn't have any proof, and no one believed him. So now he just has to watch while this criminal gets away with what he did. And the worst part is, the person who did it … he's right there at school with him, so my friend has to see this guy every day, and there's nothing he can do about it."

"I see," Mr. Jones said, bobbing his head up and down for a moment as he pondered the problem. "Well, it seems to me that if I were to give your *friend* advice, I would tell your friend that if the police need proof, he's just going to have to find the proof."

"Really?"

"Absolutely." Mr. Jones peered at me compassionately, "I didn't get to be the CEO of one of the top technology companies in the world by taking no for an answer. Whenever there was an obstacle, I bulldozed my way through it. If I were your friend, and the authorities didn't believe me, I would make them believe me. I would become my own detective and find the answers that I needed. You're a smart guy. I'm sure you and your friend will find the answers you need."

"Wow," I said. "Thank you."

"Anytime, Kalib," Mr. Jones replied with a smile. I could see it then, the resemblance between him and his daughter. They both had the kind of winning smile that made you feel like everything was going to be okay. "Be safe on your walk home, okay?"

"Thanks, Mr. Jones." I nodded. "Have a good day."

Mr. Jones was right. I really couldn't take no for an answer, not when my life might be at stake. I was going to have to take some risks. I pulled out my cell phone as I rushed through the glass doors of RavenTech, typing out a message to Triston.

Kalib: *Meet me in the woods outside of James Street. Tell no one.*

7

I Spoke Too Soon

"The open house at school tonight goes until eight o'clock," I explained, while looking at the old Victorian house where Macelton lived. "That should give us enough time to get in, find the necklace, and get out."

"This is a really bad idea," Triston warned.

"You don't have to go in," I told him.

"You say that, but if I don't, you're going to do something stupid and get caught. Then I'm going to feel guilty for not helping, and I don't want to have to live with that for the rest of my life."

"So then, we're doing this?"

"Is there any way I can talk you out of it?"

"Not really."

Triston took a deep breath. "How do you know it's even here?"

"It's here," I said. "I can't explain it. I just know it's here. It's like I can feel it."

Triston shot me a long meaningful look. Undoubtedly, thinking about all the ways this could go south. But eventually he puffed out a large breath, rolled his eyes and said, "If this is something you have to do. I got your back."

"Thanks Triston," I said, patting him on the shoulder and scanning the house for a way inside.

The Old Vic' was probably really nice once, but the enormous old house had long since lost its dazzling allure. The yellow paint was faded and chipping away. Ivy had overtaken most of the outer walls in a snarl thick enough to tangle a horse. Several stains and watermarks gave the impression that the stubborn structure had undergone severe water damages over the years.

It wasn't long before we noticed a window ajar leading to a downstairs bedroom on the side of the house. It was propped open by a small piece of wood jammed into the groove of the window.

"Looks like someone was expecting us," Triston joked. We checked to make sure the coast was clear before we crossed the street and climbed into the room through the open window. It was immediately clear that this was not Macelton's bedroom. The room had a full-sized bed. A fairly large stereo rested on an oak dresser, and the walls were covered with movie posters and pictures of sports cars. It was clearly a teenager's room.

"I didn't know Macelton had a kid," Triston whispered.

"I think there's a lot about Macelton we don't know," I said. "That's why we're here."

The door creaked as I pushed it open. I shuddered. *I hate creaky houses.* Triston and I stepped out of the room and entered the hallway. On one end, there were several doors and a long stairway. Something about the old house made the hallway seem extra dark and creepy. I imagined all the things that could be behind those doors, each door leading to something more horrible than the last.

"I think that's the living room over there," Triston said, pointing in the other direction. I saw the edge of a red sofa and a coffee table at that end of the hall. "Let's go that way."

We started down the hall toward the living room. For an assumed bachelor, Macelton's house was furnished much more nicely than I would have imagined. The living room alone was decorated with classical paintings and vintage furniture. On the walls were models of medieval weaponry, and on the mantle were busts and statues.

"I wonder how much Macelton spent on all this." I ran a finger over a statue that must have been crafted from pure gold.

"What, no television?" Triston said. "What does he do all day?"

A glimmer of gold caught my eye. Light reflected off a plaque on the mantel above the fireplace. Triston immediately went to it.

"Whoa!" The plaque held a double-edged sword, crossed with a small spear. Triston ran his hands over the sword. There were words engraved in it, but they weren't in English. "Anseo scith Fragarach an claíomh sin riamh caill sé sprioc," Triston read as if he knew the language.

"Fragarach," he repeated.

Bewitched and unable to resist any longer, he grabbed the sword sliding it from its resting place beneath the spear. At that moment, I would have sworn he was a different person. He still looked like Triston, but more confident, powerful, elegant even. He swished the sword back and forth as if preparing for battle.

"Aha!" He scowled, sparing with invisible enemies. "Did

you really believe that you can take me, Sir Triston the forty-fourth? Then step right up you good for nothing scallywag!"

He was definitely still Triston.

"Stop playing around," I said. "We don't have that much time."

Triston reluctantly returned Fragarach to its place on the mantel and followed me to explore other parts of the house. Before long, we'd spotted a staircase on the other end of that hall we had avoided walking through earlier. This time, we cautiously crept passed the seemingly ominous doors toward the stairs on the other end.

The hallway felt colder and creepier than the rest of the house. Macelton didn't have photos on the walls, only drawings and old paintings that looked like they dated back to the thirteen hundreds. There were also a lot of strange collectible items, old busts, peculiar artifacts, and bizarre relics. This house was like a museum of things forgotten.

"Do you remember in school when we learned about how the ancient Egyptians would hide body parts in old relics because they thought it would preserve the souls of holy men?" Triston recalled once we'd begun ascending the stairs and eying the old relics that sat in individual niches on the wall. "I really hope Macelton isn't trying to preserve any holy souls in these."

He shuddered. The upstairs aesthetic was different than downstairs. Whereas downstairs felt more like a museum, upstairs actually felt like a place people could live. It was homier. On the walls were more portraits. Macelton really had a thing for the Renaissance portraits. At the end of the hall, in front of a window, was a vase with flowers in it. I found it odd. Macelton never struck me as a *flowers* kind of guy.

I turned to Triston to point out the flowers, but he was

gone. "Triston?" I called, wondering which door he could have disappeared through.

Triston popped his head out of a nearby room and said, "Hey Kalib, come over here. You've got to check this out."

I followed Triston into a cluttered room filled with more interesting objects. The walls were lined from floor to ceiling with books, mostly in different languages, but there were a few that I recognized: *The War of the Gods*; *The Retreat to the Isle of Man*; *The Lady of the Lake*. They all looked pretty boring to me.

"Merlin and King Arthur's Court," Triston whispered excitedly. "My mom used to read this to me! I love this book!" Triston smiled as he flipped through the pages, recounting the times his mother would tuck him into bed and read the stories to him. "I used to love the way she did the voices for the characters." Triston took a deep breath. I could tell that the memory of his mother made him a little sad. They had been really close before she died.

"There's a lot of weird stuff in here." Triston gestured around the room.

There *was* a lot of weird stuff, including a mannequin with chainmail and a long spear, several more Renaissance paintings, and more weird busts. Why would Macelton own this stuff? How long had he had it all?

"Come on. We've gotta get out of here. Macelton might …"

But Triston was no longer listening. He stared at himself in a mirror, which hung on the wall, like he'd just seen himself for the first time in years.

"Triston," I began, moving toward him to see what had been so interesting to have stopped him so suddenly. But before I could drag Triston away from the wall mirror, a different item caught my eye. It was an old book. Real old. The cover was wrapped in pure leather. Inscribed in gold on the front cover, was the title:

The Book of Ambrosius

The book was somehow familiar, though I was certain I had never seen it before. I opened it, and strange words were handwritten on the first page.

Famgravæh ba drulf gaklæklæ drulfgalklek ba dramgr

I didn't know how, but I recognized this language. The words were familiar. But I couldn't figure out why. I turned the page. The pages felt odd. They didn't feel like paper. It felt more like... skin. Maybe not human skin, but skin nonetheless. I flipped through the book. The entire thing was handwritten and appeared to be scribed in that same language.

I turned back to the first page but to my surprise the strange handwritten words had changed. Instead of the mysterious language I had read earlier, the words now read— *Seek, and you will find. Find, and you will seek*—in perfect English!

I blinked. I could have sworn it had been in a different language earlier. The room around me began to swirl and dissolve until I was somewhere else entirely. I was standing in a river amongst a group of people. Their clothing sure didn't look like anything a person would wear these days. They were wearing cloaks made of white linen. An elderly woman stood at the center of the group, and next to her, a young couple held a baby. A young boy clasped his father's tunic. He looked vaguely familiar.

"The child," the elderly woman said, holding her hands out. The young couple transferred the baby from their arms into hers. The woman's eyes looked so joyful. She kissed the child on the forehead and chanted:

> *The lost boy, born from the blood of the past,*
> *Will return on the eve of war.*
> *Though death, magic, and fire rehashed*
> *The last Angel Warrior shall be reborn*
>
> *The golden blood shall be paid at last*
> *On the night of his sixteenth sun*
> *By letter, symbol and liquid unlatched*
> *The Last-Born Angel Warrior will forever be won*

The elderly woman dipped the baby into the river, and the people cheered. Then the world swirled and dissolved again, and I was in a house. The young couple from before paced back and forth in the candlelit room. They were in a heated discussion.

"He is the last Angel Warrior," the man said.

"We cannot let word spread about his identity," the woman added. "Nothing but bad can come from this. It's an omen hanging over our heads."

An urgent knock came from the door. Before the young man could open it, a large brown-haired man wearing a feather pelt burst in.

"Brother!" the man with the feather pelt said urgently. "We don't have much time to speak. I need you to do exactly as I say! The demons know about the Angel's Kiss. You must flee this place. You must take your family and leave—tonight."

The room swirled and faded, and moments later, I was on a hill in the middle of a war. In the valley below, I saw an army of soldiers in horned helmets racing toward the young man and his family. They appeared to be fleeing toward the ocean on the other side of the hill. There was a flash of light, and a scream ripped through the air. As if I was pulled from the hill, I was suddenly in the water. The little boy raced toward me. *Was he reaching for me?*

"NOOOOOOOOOOOOOO!"

I wasn't sure if the scream came from the boy or from Triston. I was back in the junk room, gasping for breath.

"Mom?!" Triston cried, "Come back! Mom?!"

8

Tattoos Really Aren't For Me

My eyes darted around the room, half expecting to see soldiers in horned helmets racing toward me with spears. But the only things in the room were the abandoned books and artifacts, and Triston, who banged his hand against the mirror, yelling, "Come back!" with tear-filled eyes. "Come back!"

"Triston!" His eyes were vacant and lifeless as he hammered on the glass. Without thinking, I shoved the book in the waistband of my pants and rushed to Triston, putting both hands on his shoulders to get his attention. "Triston, what's wrong? Triston?" I shook him, but it was like he was looking right through me. "What's happening?"

A second later, he gasped, and life rushed back into his blank face.

"What happened?" he asked, looking around the room.

"I ... I don't know," I said. "You were staring into that mirror, and then you started yelling."

Triston frowned. I wondered if Triston had seen the same things I had.

Before I could ask, Triston snapped his head toward the door.

"Someone's coming," he hissed.

I heard it too, footsteps ascending the stairway. For a moment I had forgotten, but then I realized we were still in Mr. Macelton's house. But he wasn't supposed to be home for hours. How long was I in that book?

"We have to get out of here," I said quietly.

"How?" Triston spoke slowly. His eyes darted around the room like he was searching for answers in the walls. I wondered what had happened in the last ten seconds to disorient him so much, but we didn't have time to delve into that.

"There's a window at the end of the hall," I remembered. "If we're fast enough, we can make it to the window, climb down the drainpipe, and jump to the next level. Do you think you can manage the jump? I know you're afraid of—"

"Everything, Kalib! I'm afraid of everything." Triston smiled. He still looked flustered, but at least his sense of humor was intact. "C'mon, let's get out of here."

Triston pushed past me, pressing his ear against the door. He slowly turned the knob, opened the door slightly and poked his head out. "The coast is clear. On the count of three, let's make a run for it."

I nodded in agreement. Locking eyes, we mouthed, "One...two..."

On three, we pushed the door wide open and sprinted toward the window at the end of the hallway. Somehow, the hall seemed longer than it was before. The creepy portraits glared at us as we passed.

As soon as we got to the window, Triston lifted the latch,

attempting to pull it open.

"It's stuck!"

This can't be happening.

"Let me try." I edged around Triston and pulled at the window. It didn't budge.

"I told you," Triston said.

"Help me then!" I gripped the ledge so tight my knuckles turned white. Triston slid his fingers next to mine.

"C'mon!" he cursed.

With our combined strength, we inched the window up until the gap was wide enough for each of us to slide through. We climbed onto the roof and shimmied down the drainpipe. Once we were on the roof of the porch, we jumped down and jetted into the woods across the street.

Triston made it to the cover of the trees first. I don't know why I did it, but I looked back and saw Macelton in the window … just standing there. He stared at me expressionlessly. His eyes locked with mine, and I stood paralyzed, trapped by his gaze. His lips curled into a half-smile before he nodded and turned away.

"Kalib, what are you doing?" Triston called. "Come on!"

I glanced back up at the house to see the window was now empty before I followed Triston into the woods.

* * *

I don't know how long we ran. We were deep into the woods before we collapsed, panting on the ground. I couldn't explain what happened. I had no idea where to even begin.

"I … I think we're in the clear," I managed between gasps. "I don't think we were followed."

"Do you think anyone saw us?" Triston's chest heaved as he gulped in air. His hair and freckles matched the autumn leaves that littered the forest floor. I cast a glance over my shoulder. Macelton had seen us. I wondered how long it would be until he called the cops and sent us both to jail?

I opted to stay silent. Triston had already forgotten the question. Ever since that mirror, he seemed distracted. I mean, yeah, he did what he had to do to get out of Macelton's house, but now he had the same look of bewilderment he had when we were back in the room.

"Hey." I nudged him with the back of my hand, "What happened back there?"

"I … I don't know," Triston said, knitting his eyebrows together and searching the sky for answers. "Kalib—I saw my mom."

I pulled myself to my elbows so that I could see him better. He couldn't have seen what he thought he saw. That would have been impossible. Ceanna McLain had been dead for years. Then again, so many *"impossible"* things had happened in the past few days, I wasn't sure where to set the barometer.

"In the mirror," he explained. "In Macelton's house. She was in that mirror, and she—she talked to me."

"Triston your mom's been—"

"I know she's dead." He sat up so that we were at eye level. "Don't you think I know that? But it was her. It doesn't make sense to me either."

Triston reached up and used a low-hanging branch to pull himself to his feet. "You think I'm crazy, don't you?" He silently kicked a tree root.

"No." I snorted, barely stifling an outright laugh. "I believe you."

"You do?"

"Yeah, I do." I smirked. *If only he knew.* I stood and rubbed some dirt off my sleeve. "C'mon, let's get out of here," I said, taking several confident steps through the trees before realizing that I had no idea where we were. The woods outside of Hainesville were a dangerous place, especially if you didn't know where you were going. One wrong turn and you could end up all the way in Jacksonville, Florida. I shuddered, pulling out my phone and looking at the GPS. *No service. Dang it!*

I looked up at the night sky and spotted The Big Dipper, then followed it to The North Star. Using every last bit of my Boy Scout knowledge, I made a guess at north and chose a direction to head out in. I ducked under the low-hanging Spanish moss and started through the woods.

Triston was silent as we walked. I knew that he was trying to take it all in. I had my own share of odd events to make sense of, but I wasn't ready to talk about it. Everything about that house was so strange and yet … familiar.

"What was it like?" The land sloped, and I held on to a branch to steady myself before letting go and surfing on the dead leaves to the bottom of the hill. "Seeing your mom? Was she different?"

Triston followed shortly. A cloud of dust billowed behind him as he skidded to the bottom of the hill.

"No." He clumsily brushed the dirt off of himself. "She looked exactly the same. Just like I remember her."

"Was she, like, a ghost?"

"I don't think so." Triston picked up a twig from the ground and pushed past me. "She didn't seem like a ghost. It was different than that. It was more like a memory—not the house, but the moment. Like I'd lived it before. Seen it before."

I knew what he was talking about. I felt the same about the book. I didn't have a clue what language it was written in, but I recognized and understood it.

"She said, 'everything I did was for the two of you,'" Triston said after a moment of silence. "I don't know what that means. Me and who? My dad? What did she do besides ..."

Triston's words trailed off; he didn't like thinking about the night she died. Triston was the one who found her. Everyone said it was an accident, but he knew it wasn't. He swore at the time that he saw someone else in the room with her. The problem was there was no way out; there was no way someone could have escaped without being caught.

I nodded sympathetically, not wanting to push him further.

A giant shadow passed over us in the moonlight. I darted my eyes to the sky, half expecting to see a dragon by the size of the shadow. But it was just hunter flying back and forth over the trees looking for food. The size of its reflection must have been magnified by the moonlight.

"What's with the book?" Triston asked, pointing at the leather-bound book I was still carrying.

"I guess I forgot I was holding it when we ran."

"You stole something else from Macelton?"

"Not on purpose!" I retorted defensively. "There wasn't much time to put it back. We heard him coming, so I just held on to it and ran."

Triston wiped a bit of dirt off his face with his shirt. "Do you think he'll notice it's gone?"

I thought about the smug look on Macelton's face when he saw me from the window. "Oh, I'm pretty sure he'll notice."

"What are you going to do with it?"

"I don't know," I admitted. "It's not like we can give it back."

"Then we keep it." Triston reached for the book. "Can I see it? Maybe we can learn something from it."

"Good luck." I handed him the book. "It's not written in English."

He flipped through the thin pages, using a small flashlight he kept on his keychain for emergencies. Occasionally he stopped to study the weird characters of the language. "What language is this anyway?"

"I don't have a clue," I admitted.

"They look ancient." Triston flipped further into the book. "This entire book looks ancient. Hey!" he said suddenly. "These symbols look similar to the ones engraved on your necklace and the ring. Maybe they're the same. Let me see the ring. We might be able to use it to decipher whatever is written here in the book."

"Okay," I said, reaching into my pocket for the ring. "Though, I don't know how one could decipher the other. If they're written in the same language, the only thing we have are two objects we can't read."

Triston flipped through the book again, selecting a page at random to decipher. The page had a drawing of a bird carrying a ribbon in its beak, hand-sketched on the top right corner of the page. He held the ring beside the hieroglyphs for comparison. The symbols were similar. Almost identical, but it was clear that each symbol meant something different. I didn't know how to begin to decipher it.

"Hey, there's something written here below the symbols," Triston whispered excitedly, attempting to pronounce the words on the page.

"Cuir plàigh an fho-thalamh gu dochann Bidh bàs gun chumhachd

le fuil gealach fíor."

As soon as Triston began reading, I began to feel dizzy. "Triston," I tried to call, but the breath had been taken right out of me. No matter how much I gasped, air wouldn't fill my lungs. I was suffocating.

The ring in Triston's hand lit up. "Triston," I tried to say again. Then a burst of pain seared across my skin, as if I were being stamped with a branding iron. I looked down at my hands and saw letters writing themselves onto my body. In bold black ink, the words that Triston was speaking were engraving themselves onto me. Each word felt as if it were being burned in. The words traveled up my arms and began to wrap themselves around my neck. If Triston didn't stop reading, he was going to kill me.

But Triston was mesmerized by the book. Had he been paying attention, he would have noticed me writhing in pain. Had he looked up from the book, he might have seen the black rift that was forming in midair right in front of me. The rift grew to about five feet high and expanded to about three feet wide. There was nothing but blackness inside.

No, I was wrong. A talon-like hand stretched out from the void, and the familiar smell of rotten eggs and burned hamburger meat seeped from the darkness. Whispers filled my head, voices chanting the prophecy from the book I had heard earlier. The hand reached out toward me. If Triston didn't stop reading, it was going to pull me in.

Soon, young Angel Warrior, a voice said in my head. *Soon the blood will be paid, and you'll be mine!*

It took all the strength inside of me to scream Triston's name. "TRISTON!"

Finally, Triston looked up from the book, and everything stopped. The rift began to close, and the bony hand was sucked back into it. Oxygen rushed back into my lungs, and I collapsed.

"Whoa! What was that?" Triston said after the rift and the hand disappeared completely.

"I—" I began, still gasping for air. "I don't know. Just stop reading that book, okay?"

I looked down at my arms and hands. The writing was gone. What was that? Some kind of spell? I looked at the leather tome still in Triston's hands. I didn't know what it was, but I was convinced, now more than ever, that the book was evil.

"We better get out of here."

9

The Sisyphean Blues

I must have studied the book and the ring a thousand times before the next day rolled around. Nothing extraordinary happened—no visions, no weird rifts, or mysterious writing. I didn't tell Triston about the whispering voices in my head. I didn't know how to explain it.

"Do you think it was a curse?" Triston asked, sliding into the lunch table next to me. "I'm just saying, nothing happened until I started reading that book. Maybe it's some kind of magic book of spells. What did it say again when you read it the first time? You saw it in English, right?"

"Seek, and you will find. Find, and you will seek," I recited. "It seems kinda obvious, doesn't it?"

"It sounds cyclical," Triston agreed. "Like the Sisyphean Curse."

I scrunched my eyebrows together. "The what?"

"The Sisyphean Curse," Triston repeated like I was going to suddenly understand what that meant. "Sisyphus? The King of Ephyra?"

I stared blankly at Triston. He rolled his eyes, miffed that

I didn't know this particular piece of mythology. "Sisyphus was a self-promoting trickster who was punished by Zeus. He had to push a rock up a hill, but Zeus enchanted the rock to roll back down the hill every time he got near the top, thus consigning Sisyphus to an eternity of useless efforts and unending frustration."

"So, you're saying that maybe the phrase in the book is like the Sisyphean Curse?" I asked. "Doomed to keep looking for something but never to find it?"

He nodded. "Basically."

"Keep looking for what?"

"Who knows?" He shrugged. "Could be anything. Maybe it's answers. Maybe it's something else. Maybe the thing you're supposed to be looking for has been right in front of you the whole time."

"Maybe it's me?" I offered.

"What?"

"Something happened when you were reading that spell," I explained.

"I know. That rift opened, and a creepy hand tried to pull you into the underworld—or wherever."

"Not just that! Something else. I heard these voices. They were all saying the same thing, '*Though death, magic, and fire rehashed, the blood of the Angel Warrior will be paid at last.*' And then I heard another voice. Even crazier, I think it was the hand from the rift. It said, '*Soon, young Angel Warrior. Soon, the blood will be paid, and you'll be mine.*' Then the rift went away, and it all stopped."

Triston stared at me for a moment. I could see him trying to decide which of the hundreds of questions—that were undoubtedly bouncing around his head—he was going to lead with.

"How come *I* didn't hear these voices?" he asked.

"Because they were in *my* head," I explained, "and it wasn't the first time I've heard them either. When I first met Macelton, something similar happened. I think these objects react to each other somehow. The ring, the necklace, the spellbook … they're somehow connected. I just don't know how. When I first met Macelton, he must've had the ring with him, and the ring and the necklace reacted to each other. That's why I heard the voice back then. And then later when I was on the street, I had the ring, and Damien was walking down the street with my necklace. And then yesterday, it was the ring and the book. They all must be connected somehow."

"But what does it mean?"

"I don't know," I huffed, dropping my head to the table. "When I went into that house, I thought I was going to get answers, but now all I have are more questions."

"Hmm." Triston put both of his elbows on the table, resting his chin on his palms. "Seek, and you will find. Find, and you will seek. Huh, we're Sisyphus."

"Yeah," I said, "I guess we are." I shook the thought out of my head, shouldered my book bag, and pulled myself out of the lunch table. "I've gotta go run an errand for Mr. Jones before work. He wants me to pick up something from MegaBite."

"The comic book store?" Triston laughed. "What does Mr. Jones want with a comic book?"

"Beats me." I shrugged. "They're not just a comic book store. They sell video games and computer hardware too. Maybe RavenTech is outsourcing. I don't ask questions. I just follow directions. Anyway, I should get going. I'll text you when I get off."

Triston and I fist-bumped, and I left.

Megabite Video Game and Computer Haven was only two blocks away from the school. Although I had never been there on official work business, I was no stranger to the store. Triston and I had spent every day there that summer, buying video games, comic books, and cheat code magazines.

The bell on the door rattled as I entered the store. Jason Tahm, the green haired cashier whose face was buried inside a comic book, looked up and flashed a toothy grin.

"Hey, what's up, demonboy?" Both Jason and his brother Brandon, who I went to school with, knew me by my gamer tag, Demonboy6871. I was going through a bad boy phase back in middle school and thought it would make me cooler. I know … embarrassing right? Jason helped me set it up. "Heard about the new Zombietack 5 release, didn't ya? Only got one left in stock."

"Oh, I forgot about that," I said. "Unfortunately, I'm here on business."

Jason raised an eyebrow. "Business? Here? For the diner?"

"Oh. Uh, no," I stammered. "Donald and Susan made me take an internship at RavenTech as a punishment for breaking into a teacher's classroom."

"So, let me get this straight," Jason said. "You get in trouble, and now you *get* to work at the most prestigious company in town … as a punishment?"

"Yeah, pretty much," I replied, shoving my hands into my pockets, and fiddling with the ring, like I always did whenever I felt nervous or exposed.

"Man. Must be nice to be you, demonboy." Jason shook his head, and his green hair fell a little further over his eyes. "What I wouldn't give to get a job at RavenTech, instead of working in the family shop."

"Anyway," I continued, trying desperately to change the subject. "Mr. Jones said you had a pickup for him."

"Oh yeah, his ticket is around here somewhere." Jason stepped back and scanned the shelves behind the counter, "Ah, there it is." He reached down and pulled out a square metal box. "This came in from China last week. Unfortunately, it's no good. Tell Mr. Jones I couldn't start the hard drive."

"Oh, that's a bummer. Mr. Jones isn't going to be happy about that."

"No, I guess not," Jason said, extending his hand to give me the hard drive. "He could always try Sue Zucki's shop down the street. She might have a better handle on this kind of stuff."

I reached to take the hard drive from Jason, but when my hand grazed his, it was no longer Jason standing in front of me, at least not the Jason I recognized. Jason's skin was black, his mouth was full of razor-sharp teeth, and his eyes were beady and red. His green hair stood straight up. Behind him were a pair of large, leathery bat-like wings. I stumbled backwards, nearly toppling over.

"You alright, bro?" I looked up again, and the monster wasn't there. It was regular old Jason, the same as he had always been. His long green hair still falling over his eyes.

What the—

"Everything, alright?" he asked, concern painted on his face.

"Yeah. I-I'm fine," I stammered, "I should … I have to go." I rushed out of the store without looking back. What was going on in this town? Did I just see what I thought I saw? All around me, people were headed in and out of stores, going on with their busy lives. I looked back at the glass storefront. If I really had seen what I thought I saw, someone else would have seen it through the window. I took a deep breath. I was definitely going crazy.

Between the hot Georgia sun, and my panicking the whole walk to work, my armpits looked like I had poured two glasses of water on them. When I finally arrived at work, I was still all jitters. All I wanted was to get to the bathroom, throw some water on my face, and wash up. Unfortunately, I wouldn't get the opportunity. When I opened the lobby door, I practically collided with Caliyah, who was walking the opposite way.

"Oh, sorry," I murmured. "Sorry, I didn't see you."

"It's alright," Caliyah giggled. "How could you have? Unless you have x-ray vision."

"That's funny." I forced a laugh, Caliyah was the last person I wanted to see me like this. I wanted to run away and hide in a shower or a deserted cave a hundred miles away. "Well, I've gotta get to—"

"Are you alright?" she asked. "You don't seem yourself."

"No. I mean, yeah! I-I'm good."

"Are you sure?" The way she looked at me was like she could see right through me. My stomach tied itself into a knot and jumped right into my throat. "Because you don't seem good. Did I do something to upset you?"

"No! No! Not at all!" I said, probably a little too passionately. "No, no, no, no. I just … it was a long walk here. And, uh, this is embarrassing. I feel kinda sweaty, and maybe a little stinky, so I just wanted to rush to the bathroom and clean up a bit."

"Oh Kalib, you don't have to worry about that." Caliyah giggled, brushing one of her tight curls behind her ear. "You look fine to me. Just as handsome as you always do."

"Oh. Well, thank you." She called me handsome. A week ago, I didn't even think she knew I existed outside of the few moments we spent together at our lockers, and now I'm working with her, and ... was she flirting with me?

"Hey, I was wondering ... are you going to the homecoming game tomorrow night?"

She was definitely flirting with me.

"I, uh, I-I mean, I was supposed to work."

"Don't be silly." She flashed her white teeth, which, and I may have been imagining this, literally sparkled when she smiled. "Daddy'll give you the time off."

Then she did something that I never would have dreamed of in a million years. She took my hand and wrote her number on my palm. "Well, if you decide to go, text me and tell me where you're sitting. I'll look for you." She kissed me on the cheek and walked away.

Just like that.

And, *just like that*, I was rendered useless. My feet wouldn't move, and after jumping back down my throat, my stomach turned to stone and sat at the base of my gut. What just happened? The monster attacks were weird enough, but had I been pulled into an alternate dimension where I was a ladies man?

I practically floated to Mr. Jones's office on the fifteenth floor. If it hadn't been for the ceiling, I might not have even needed the elevator. I had forgotten about everything I had seen at MegaBite, winged Hell beast and all. Caliyah Jones kissed me! Sure, it was on the cheek, but still, her lips were on my skin. Mine. This was the best day of my life!

My bliss was short-lived when I remembered that I had to give the hard drive to Mr. Jones, who was intimidating even when you hadn't just kissed his daughter. Fortunately, when I made it to his office, he was occupied with a client, who seemed less than satisfied. They must have been a pretty high-profile customer because when I arrived at his office, two large gentlemen in black suits and ties stood on either side of the door—personal security, I assumed. I sat in one of the plush, velvet chairs outside of Mr. Jones's office to wait.

I couldn't help but listen a bit, and I thought I caught the tail end of an argument because I heard a woman shout, "Time is running out, Patrick." Her voice was cold and stern. "You've got three days to make the payment, or else the deal is off."

I felt it again. Goosebumps rose on my skin. And the hair on the back of my neck stood on end. The door swung open, and a blonde-haired woman in a fur coat stormed out. Without speaking or awaiting instruction, the two security guards followed her, flanking either side. A chill ran down my spine as she passed. She was a beautiful woman who radiated power and authority. I slid my hands into my pockets. My nervous habit. For a moment, I actually felt sorry for *Mr. Jones*, the most powerful man in town. I knew in an instant that her bad side was a dangerous side to be on.

"Oh, Kalib, you're here," Mr. Jones said, peeking his head out of his office, a hint of aggravation still on his voice. "Come on in and take a seat."

I did as Mr. Jones instructed, sitting in the seat across from his desk. "I apologize for that. That is one of RavenTech's biggest clients, and she's unimpressed with the speed in which her order is being processed. Nothing to be concerned about. Did you run that errand for me?"

"I did, sir." I hesitated. The last thing I wanted to do was give him more bad news after he had just gone toe-to-toe with *that* woman. "Unfortunately, Jason says the hard drive is shot."

Mr. Jones let out a deep breath. "I was afraid of that."

"I'm sorry."

"Not to worry," he said with a smile, "Do you have it with you?"

"Yes sir." I reached for my bag clumsily, accidentally picking it up from the wrong side and spilling all of its contents. "Oops. Sorry," I mumbled, scrambling to retrieve the drive from among my schoolbooks. I picked up the hard drive and slid it across Mr. Jones's desk. "I hope I didn't damage it more than it already was."

"Nonsense." Mr. Jones smiled. "These things are durable; a little bump won't hurt it."

I hurriedly gathered the remainder of my books, and the leather-bound book was among the textbooks being shoved into my bookbag.

"That's a fancy-looking book," Mr. Jones noted. "What is it?"

"Oh, that's just a book I got from a friend," I lied. "Unfortunately, it's in a different language. You wouldn't happen to know any other languages, would you?"

"No. Unfortunately, I don't." Mr. Jones picked up the hard drive, looked at it for a moment, and then stuffed it into the top drawer of his desk. "By the way, how did your friend's '*issue*' work itself out?" he asked, folding his hands on the desk. "The one you were concerned about the other day. Did everything work itself out?"

"Oh, no," I said with a defeated chuckle. I felt so foolish thinking I would be able to outsmart Macelton. "It didn't. My friend thought he would get more answers, but now he just has more questions."

"I'm sorry to hear that, Kalib." Mr. Jones leaned forward over the desk. "You know, sometimes when things don't go as planned, you just have to keep trying. Often, when things get in the way, they aren't really roadblocks, but obstacles. You just have to find your way around them."

"You're right." I nodded. "Thanks, Mr. Jones."

I may not have found the answers that I was looking for, but I did find that strange book. All I needed to do was figure out what it was and why Macelton had it. I shook Mr. Jones's hand and started for the door.

"Hey, Kalib?" he called. "Caliyah tells me your birthday is this weekend. Is that right?"

How did she know that? I smiled, *I guess she's been paying attention longer than I thought.*

"Yes sir," I answered. "It's in three days."

"Why don't you take the whole weekend off, starting tomorrow. You can go to that football game my daughter just asked you to," he said with a wink. My cheeks flushed red and hot. Approval from the CEO of RavenTech to go on a date with his daughter? Now I *knew* I was dreaming or in an alternate dimension or something!

"Are you sure, sir?" I asked. "I could still come in and—"

"Happy birthday, Kalib." He picked up a glass of water from his desk and swirled the liquid around inside of it. "Enjoy it while you can. You only get so many birthdays before … well, before they just don't mean anything anymore."

"Thank you, sir." I tilted my head appreciatively before turning for the door.

10

I Met A Kitty From Hell

I rushed home after work that day. My world had been turned upside down. Up until a few days ago, I was just a normal kid, working at the Georgia Peach, and the only person who ever made any effort to spend time with me was Triston. Now, I was working at the town's largest company, Caliyah Jones asked me to sit next to her at the homecoming game, and her father, perhaps the most important person in town, was alright with it. What crazy bizarro world had I stepped into?

I closed the door behind me as I stepped into the house. I just wanted to go to sleep before anything could happen to wake me up from the dream that I was living in, but of course, that was too much to ask.

"Kalib? Is that you?" Susan popped her head out of the kitchen.

"Yeah, it's me," I said, leaning my head back against the door.

"Good. I'm making supper. Why don't you go upstairs and wash up?"

Dinner at the Donovan's was one of the few attempts Susan

made to keep normalcy in the household. With Donald always working, and Susan doing all of his heavy lifting, things got pretty busy. But at least once a week, Susan insisted we would eat dinner together.

Again, don't be fooled into thinking this was about family. Trust me; it wasn't. Susan read somewhere that politicians who had a healthy home life with a loving family were ten percent more likable in the polls. So, Susan resolved that if we at least appeared to be a happy, loving family, it would raise Donald's chances of being elected to Congress.

Upstairs, I splashed water on my face, changed my shirt, and came back to the dining room for dinner. The three of us picked at our food in silence. As was customary in the Donovan household, we didn't speak while eating. We weren't much of a talking family unless we had company, in which case, Susan would give Donald and me notecards with talking points and forbidden topics.

There was a buzzing like a thousand bumblebees in my head. So much had happened in the last few days, and my brain just didn't know how to process it. The visions at Macelton's house, the book, the hand, the voice. It all seemed too crazy to be real, but still, a part of me wondered if there was more to the world than I knew. I suppose, a part of me had always wondered. I guess that's why I put up with Triston's crazy conspiracy theories. Deep down inside, a part of me wanted his conspiracies to be true.

When we were kids, Triston would make up these crazy fantasies about our parents. We would pretend that they were pirates, or superheroes, or ancient gods. Back then, I wanted it to be true. I wanted to believe that they were out there somewhere, that they were coming back. But they never did.

And all I had left of them was my necklace and a tattered, old picture of the man who dropped me off at the orphanage. I had looked him up once I'd learned his name. I didn't find much, just my adoption information and that old picture. Mrs. McLain, Triston's mom, used to call him my guardian angel. Sometimes I wondered if—

"Are you alright, Kalib?" Susan asked, interrupting my thoughts. "You've hardly touched your food. That salad isn't going to eat itself." I had just been poking at the same piece of lettuce on my plate for the last ten minutes.

I finally brought a salad filled fork to my mouth but stopped short. "Do you think angels are real? Like, could they be living here on earth, just blending in with everyone else?"

Susan and Donald shared a meaningful look. For a moment, they looked surprised, worried even. But a moment later, they both let out a chuckle.

"Where does he come up with this stuff?" Donald laughed.

"Don't be ridiculous, Kalib." She stabbed a piece of lettuce with her fork and moved it around her plate to get more dressing on it. "Perhaps you've been spending too much time with Triston. Angels don't exist."

Donald and Susan shared another humored look and returned to their plates. That was the end of that conversation.

* * *

That night my dreams were wild. At first, I was back on the hill by the ocean, and an army of horned helmets raced toward me from the valley below. I ran toward the water, but I was too late. A spear cut through the air and embedded itself into my abdomen.

Next, it was present day. People walked aimlessly through the streets of Hainesville with blank expressions on their faces.

I noticed a crack in the ground that was growing wider every second, and translucent spirits seeped into our world from the crack. The fissure grew, devouring everything in its path. The people were walking straight into the crack, and I tried to stop them, but I couldn't. It was like they were being pulled to it. I began to run toward the growing gap. There was something there, though I couldn't tell what it was—a box maybe—teetering on the edge of the widening crack. I had to get to it before it fell in, but I was too late. The box fell and disappeared into the abyss.

Suddenly, I was in a—was it a desert wasteland? No, there was a destroyed city all around me: the ruins of Hainesville. A monster rampaged in the distance, devouring the earth until there was no life left. Everything was destroyed.

"Yeah, priv," a voice said beside me. It was Damien Daslic, sitting with his feet kicked up on my bed. "I see it too. Open your eyes."

Beep, beep, beep, beep.

I woke to the persistent beeping of my alarm clock and sat up in bed. No Damien. I looked around my room. There were no demons, no death or destruction, just an ordinary room. I rubbed my hands over my face. I had to get a handle on this.

I rolled out of bed and dragged myself to the bathroom for a shower. I didn't feel like I had slept at all. In fact, I think I felt more tired than I did when I had gone to sleep. I forced myself through the steps of my normal morning routine and headed to school. Despite the crazy dreams, nothing out of the ordinary happened that day. It was a normal day, with normal teenaged problems.

"And you didn't ask her to the dance?" Triston asked incredulously after I'd told him about Caliyah.

I shrugged. "I didn't think she wanted me to."

"She obviously wanted you to!" he said, smacking his forehead in disbelief. "Who asks someone to the homecoming *game*? She was opening a window."

"Well then, why didn't she just say that?"

"Because she wanted you to ask! Do I have to teach you everything?"

"Okay!" I conceded, putting both hands in the air, half expecting Triston to hit me. "I'll ask. I'll talk to her at the game tonight." Triston seemed satisfied with that. Though, I detected a hint of jealousy.

That night, the school stadium was packed. Everyone in town came to the game. Football was probably the only thing the entire city agreed on. Even Damien came to the game, which was kind of a surprise considering Damien had never shown any interest in participating in school events before or any social gathering for that matter.

I arrived a bit earlier than I might have otherwise. I sent Caliyah a text, telling her where I was sitting. She was running a bit late but asked me to save her a seat. Triston sat on the other side of me, because what's a date without your best friend, right? He insisted that he wouldn't bother me *if* Caliyah actually showed up. I know, so supportive.

I caught a glimpse of Damien Daslic pointedly staring at me several feet away in the crowd. What did he want? When he got my attention, he mouthed something. I couldn't be sure, but I thought he said, *"open your eyes."* Just like from my dream. I blinked. I was probably being paranoid, but when I looked back at Damien, his eyes were still on me. He slowly turned his head toward the school, nodding for me to do the same. My eyes followed his, until I saw a cloaked figure walking away from the crowd and into the school.

That's when I remembered the box from my dream. The one that fell through the crack before I could get to it. I realized it wasn't a box at all. It was a book. The same book that I had stolen from Macelton. The book that I kept in my bookbag, which was currently locked away in my locker. Inside the school. Where that cloaked figure was now headed.

"It's after the book," I said audibly, startling Triston.

"What?"

"I'll be right back," I said. "If Caliyah shows up, give her my seat."

"Where are you going?" I heard him shout as I ran into the school. I didn't know the significance of the book, but if Damien had gone through all that trouble to warn me about it, I knew it had to be important. I had to get it before someone, or something else did.

I tore open the double doors of the school and sprinted down the hallway, half expecting to turn a corner and find an army wearing horned helmets, but when I got to my locker, the hall was empty. *Yup, definitely paranoid,* I thought, hands on my hips, catching my breath. *I'm losing my mind.* A cheer came from the crowded stadium outside. *The game must be starting. I gotta get back out there.* I decided to be safe and take the book with me. I didn't know why, but I felt like I needed to keep it close. I put in the combination of my locker and reached in to grab the book.

Out of the corner of my eye, I saw something move in the shadows, but when I looked closer, nothing was there. *That dream and Damien must have really gotten inside my head.* I turned back to the locker and grabbed the book, stuffing it securely into the waistband of my pants. As I started to shut the locker, I heard a low growl. I turned quickly, looking in both directions, but all I saw were the rows of lockers stretching down the hall and disappearing into the darkness.

Then I saw it, two glowing eyes staring at me from the end of the hall. They weren't like Macelton's eyes which reflected light; these eyes were producing it. I saw the silhouette of a broad-shouldered beast standing between me and the exit at the other end of the hall. I could hear the tapping of claws on the concrete floors as the beast stalked me, pacing back and forth in the hallway.

With an explosion of speed, the creature barreled down the hall, scraping against the lockers as it sprinted. I took off running in the opposite direction, but the creature was too fast. I could feel its warm breath on my neck as it dug its claws into the lockers and the ceiling. Gravity meant nothing to this beast. I dodged into a nearby science lab just as the beast was about to sink its claws into me, but the creature followed me through the door. Test tubes and beakers clattered to the ground as the monster bounded onto a nearby lab table. I looked around for something to distract the monster. I picked up a glass measuring cup and threw it at the monster. It swatted the glass cup with its huge paw, sending it flying toward the wall. I ducked out through the door on the opposite end of the room and back into the hallway, closing the door behind me. Seconds later, the monster burst through the door, tearing it off its hinges and smashing into the lockers on the other side of the hall, leaving a ginormous dent. Before I knew it, the monster leaped onto the ceiling and clawed its way over my head, landing directly in front of me and blocking my path outside.

I stopped just short of the razor-sharp claws that slashed the air mere inches away from my face. The creature growled and went back to pacing in front of me. Only then did I get a good look at it: a giant cat that looked like it had come straight from Hell. Its black fur was matted and stretched over unnatural flesh and bones. Its insides could be seen through its bare ribcage. Its right paw and spine were lined with green scales, while the other paw remained mangled with fur and flesh. Its claws were pure bone sharpened to deadly points. And its tail, which swayed back and forth behind it, tapered from flesh into a singular boney spike. It lowered its ruined face, and its right eye looked as if it had been slashed by its own claws. I could see now that its eyes weren't glowing at all. The demon cat's pupils flickered with actual flames.

"Nice, kitty," I whispered, "Nice, kitty-kitty-kitty."

For a second, I thought my non-threatening tone was actually calming the demon cat. It purred as it continued to pace, but then it bared its long, sharp fangs and lunged at me, teeth and claws extended. I stumbled backwards and fell flat on my back. I knew I was a goner; there was no way I was getting out of this. But before the demon cat landed, a person with a fire-engulfed sword jumped over me and slashed at the monster. The cat exploded into smoke and disappeared.

11

Silly Rabbit, Cults Are For Psychopathic Killers!

amien Daslic stood over me, both hands still gripping the hilt of the smoking blade he had just buried into the demon cat. When he was sure the monster was gone, he straightened up and lowered the sword.

"What can I say?" He smirked. "The bullies at this school can be pretty hellish."

"What the—" I scrambled to my feet. "What was that?"

Damien wiped the back of his hand across his forehead. "A hellcat," he said matter-of-factly. "Someone must have sent it after you."

"What? Wait ...what? Someone *sent* that thing after me?" I looked around as if the perpetrator might be there in the hallway. "Why would anyone send that thing after *me*? Who would do that?"

"Probably your buddies at RavenTech."

"RavenTech? What do they have to do with any of this?" I brought both hands to my head, messaging my temples. "I'm so confused. What's going on here?"

"Not enough time to explain," Damien said shortly, glancing over his shoulder. "We've gotta get out here. Macelton will want to talk to you. Come on."

"Wait, wait, wait. I'm not going anywhere until you tell me what's happening."

"That's a bad idea, priv," Damien said, wiping the blade of his sword with a cloth and shoving it into a bookbag that seemed entirely too small to hold a sword. "You're going to want to get out of here."

"Wait, how did you—" I shook my head. I was going crazy for sure. "Why would I do anything you say?"

"Because—" At that moment, the wall where the science lab had just been exploded into the hallway, and smoke began to billow out of the now-demolished science lab "—that," Damien finished.

"Holy cow!" I gasped.

"What do you get when you unleash a hellcat in a room full of flammable chemicals?" Damien held both hands in front of him and expanded all ten of his fingers. "Kaboom."

I could already hear the footsteps of people coming to investigate the explosion. If I was found there, they would assume it was me who had blown up the science lab. I had to get out of there. Damien was already one step ahead of me. He raised an eyebrow with a look of *are you coming or not?* The two of us ran out of the building until we were a safe distance from the school. I bent over on my knees, struggling to catch my breath.

Damien laughed. "What a way to make an exit."

"I have to go," I said, starting down the street. I needed to clear my head.

"Wait!" Damien grabbed my arm. "You need to come with

me. All of this will make sense when you talk to Macelton."

"I don't want to go anywhere with you." I pulled my arm away from Damien.

"Okay, okay," Damien said, putting his hands up in surrender, "Look, priv, I'm not going to make you do anything. No matter how much joy it would bring me to twist your puny little arm and drag you down to Macelton myself, you gotta figure things out on your own. Just give me the book, okay? That's what they're after."

"What book?"

"Don't play dumb," Damien sighed. "You stole the book from Macelton's house. You know it; I know it. Just hand it over before they come for it again."

I stared at Damien for a moment. I didn't know if I could trust him. Why would I give him the book? Then again, he *had* just saved my life, although he was the reason I'd gone into the school in the first place. *Why was this book so important anyway?* I thought, reaching for it in my waistband. It wasn't there. I patted myself as if patting would bring the book back, but I definitely didn't have it anymore.

"Are you gonna give it to me or not?" Damien asked in a tone that told me he was prepared to fight for it.

"I don't have it."

"What do you mean you don't have it?"

"I mean, I don't have it. It must have fallen out when I was running."

"... Or the hellcat got it." Damien paced back and forth. "This is bad, priv. Macelton isn't going to be happy about this."

"Wait, you killed the hellcat, didn't you?" I asked. "So then it couldn't have gotten it."

"No. I *vanquished* the hellcat," Damien replied irritably.

"There's a difference. All I did was send it back to wherever it came from. So, if it had the book, I just sent it express to its master. Look, just come with me, and we'll figure all of this out with Macelton."

Damien reached for my arm again, but I pulled away. "I'm not going with you. I don't know what any of this means. None of this makes any sense. Just leave me alone!"

I ran away, half expecting Damien to chase me down, but he didn't move. He stood in the street and watched me until I disappeared from his sight.

* * *

My head was spinning. The more normal I tried to be, the crazier things became. Damien and Macelton were going to kill me. I heard them say it that night in the woods. *Kalib's blood will be spilled.* But if they were trying to kill me, why did Damien save me? Why not just let the hellcat tear me to shreds? Damien said that someone must have sent the hellcat for me. But why? And who? Was all of this really just for the book, or was there something bigger going on?

A squawk came from the sky above me, and I glanced up to see Hunter circling overhead. It wasn't uncommon for me to see Hunter off in the distance. I could normally catch sight of him from my bedroom window, gliding over the trees, searching for food. But every once in a while, he showed up right when I needed him. He settled on a lamppost halfway down the street.

What do you think, Hunter? Should I leave it all alone, or should I figure out what's going on? I didn't expect Hunter to answer or anything, but knowing he was there comforted me in a way I couldn't explain. Damien said that my friends at RavenTech probably sent the hellcat. That made zero sense to me. Mr. Jones had never been anything but kind. He gave me a job. He gave me the night off to celebrate my birthday. Besides, I heard Damien and Macelton say they were going to kill me that night in the woods. How could I be sure he wasn't just trying to distract me, by making me suspicious of RavenTech?

I pushed out an exasperated breath, banging my head on the lamppost. *Ow.* Okay, that actually hurt. Hunter leaped off the lamp and soared over the trees into the distance. That's when I noticed the RavenTech building. I had never noticed before, but from where I was standing, I could *just* see the building peeking over the trees. Had I been standing anywhere else, I wouldn't have noticed that the lights were on, which was strange, because it was after hours. But I could clearly see there was something going on inside the building.

I shook the thought out of my head. Damien was probably trying to distract me by making me suspicious of RavenTech. I started back toward the school. I needed to find Triston. He'd be worried about me after the explosion, but something made me stop. What if Damien was telling the truth?

Ugh. I groaned, turning around and forcing myself down the street that led to the RavenTech building. If they were up to something, I needed to know for sure. As I passed the long driveway, I could see a couple dozens of cars in the RavenTech parking lot. There was definitely something going on. I ducked into the trees to get a closer look. Several men and women were still arriving. There was someone at the door, greeting each person as they entered. They were saying something, but I couldn't quite make it out. It was some kind of chant or something. I stepped a little closer so I could hear. A man and a woman wearing gray suits approached the door.

The man guarding the door extended his hand, clasped the other man's forearm, and said, "Peace to the Order."

The second man clasped the first man's forearm in return and answered, "As She wills it." They tilted their heads simultaneously, then the man guarding the door stepped aside, allowing the couple to enter the building. This routine repeated as a few more arrivals entered. There was no way this was official RavenTech business.

I needed to get inside. If it *was* RavenTech that sent that hellcat after me, like Damien suggested, I needed to find out why. But I knew I'd never make it through the front door, not without being seen. I had to find another way inside.

I scurried back into the trees. There was a fire escape on the east side of the building, and if I was lucky—and I rarely was—I might be able to find an open door or window. I scanned the wall as I made for the metal stairs. Score! A window *had* been left open on the fourth floor. I hurried up the fire escape and lifted the window.

I stepped into what looked like a robotics lab. I maneuvered past a pair of robotic arms that looked like they could rip through steel. *I thought they only did schematics and design here* ... I peeked out into the hall to see if the coast was clear. RavenTech had fifteen floors of laboratories and testing rooms, half of which I'd never even seen. At the center of the building was a giant warehouse where most of the action took place.

When I was sure no one was around, I crawled to the railing and looked over to the ground floor. Instead of the separate workstations I was used to, all of the desks had been replaced by rows of chairs, all facing a platform at the end of the room. Dozens of people filed in and took their seats. I recognized several of them: Mr. and Mrs. Stevens, who frequented the diner; Ted Greenby and Paul Newman, who owned the floral shop in town together; and Julie and Thomas Withers, whose daughter I went to school with. Everyone in the room wore the same gray suit.

Mr. Jones stepped to a podium on the platform, and the crowd silenced.

"Peace to the Order," he said, and the entire crowd responded, "As She wills it."

I shuddered. Large groups speaking in unison gave me the willies.

"Brothers and Sisters of the Order," Mr. Jones began. "We have waited long for our time to come. We are tired of being pushed around by those that call themselves 'divine.'"

Divine? What's he talking about?

"Since the beginning, mankind has been caught in the middle of a war that isn't our own. The angels and demons have recklessly fought, leaving entire civilizations helpless in their wake. They have used us, abused us, enslaved and betrayed us, and told us lies of their divinity, calling themselves gods and forcing us to worship them."

I scanned the faces in the crowd. What was he talking about? Were people actually buying this? But every person on the ground floor was engaged in Mr. Jones's story. They nodded and agreed, muttering praises and affirmations as if he were reciting history.

"Finally, Brothers and Sisters. We have said no more!" Mr. Jones declared. "We refuse to be outmatched by their supernatural abilities. We will fight back. For centuries our weapons and technology have matched their abilities, but it is not enough. We need to fight fire with fire. We need a goddess on our side."

The crowd cheered. These were people that I knew, people that I've seen every day at the diner, at school, or simply walking down the street. Normal people. But what Mr. Jones was saying was crazy. This didn't sound like *normal* people talk. This sounded like a cult.

"Alatayi has always been on our side," Mr. Jones continued. "Since the beginning of time, she has vowed to protect Humankind. And her very own people imprisoned her for it. No more."

The crowd cheered again. "We say no more!" they chanted.

"We will raise our Goddess of Justice, and she will fight for us, restoring what is rightfully ours!" Mr. Jones spoke as if he were rallying the troops. "Earth for humans! For mankind!"

The crowd began to chant after him. "Earth for humans! For mankind! Earth for humans! For mankind! Earth for humans! For mankind!"

Mr. Jones held a hand up, and the crowd quieted. "We needed three items in order to raise our Goddess of Justice. The spell from the book with which her prison was created, the magic from the stone that sealed the gates, and now the blood of an Angel Warrior, to pay the price for her freedom."

For the first time that night, the crowd fell silent. They sat at the edges of their seats, anxiously awaiting whatever news he had to report. Mr. Jones stared at his people for an eternity. He loved the suspense building in the room. "The task is near completion," he finally said.

The people in the room stood and cheered. This was the moment they'd been waiting for. I wasn't sure what it all meant as Mr. Jones pulled out a small metal box. It was the broken hard drive I had picked up from Jason's shop. He held the hard drive in the air before smashing it on the ground. With a smile, he reached down and pulled something from the wreckage: a black and red arrow-shaped talisman. And at its center was a blue stone with ancient lettering engraved on it, just like the stone on my necklace and the stone on Macelton's ring. "We have retrieved a fragment of the stone."

The crowd cheered again, this time even louder than before. Mr. Jones extended another hand to hush the crowd. Next, he reached into the breast pocket of his suit jacket and pulled out a leather-bound book. I gasped. As soon as I laid eyes on the book, I knew that Damien had been right.

"Tonight, we claimed the Book of Ambrosius for ourselves."

The crowd cheered again. I was so angry. It *was* Mr. Jones who sent the hellcat after me. He must have seen the book in my bag. But why was the book so important? That hellcat could have killed me. Didn't he care? I thought he was my friend. I sighed. It was foolish of me to think someone like Patrick Jones actually cared about *me*.

"You may think that the final ingredient of our divine resurrection is out of reach," Mr. Jones continued. "After all, no one has seen an Angel Warrior for almost two thousand years. How could we find the blood of an Angel Warrior to release the bonds of Alatayi? Well, Brothers and Sisters, question no further. There is an Angel Warrior dwelling among us here in Hainesville. He will be brought to me so that Alatayi will rise again! Tonight, that Angel Warrior will be captured, and on the night of his maturity, we will sacrifice Kalib Andrews."

12

Raise Your Hand If You Want Me Dead

My eyes widened. My lungs felt like they were made of lead. *The blood of Kalib Andrews will be spilled tonight?* They were going to sacrifice me! I gasped. Probably a little too loud. Several Order members turned their heads to where I was standing. I ducked out of sight and hurried into the room I had crawled out of. Was I seen? I had to get out of there. I had to get out of town and call the police.

I climbed back through the window and down the fire escape, my mind racing. First Macelton and Damien, now Patrick Jones and the Order. Was there anyone in town that didn't want to kill me? I couldn't believe it; there was a whole cult that believed I was the perfect sacrifice to bring their goddess back. I didn't know what I was going to do, but I knew I couldn't let them catch me.

I sprinted the whole way home and burst through the front door, slamming it behind me. I turned the deadbolt and looked through the peephole out into the front yard just to be sure I wasn't followed.

"Donald?" I shouted. "Susan?" If there was ever a time I needed my parents to be home, it was right then. Donald would be able to get the sheriff's department over right away. He *was* the mayor after all. I searched the entire house, but they weren't home. The one time I actually wanted them to be home, and they weren't.

I ran back down the stairs and picked up the phone to call the police.

"Kalib?" Susan called from the garage door. "Are you okay?"

I heard footsteps, then saw Susan standing in the doorframe of the kitchen, peering at me cautiously. They must have just gotten back from a city council meeting or something because Donald was hanging his suit jacket in the laundry room that connected the garage to the kitchen, and Susan looked like she'd had a long day.

"What's going on, bud?" Donald said, unbuttoning his white sleeves and rolling them up so that his forearms were exposed. "You look scared."

I rushed to them. "Donald, you have to call the cops!" I shouted, shoving the phone into his chest, "Patrick Jones is trying to kill me."

"Whoa, whoa, calm down now." Donald and Susan ushered me to the table. "Take it easy."

"We have to get out of here," I insisted. "They're coming to get me."

"Kalib, what is all of this about?" Susan replied hesitantly.

"That's what I'm trying to tell you!" Why were they being so calm about this? "I overheard Patrick Jones tell a group of people that he was going to sacrifice me tonight."

"Don't be silly, Kalib." Susan smirked. "That's ridiculous. Here, I'll put some tea on for you."

"Is this like the meeting in the principal's office, when you thought your teacher was stalking you?" Donald laughed.

"No, I'm telling you the truth. I heard it. You've got to believe me!" I was desperate. "There was a meeting at RavenTech, and hundreds of people were there. Patrick Jones told everyone that I would be captured tonight. He called me a … an Angel Warrior? Please, you've gotta believe me. They were all there. People we know. The Withers. The Stevens. They were all wearing …" I paused. For the first time, I realized the color of the suit jacket Donald had hung in the laundry room. I glanced down at their gray slacks beneath their white button-up shirts. Donald and Susan were both wearing gray … suits.

"Where did you just come from?" I whispered.

The kettle on the stove whistled. "Tea's done," Susan said cheerfully, hopping up to tend to it. Through the large bay window in the living room, I could see a couple dozen cars pulling up outside our house. They were working with the Order.

"Donald? Susan?"

They both turned toward me, guns drawn and pointed directly at me.

"This could have been easier for you, Kalib," Susan's voice was cold and emotionless. "If you hadn't started snooping around, it would've been quick and painless. But that despicable halfling had to show up and start messing everything up." The Order members were now banging on the front door, brandishing guns of their own, and occasionally peering through the bay window.

"You knew?" I asked. "All this time? I've lived with you, and you knew what Mr. Jones was planning?"

"I didn't always know," Susan admitted. "Of course, I

suspected. When Patrick Jones asked us to adopt you all those years ago, I wasn't foolish enough to think you weren't important. Donald was simple—all he needed was the assurance that Patrick Jones would raise his political standing. But I needed to know what you were for. When he told me that you might be an Angel Warrior, I knew it would be my responsibility to prepare you for the sacrifice."

Her words cut deep. I knew that we had never had a close relationship, but she was still the woman who had raised me. How could she be okay with this?

"So that's all I am to you?" I asked. "A pig raised for the slaughter?"

"Oh, Kalib, don't be so sentimental." Susan kept her gun trained on me. "I really did hope it wasn't you."

Then things started to get *really* weird. Susan cocked her gun and took aim. I instinctively put my hands in front of my face to shield myself, and I felt a small tug in my stomach, right behind my navel. The kettle on the stove flung itself from the burner and smashed into Susan, covering her with boiling hot water. Susan screamed as the water seared her face, and her gun clattered to the ground.

I stumbled backward and ducked behind the island in the center of the kitchen. *Did I do that?* I didn't have time to think about it, however, because at that moment, the other Order members shot the lock off the front door and entered the house, guns blazing. Susan scrambled to find her gun on the floor and joined Donald and the others shooting at the island that I was now hiding behind. I ran for the garage door, through the laundry room, but there were more Order members waiting for me there. Guns blazed as I scrambled once more behind the island.

What do I do? The house is surrounded. If I didn't think fast, I was going to die. A bullet whizzed over my head—way too close. I shielded myself with my arms and felt another pull behind my navel, and a flash of white light burst from me, blinding everyone in the room and somehow knocking Donald and the others to the ground. What the heck was happening? I leaped to my feet and made for the front door. Another bullet whizzed past me. It was Susan. How was she shooting at me blind?

As I reached the front door, I was met with another round of blazing bullets. I slammed the door shut and rushed upstairs, bullets shattering pictures on the wall and sent chunks of plaster flying. I didn't know what was happening, but I could feel energy radiating from my body. My skin tingled like it was full of electricity.

Whizz.

Another bullet sped past my head, and I ducked, flinging my hands over my head for protection. A bolt of electricity shot from my hands and into the wall in front of me, leaving a smoking scar in the upstairs hallway wall. *What the—?* There was no time to investigate as another string of bullets whizzed past me. Half a dozen members of the Order had made it up the stairs with Susan heading the charge. *She just won't give up, will she?*

Another flurry of bullets buzzed past me as I made it to the end of the hall. I rushed inside my room and slammed the door. More bullets peppered the door, but it held.

I looked around the room. *What do I do? What do I do?* I needed to get out of there, but how? The house was surrounded by people. I heard a noise in my room and snapped my head around.

"Damien?" I said, looking around the room in case he was also working with the Order. "How did you get in here?"

"I really wish you'd stop getting yourself into trouble, priv," he answered, looking out the window at the scurrying cultists. "This whole saving your butt thing is getting old."

"What are you doing here?" I asked again.

"What did I *just* say?" Damien scowled. "I'm rescuing you."

"Why should I trust you?"

Damien raised an eyebrow, looking back out the window. "Really? A couple dozen Gray Suits are outside your window with guns, and you're still wondering who you can trust?" He beckoned me toward the window. I looked out and saw a dozen of them rushing through the front door.

"It's now or never, priv," Damien said, crouching on the sill and squeezing through the window.

I didn't have time to think. I grabbed my book bag and followed Damien onto the ledge. Order members surrounded the house.

Bang!

The bedroom door flung open. Someone had kicked it down. Susan and several Order members flooded into my room as I pressed myself against the wall outside my window.

"Where did he go?" one of the Order members growled.

"He wouldn't be stupid enough to jump, would he?" another member asked, pointing at the open window.

I stole a glance at Damien, who smirked. "You're going to be that stupid."

"What?"

"Jump." Before I could protest, Damien pushed me off of the ledge. As I fell, I heard a flurry of gunshots and screams. I closed my eyes and braced for impact, but my feet never touched the ground. *Was I shot? Am I dead?* When I opened my eyes, the house was fifty feet below me.

"What the—!" I yelped. Order members rushed outside, firing their guns into the air. Bullets zipped past me as my body flung to the left and right unwillingly but not ungratefully, dodging every bullet. Damien Daslic was still on the ledge, shooting ... fireballs? Yes, he was shooting fireballs out of his hand and into my bedroom full of cultists who wanted to kill me to resurrect an ancient goddess, and I was flying—normal teen stuff.

Wait! I'm flying?! I looked up to see Macelton levitating in midair, carrying me away from the house. Holy crap, we were high up!

Macelton sped away out over the woods surrounding the city.

"Let me go," I shouted, still unsure of who I could trust. "Let go of me!"

I flung my arms and legs, trying to break free.

"Keep still," he grunted.

"No!" I screamed. "Let go of me."

"You're going to make me drop you," Macelton warned, but I didn't stop flailing. Macelton lost his balance, and we both tumbled to the ground.

I fought my way out of Macelton's grip and scrambled to my feet. "Get away from me!" I shouted, "I'll call the cops."

"I realize there's a lot we need to talk about, Kalib," Macelton said cautiously, holding both hands out as if trying to calm a rabid dog. "Unfortunately, this is not the place to do it. We're only a quarter-mile away from your house, and the Gray Suits will have seen us fall. Damien won't be able to hold them off for long, and I'd like to discuss this with you somewhere safe."

"I'm not going anywhere with you." My voice cracked as I spoke. "For all I know, you're one of them. You probably took me here to kill me yourself."

"There they are!" a voice shouted from a distance.

"They're coming," Macelton said calmly. "I assure you that I do not want to kill you, but we have to leave now."

"You're lying—" I started to say, pointing a finger in Macelton's face. Pain shot through my right shoulder, and my hand instinctively flew to the source of the pain. My shoulder was wet. I brought my fingers back covered in blood. I'd been shot.

"A bullet must have grazed you as we fled," Macelton explained. "Normal bullets can't, but Order-issued weapons *can* harm you. It could be lethal. I need to get you to safety."

My legs began to wobble, and my vision began to blur. "I don't feel so good."

"We need to get out of here," Macelton cautioned, looking over his shoulder as the first Order member emerged from the trees.

"What did … what's … what's happening?" The trees spun around me.

"Put your hands up!" another Order member commanded, but they were spinning so fast, I couldn't figure out where the voice had come from.

"You're going into shock." Macelton's voice sounded distorted. "I need you to trust me so that I can get you out of here and get you the help you need."

"LEAVE ME ALONE!" I shouted. A wave of energy left my body, and then everything went black.

13

A Small Matter Of Wars And World's Passed

CRUNCH. CRUNCH. CRUNCH. CRUNCH. Each noise was an explosion in my head.

"What happened?" I struggled to open my eyes. My body felt like it was hit by a semi, smashed through a brick wall, and then crushed by a 747.

"It's about time you woke up, priv." a voice sneered, a little too loud.

Instinctually, I jumped off of the sofa I found myself lying on, and immediately, the room began to spin. My knees wobbled, and I flopped back onto the couch.

"Careful," the voice said, with a mocking laugh. "You were being stupid last night and passed out like a baby."

I recognized that voice. *Damien?* Still a bit disoriented, I rubbed my eyes to get a better look.

Damien had pulled a chair to the sofa and was eating cereal out of a mixing bowl directly over my head. What was happening? Why was my childhood bully eating cereal from a mixing bowl and watching me sleep? A question I never thought I'd have to ask.

My eyes glossed over the red sofa and the wooden mantel over the fireplace. "Where am I?"

"You're at home," Macelton's voice came from somewhere behind me. "Well, my home anyway."

I tried again to get to my feet and tumbled down once more onto the sofa, my knees refusing to support me. Macelton leaned on a counter that divided the kitchen from the living room, his arms folded, and his eyes fixed on me.

"You really should rest, Kalib," Macelton continued. "You exhausted yourself yesterday. Between fighting during the home invasion, getting shot by an Order issued bullet, and what happened in the woods last night, you expended more energy than you were ready for, both mentally and physically. It was really quite impressive, but extremely dangerous." Macelton grabbed a glass as he spoke, filling it with water from the faucet. "You're lucky you didn't die."

"Noob," Damien snickered.

"What ... happened last night?" I strained to remember the events of the night before, but my memory was fuzzy. The whole thing was like a dream.

"You don't remember?" he asked, considering me cautiously. "We were surrounded by Gray Suits. I tried to save us, but you were uncooperative, and then ... you ... exploded. You sent a shockwave in every direction, a radius of about a half a mile. You stunned every Gray Suit in the vicinity, and you would have stunned me too if I hadn't leaped into the air."

"Wow," I said. I didn't remember any of it.

"It was remarkable," Macelton added, handing me the glass of water. There was a hint of pride in Macelton's tone, though I had no idea why. I sipped the water cautiously, taking in more of the room. "Why am I here?"

"Well, after you stunned all of the Gray Suits, you passed out," Macelton answered. "I took you home, tended to your wounds, and made sure you were comfortable,"

I looked down at my right arm. It had been cleaned and bandaged. I was wearing a different shirt too. I closed my eyes, trying to remember, focusing on the rise and fall of my chest. It was all coming back to me. The reality of what happened finally started to sink in. My parents had tried to kill me, and they might have managed it if these guys hadn't been there. I braced myself on the arm of the sofa as I stood slowly.

"Why did you save me?" I asked, fighting to stay standing.

"Isn't it obvious, Kalib?" Macelton spoke plainly. "I wanted to protect you."

I shook my head. "But you tried to kill me that night on the street. You weren't trying to protect me then, so why now?"

Macelton narrowed his eyes. "Is that what you think happened, Kalib?"

"I mean, I was there," I said. "I saw you. You followed me home after I left the diner, and then you attacked me."

Macelton moved around the counter, getting closer, placing both hands on the back of the sofa. "You saw *me?*"

I kept my distance, careful not to make any sudden movements and accidentally end up on my face again. "Yes. I saw you."

"You saw my face?" he clarified, "You saw my *face* while you were being attacked?"

"Yes, I—" Macelton inclined his head knowingly. "Well, no. It was all cloaked in shadows, but I saw the ring. And then that night I saw you outside my window, and the next night too, when you were meeting with Damien in the woods. I heard you say my blood would be spilled."

Damien snorted, muttering something else beneath his breath.

"You're right." Macelton leaned back against the counter, crossing his arms. "It *was* me you saw through your window and in the woods. But I give you my word, Kalib, that I did not attack you that night."

He spoke plainly. He didn't try to hide his intentions or defend himself. He simply answered my questions.

"Well if you didn't attack me, who did?" I asked skeptically.

"I don't know," Macelton admitted. "I have my suspicions, but it could have been anyone. A demon. A shapeshifter. Whoever it was, wanted you to suspect me."

"Well, it worked." I still wasn't sure I could trust him, not after everything I'd seen. "Why did you say you were going to kill me?" I asked. "That night in the woods, you said you were going to kill me."

"I didn't say I was going to kill you, Kalib," Macelton answered. It was still hard to read him. His face didn't betray any emotion.

"Yes, you did," I protested. "I was there. I heard you. You said the prophecy would be fulfilled, and my blood would be spilled by the night of my sixteenth birthday. That's tomorrow."

"Kalib, have you not figured it out yet?" Macelton said, "Can you not see what I've been trying to do? The necklace. The ring. I've been trying to protect you."

"You keep saying that," I snapped. "But I wasn't in danger until the night you showed up, so what are you trying to protect me from?"

"From the prophecy, Kalib!" Macelton answered passionately. He furrowed his brows, dropped his gaze, and scuffed his oxford shoes on the wooden floor. "I am trying to protect you from your destiny."

"My destiny," I repeated. "What does that even mean?"

"You're supposed to die tomorrow," Macelton explained. "The night of your sixteenth birthday."

"Yeah, no kidding. Those psychos in gray suits literally just tried to kill me."

"They're not the only threat," Macelton said grimly.

"What?" Panic began to rise in my throat once again, "More people want me dead?"

"Only if you count all the cities, civilizations, and followers of Xothog, who believe that the blood of the Angel Warrior will aid the Big Three in the War." Damien answered from the kitchen. He was pouring another bowl of cereal. I hadn't even noticed he'd left the living room. "You know, putting it lightly."

"The what?" I could feel the blood draining from my face. Entire civilizations wanted to kill me? Macelton shot Damien a warning look, which I assumed meant, *shut the heck up, boy*. Damien chuckled a bit. He was enjoying seeing me panic.

"It's probably nothing you have to worry about," he added, though I could tell it was completely for Macelton's sake. "I'm sure it's all just a myth."

Damien carried the bowl of cereal to the kitchen table, a box of Frosted Flakes tucked snugly under his left arm. He gestured for me to come sit and eat, as if eating were anywhere near my list of priorities after what I had just heard. My stomach growled. I guess I *was* still hungry despite my terror.

"What war?" I asked, making my way toward the table.

"The Great War." Damien repeated. "It's a war between the Anzichioians and the Xothogians. It's been going on for centuries."

"I'm sorry, the what and the what?"

"The Anzichioians and the Xothogians." This time it was Macelton who answered. He didn't follow me to the table. Instead, he sat on the barstool in front of the kitchen counter. His argyle socks peaked from beneath his slacks. "They are the two oldest civilizations. You know them by a different name: angels and demons."

"So, wait, it's true?" I asked. "Everything Mr. Jones said last night about the war and how angels and demons were using humans for their own gain. All that is true?"

"Unfortunately, yes." Macelton shifted uncomfortably in his seat. "Angels and demons have been fighting this war since the beginning of time. Sadly, humans and other halfling species found themselves caught in the middle. Some joined the war, while others ... well, there have been many causalities."

I thought about what I experienced at MegaBite the day before. "So, the other day when I saw Jason Tahm turn into that ... thing? I wasn't just—"

"You're not crazy, Kalib." Macelton confirmed. "The Tahms have lived here in Hainesville ever since their home was invaded during the war."

"So, angels and demons actually exist?" I couldn't wrap my head around it.

"Yes, priv," Damien let out an exasperated sigh. "All kinds of them, Aseths, Zarofes, Shanti, Koalas."

"Koalas?" I asked.

"They're cute ... but they're evil," he said, scarfing down *another* large bowl of cereal. I wondered what Macelton's cereal budget was like.

"The Halfling Ring that you stole from my desk last week,"

Macelton began, crossing his legs as he spoke. "When used correctly, the stone on the ring, allows you to reveal the truth. That's why you may have been seeing people in their true forms." I felt a tinge of embarrassment at Macelton's mention of my thievery.

"So, which are you: angel or demon?" I asked. I noticed Damien roll his eyes from across the table where he sat.

"Neither," Macelton replied.

"So, you're Human?" I pressed, wondering how he'd managed to levitate the night before.

"No."

"So, what are you then?"

"Kalib, you and I are ..." Macelton chose his words delicately. "We're a halfling race known as Nephilim."

He held me in his gaze, his expression still. *Nephilim?* He included me in that grouping. I was not human, but a Nephilim. I waited for the punchline, for him to break into laughter and say, "I gotcha, Kalib. It's all one big joke! Boy, I got you good!" But that moment never came. There was no punchline, no hidden cameras, nothing. Macelton was serious.

"And a Nephilim is ...?" I asked after a lifetime's silence.

He took a deep breath as if considering how to explain. "Nephilim are the fifth civilization of the great union of Pangaea."

"Pangaea," I repeated. I'd learned about Pangaea in school. "You mean like the supercontinent?"

"Yes," Macelton said hesitantly, "but not as you know it. Pangaea was more than just a supercontinent; it was a unified world. At the beginning of time, each species—angels, demons, humans, and halflings alike lived in one place: Pangaea."

122

Macelton flipped his hand, and the box of cereal floated toward him at the counter. I blinked in disbelief as the box flew into Macelton's hand like it had been there all along. He grabbed a bowl from the cabinet above him and poured himself a bowl of cereal as he spoke. Damien nudged me humorously, noting the shocked expression on my face.

"When the war began between angels and demons," Macelton continued, "we were forced into cities, fortified by magic, and were unable to be located from the outside. Which is why many never leave their city. Most civilizations forbid it. It's been this way for thousands of years."

"But … I'm confused," I replied. "If it was against the law to leave those fortified cities, why are there supernaturals here now?"

"That has a lot to do with the Big Three," Damien interjected. "Before the war began, three demon siblings became jealous of the Anzichioians' influence on the rest of Pangaea and started a revolt. They were the reason the war began. They wanted to reshape Pangaea in the image of Xothog."

"Xothog?" I asked. There were way too many names to keep track of.

"Demons, priv," Damien clarified through a mouthful of cereal.

"Right."

"Xothog, was the Homeland of the Xothogians," Macelton explained. "They believed that all other species should bow to them. So they started a war. The Anzichioans—er, the angels, were the only civilization large enough and strong enough to fight back."

"But that still doesn't explain why there are demons in Hainesville," I pointed out. "Why did Jason Tahm transform in MegaBite, and why did that demon cat thing attack me yesterday? If these supernaturals are forbidden to leave their realm, then why are they here?"

Macelton looked at me. "Because, despite the Big Three being imprisoned, the war for control of Pangaea is still being waged, leaving many people—like the Tahm Family—without a homeland."

"They're homeless?" A pang of guilt and sadness pierced my side as the revelation hit me.

"They've made the human world their home," Macelton affirmed.

I couldn't imagine being in that situation, watching everything that I knew destroyed and having to find a new home in a world I never even knew. "Why have I never seen or heard of any of this before this week?" I asked

"Because a decision was made to keep the knowledge of Pangaea from the humans," Macelton answered. "They were helpless against the supernatural races. Anzichioians saw them as a liability, and the Xothogians, well … they were not useful to their cause. So, an agreement was made that the boarders of Pangaea would be invisible to the human race, and all were forbidden to cross the boarders into the human realm."

"But then the renegades happened." This was the most I'd seen Damien speak in … well, ever. It was like Macelton was telling his favorite bedtime story.

"The renegades?" I repeated.

"Yes, the renegades, of course," Macelton said. "There were those that disobeyed the decree and crossed into the human world. Some came searching for independence, others for treasure, and some for power."

"Power?" I asked. "What do you mean? You just said humans were non-magical. Why come to the human realm for power?"

"No one is special where everyone is, priv." Damien snorted.

"Damien is right," Macelton agreed. "In the human world, supernaturals were seen as gods, powerful and divine. They made an impression on the humans. You may have even heard of some: Zeus, Thor, and Osiris."

"They were all from Pangaea?"

"A lot of human mythology intersects with our history," Macelton explained. "Unfortunately, not everyone viewed humans as equal, especially those that opposed the Anzichioian order. The humans were used, often unwillingly, as pawns in supernatural disputes."

I remembered what Mr. Jones had said in the meeting, how they were tired of being pushed around by those who called themselves 'divine.' "So that's why the Order wants to defend themselves? They don't want to be inferior to other species? That's why they're trying to raise that goddess … er … what was her name … Alatayi? The Goddess of Justice?"

"Trust me; she's no goddess." Macelton's eyes grew dark and intense. "And she does not want justice. Alatayi is a Xothogian. Likely, a high-profile Xothogian, and possibly one of the Big Three. I don't know why the Gray Suits want to raise her, but I suspect it's a trap. The Order has been infiltrated by demons for a long time."

"Really?" I scrunched my face up. "Why would the demons want to infiltrate the Order? I thought you said humans weren't useful to them?"

"They weren't," Macelton admitted. "Not when the war began. However, humans have evolved since then, and their thirst for knowledge has made them susceptible to deception."

I thought about that for a moment. This was all so much to take in. A whole world I didn't even know about, and yet somehow I was a part of it. A few days ago, my biggest worry was how to ask Caliyah to the homecoming dance. Now, I found myself in the middle of a war.

"Why do they need *me?*" I asked.

"Because you're an Angel Warrior, Kalib," Macelton said compassionately.

"An angel? But I thought you said I was a Nephilim."

Damien snorted again. I was really getting tired of his condescending quips.

"You *are* a Nephilim," Macelton explained patiently, "but you are also an Angel Warrior. After the war had persisted for some time, a new type of warrior began to rise. They were called the Children of Michael, also known as the Angel Warriors. These warriors were born with heightened abilities. They were natural fighters, in tune with the forces of the universe. From the largest tree, to the tiniest microbe, their powers were connected to life itself."

"So basically, they were like Jedis," I said.

"Basically," Macelton confirmed. "The Angel Warriors defeated and imprisoned the Big Three, turning Xothog into a prison world."

"So, what happened to them?" I asked. "If the Gray Suits—or whatever you call them— are trying to raise a Xothogian, couldn't the Angel Warriors just stop them like they did with the Big Three?"

"They're gone," Damien grumbled; I couldn't tell why, but there was a bite of anger in his voice.

"They disappeared," Macelton continued, "One by one, every Angel Warrior went missing. No one knows what happened to them, and no one has seen an Angel Warrior in nearly two thousand years.

"That's where you come into the story," Macelton added.

"Me?" I asked

"Yes, you." Macelton joined us at the kitchen table, leaning forward on his elbows. "When you were born, the Angel Warriors had already been missing for centuries. The day you were born, my great-grandmother, Donn, had a vision. She saw you rising up in battle to claim your place as the last Angel Warrior, and she spoke this prophecy":

> *The lost boy, born from the blood of past,*
> *Will return on the eve of war.*
> *Though death, magic, and fire rehashed*
> *The last Angel Warrior shall be reborn*

> *The golden blood shall be paid at last*
> *On the night of his sixteenth sun*
> *By letter, symbol, and liquid unlatched*
> *The last-born Angel Warrior will forever be won*

A chill ran down my spine. The last Angel Warrior? That seemed like a lot of responsibility.

"Your parents knew that if word got out about the prophecy, you would never be safe. The Angel Warriors may have imprisoned the Big Three and turned Xothog into a prison world, but that didn't mean there weren't other followers who intended to carry out their plan. They had already conquered several cities, looking for something. If they found out you were the Angel Warrior, they'd come looking for you. Your blood would be seen as precious, valuable, and worth killing for.

"Your parents planned to run, to raise you in a remote location, away from the knowledge of people, but they never got that chance. Someone told. Someone in our family. The day after your baptism, a Xothogian army showed up ready to take you away. Your parents fled toward the ocean, but it was too late. A spear flew through the air and killed them both. As soon as the spear pierced their skin, there was a white light, and you were gone, nowhere to be found. There was nothing left but the cloth in which you were wrapped. I thought I'd never see you again."

"What do you mean? *You* thought you'd never see me again? How do you know all of this stuff?"

"Because I was there," Macelton said, his voice shaky. And then I recognized him. In my vision from the book, there had been a young boy who looked familiar. The young boy reaching for his parents, screaming as the spear pierced their bodies. I now realized Macelton was that boy, grown up. "I'm your brother, Kalib."

14

Oh, Brother!

I couldn't believe I hadn't seen it sooner! Macelton was identical to the boy in the vision. He had the same brown eyes and messy hair, but he couldn't be that boy any more than I could be that baby. That prophecy was given thousands of years ago, long before either of us were born. Macelton had to be mistaken ... or worse ... insane.

"Oh," I said, my voice raising a few octaves. "I see ..." I looked around for the door. I needed to get out of there. I didn't know where I would go, but I needed to be anywhere but with the clearly insane person. "I-I probably should be getting out of here, you know, and let you ..." *Hallucinate or whatever crazy people do.*

I stood from the table and started for the door. Macelton made no attempt to follow me. He didn't need to. "You know it's true, Kalib," he said, his hands folded neatly on the kitchen table. "I think you've suspected for a while now. Ever since the first day we met in the diner, you've been different. The reason you couldn't stop thinking about me, why you kept obsessing over who I am? It's because you felt our connection.

129

We are bound, Kalib, bound by blood and by destiny. Both our pasts and our futures are intertwined. You *are* my brother, and I've been waiting to see you for a long time."

There was something in his voice. Maybe it was the conviction, maybe it was the way his eyes seemed to bore into me, but I couldn't leave. I needed to know the truth. I turned on my heels. "How could you be my brother?" I asked, "I mean, look at us." I gestured at my brown skin in contrast to his white skin.

"We look different; I know," Macelton admitted. "We have the same father, Dylan, but you and I have different mothers."

"You're wrong. My father's name is Aedyn Andrews. He dropped me off at the orphanage when I was a baby. I have his picture right here," I said, pulling out the crumbled picture of my biological father from my wallet.

"I know that you think Andrews is your father, but your story did not begin with him. Aedyn Andrews is the man that found you and brought you to the orphanage. He gave you his name because he didn't want to leave you with none. I'm sorry that you had to find out this way."

None of it could be true. For so long, I had believed that Aedyn was my father, but it also explained so much: why he never came back and why he left me in the first place. But then who was I? Where did I come from? "Okay, so … where did it begin?"

"With us," he said plainly. "With our father, Dylan. Your mother, my stepmother, Oshun, the kindest and most power-ful woman I have ever met. And me, your brother."

The way he said it, like he was remembering better times, upset me. How dare he? It was like being abandoned all over again. "That prophecy couldn't be about me. You've got it wrong. That was thousands of years ago. That baby would be ancient by now."

"We're Nephilim, Kalib," Macelton reminded me. "We live much longer than humans, and we age remarkably slower." Macelton rubbed his eyes with his index finger and thumb. "Admittedly, when I found you, you weren't exactly what I was expecting."

"What do you mean? What were you expecting?"

"I was expecting something more ..." Macelton paused as he searched for and failed to find the right word, "well, more."

"Gee, thanks."

"You disappeared so long ago; I didn't expect to find a defenseless child."

"Hey!" I defended, "I'm not a defenseless child."

"Kalib, when you first disappeared, I thought you had perished like our parents. But then I learned more about what the prophecy meant. It said *the lost boy would return on the eve of war.* It gave me hope when I realized that you weren't dead, but simply lost. I have spent a thousand years pondering the meaning of the prophecy. I expected to find—well, an Angel Warrior, but when I finally found you, you were just a little boy, eight years old by all appearances. You knew nothing about your heritage, you showed no signs of power, and certainly didn't appear to have lived a thousand years."

"Whoa, whoa, whoa, whoa, whoa!" I put both hands in the air, pumping the breaks for effect. "Did you say a thousand years? How old *are* you?"

"Like I said, Kalib," Macelton stood up from the table, pressing the wrinkles out of his pants, "Nephilim age differently than humans."

"Well, if you're over a thousand years old, how old am I?"

"*You* are sixteen," Macelton scoffed.

"How can you tell?"

"Your attitude."

I shook my head. Unbelievable. In the last few hours, I had gone from being the son of the mayor, to being the lost child of some ancient race I never knew existed.

"Why did you wait so long to tell me?" I asked.

"What do you mean?"

"You said that you first found me when I was eight years old. Why didn't you tell me back then? Why did you wait so long to tell me the truth?"

"You weren't ready," Macelton said plainly. "When I finally found you. I wasn't sure it was even you. You were younger than I expected by nearly a millennium, but I recognized your eyes and curly hair, and the necklace that your mother gave you." Macelton stared off into the distance as if he were reliving the moment. "That's when things started to make sense—a thousand years of searching and only then did I fully understand. Our parents didn't just hide you from the war; they hid you in time. I had been searching for a thousand years, but for you, it had only been eight. You weren't alone, though. I didn't know who, but I was sure someone was protecting you. A Magicborne."

"How could you tell?" I asked. Someone was looking out for me? I never thought anyone cared.

"Magic from a Magicborne feels different than the energy that Nephilim or even angels and demons expel. It's more subtle and harder to pinpoint. I could sense the magic around you, but not the source. But you were safe, and I wanted to keep it that way. I checked in on you every few years, but as long as you were safe, I kept my distance instead of risking exposing you to the world."

"And that's why this year was different." I nodded, putting the pieces together. "The prophecy says that my blood will be shed on the night of my sixteenth birthday. That's tomorrow. That's why you came into the diner that night. Why you sat in my section."

"A Nephilim reaches maturity at sixteen," Macelton explained. "That's not to say that your power isn't always evolving, but if you reach sixteen, and you have not displayed any power, you likely never will."

"You were hoping that I wouldn't, weren't you?"

Macelton dropped his head. "It would have made things … easier."

"For you?"

"No, Kalib, for you." Macelton dropped onto the sofa, inviting me to do the same. I hesitated, but I needed to know the truth. I crossed to the other end of the sofa, sitting a safe distance away from Macelton. "Kalib, if you truly are the last Angel Warrior, then your life is in danger. The prophecy states that the Angel Warrior will return on the eve of war. The Big Three have been imprisoned for thousands of years. But if the prophecy is correct, and I hope it is not, then the day you accept your role as an Angel Warrior is the day the Big Three escape their chains. And your blood. The blood of the Angel Warriors. Will aid them to their victory. That is the real reason the Order has been directed to choose you as their sacrifice. They've been manipulated. I don't know who is calling the shots, but I suspect there is a force greater than Patrick Jones pulling the strings."

I ran my hands over the sofa cushion next to my right leg. I really didn't want to be sacrificed. "This year, your powers grew stronger," Macelton continued, "I felt it that night in the diner. When I shook your hand, there was a power exchange between us. I feared others would sense it too. That is why I was outside your house that night and the reason I had Damien take your necklace. I thought if I collected the items that would make the sacrifice possible, perhaps I could prevent it from being fulfilled. When you told me you were attacked, I knew that the prophecy had been set in motion."

"Who do you think it was?"

"It could have been anyone," Macelton explained. "You don't lack enemies here in Hainesville. Like I said before, there are demons everywhere, especially in the Order. Their mantra may be *Earth for Humans,* but their ranks have been overrun by demons for centuries. The humans are being used."

"Used how?"

"Humans are powerful now," Macelton replied. "You've heard the term, knowledge is power? Well, for humans, that is quite literal. The human race has the power of knowledge and innovation. Their advancements in technology make it possible for them to not only kill stronger species but compete with them as well. And that power is perhaps the most dangerous of them all. Either way, it's not good for you."

We sat in silence for a moment. In the past few hours, my parents had tried to kill me, I learned that I was a Nephilim, I'd found out that my biological father wasn't my biological father, and that I was apparently some kind of *Prophecy Child* that everyone wanted to kill. Oh yeah, also that my history teacher was my brother. It was a lot to take in.

There was a thud on the door.

"Damien." Macelton shot the platinum blonde an urgent look. Damien jumped up and headed to the front door. A few seconds later, he returned with a newspaper.

"Uh, Mac?" he said, "You might want to see this."

"What is it?" Macelton grabbed the paper and opened it to the front page. He didn't have to say anything. There on the front page was a picture of me.

Tragedy at Woodcreek!

This morning, the city is thrown into mourning over the death of Vincent Gonzalez (15), a soft-spoken Sophomore at Woodcreek Academy. Last night, during the much-anticipated football game between longtime rivals Woodcreek Academy and Glynndale Preparatory School, an explosion took place in the Woodcreek Chemistry lab, taking the life of Gonzalez. Officials suspect the explosion was not an accident and are investigating the matter as a homicide.

Witnesses say that fifteen-year-old Kalib Andrews, the adopted son of Hainesville's Mayor, was seen fleeing Woodcreek shortly after the explosion. The mayor and his wife released a statement this morning indicating that Kalib had been showing signs of instability and that they were in the process of getting him the help he needed. They informed officials late last night that their adopted son had not come home. "We just want you to come home, Kalib, so we can get you the help you need," a devastated Susan Donovan said through tear-filled eyes during this morning's press conference.

Anyone having information about the whereabouts of Kalib Andrews should contact city officials immediately. Kalib Andrews is still missing and considered dangerous. But even more dangerous is the effect this will have on Mayor Donovan's congressional campaign. Will he be able to recover from this scandal?

I snatched the paper from Macelton's hands. "None of this is true! There was no one else in the school that night when the lab exploded. It was just Damien and me. They're making me out to be a terrorist, but I—I didn't."

"I was afraid of this," Macelton muttered. "They've put a very public target on your head."

"Okay, so ... what does that mean?"

"It means we can't move around the city without you being spotted by someone." Damien snorted. "There's a giant flashing neon sign on your back."

"The Order is killing two birds with one stone," Macelton explained. "On the one hand, they're explaining your disappearance, on the other hand, if anyone sees you, the Gray Suits will know."

"It was a real stupid move to blow up that science lab, priv," Damien sneered.

"But I didn't," I insisted. "You know I didn't. You were there."

"Out of all the rooms you could have run into, you ran into the science lab?" Damien said, "What did you think was going to happen?"

"Well, I didn't see you fighting off the hellcat."

"That's literally what I did. I saved your life."

"*After* it chased me into the science lab!"

"Boys!" Macelton shouted. "Now's not the time to cast blame. We've just got to figure out our next move."

"We?" I asked. "There is no 'we.' All of this is too much. I didn't ask for any of this. Before you came into town, everything was normal. Now, all of a sudden, I'm getting attacked on streets that seem empty but are crowded a second later. I'm getting choked by magic books, hands are coming out of rifts and trying to pull me in, and I'm hearing voices, for crying out loud! I'm going crazy! Plain and simple."

"Wait a minute. What did you just say?" Macelton interrupted, his face lit up with alarm.

"I said I'm going crazy."

"No, before that." He rolled his hands toward himself as if rewinding time. "You said a hand came out of a rift?"

"Yeah," I scratched the back of my head, suddenly realizing the story involved breaking into the very house I was standing in. "When Triston and I first took the book, he was reading something, and this rift opened up in midair. I felt like I was choking, and then it tried to pull me in."

Macelton shared a meaningful look with Damien. "Kalib, I need you to tell me everything. Don't leave anything out."

I recounted everything that I could remember from that night in the woods. How the writing from the book started writing itself on my skin, how the gray hand reached for me from the rift, and the voice that said my blood would be paid. Macelton and Damien looked at each other pointedly.

"You never told us that you were hearing voices," Macelton said.

"I didn't know it was weird."

"Hearing voices is weird in any world, priv." Damien rolled his eyes.

137

"Was there a smell?" Macelton asked urgently, "Did it smell like anything?"

"Yeah," I said, still a little confused, "It smelled like rotten eggs."

Macelton looked like he had been hit in the gut. "Harbinger," he said.

Immediately, the two got to their feet and began rustling through drawers in the various cabinets and desks throughout the room. They pulled out papers and books and strange trinkets.

"A what-i-ger?" I said.

"A Harbinger of Death," Damien answered. "You should have said something sooner."

"Oh, I'm sorry, Damien," I scoffed. "I was caught up with trying not to get killed by my parents."

Damien ignored me and continued helping Macelton.

"Wait, what's happening right now?" I said. What about the Harbinger made things different?

"A Harbinger of Death is a headhunter demon from Hell," Macelton explained. "There are many, but the most famous is Ogbunabali, the Demon of the Rift. He is known for tricking desperate humans into selling their souls and then dragging them to Hell."

Damien rushed to the hallway closet, pulled a cardboard box down from the top shelf, and retrieved a canteen to put in his book bag. The same one that seemed to hold more than it should. I wondered where he'd gotten it.

"Harbingers only work for the most powerful demons in Xothog, Kalib." Macelton continued, "If you did see the Demon of the Rift or any Harbinger for that matter, Patrick Jones is the least of your worries."

"What does that mean?" I felt the panic building up in my throat again.

"It means, that at the end of the ritual, you'll be dragged to hell," Damien said, rustling through one of the kitchen drawers. "They don't just want your blood, priv; they want your soul."

"I'm not going to let that happen." Macelton turned, continuing to throw things on the counter. "We have to get out of here. I need to consult a friend about the demon you saw. A scout who sees things before others get the chance. He'll help me decide our next step."

"Wait, we're leaving?" I asked. "Right now? Are you serious?"

"Kalib, there are creatures out there that are a lot more dangerous than the Order," Macelton explained quickly. "And if they know that you're here, you won't be the only person in danger."

"So, I'm supposed to just leave everything behind?" I asked, "My friends, my belongings? Triston? Caliyah?"

"We've all made sacrifices, Kalib." Macelton didn't look up from the drawer he was rummaging through. "This one's yours."

I slammed my fist on the coffee table, sending a fresh wave of pain through the wound in my shoulder. "This isn't even my fight. This morning I didn't even know what a Nephilim was; now I'm supposed to fight for them? I'm just a kid. I'm not some Angel Warrior like you think I am."

"Kalib," Macelton soothed, "I know that this is overwhelming. It's not the life I would have chosen for you, but—"

"They'll kill everyone in Hainesville if you don't leave, priv," Damien growled, "Including your friends. So, leave or watch them die; it's your choice."

I pressed my lips together. Would they really kill everyone?

Destroy a whole town just because they were looking for me? "What about the angels?" I asked, "If I'm an Angel Warrior, like you say I am, wouldn't they help?"

"Angels are worse than demons," Damien answered, his voice quivering a bit. "At least demons might leave survivors."

"What does that mean?" I asked.

Macelton shot Damien a compassionate glance. Damien did not look up. "Not every angel is good," Macelton explained. "Just like not every demon is bad. We all have choices that we have to make, and we choose to be the best or the worst parts of ourselves. For some, the worst parts haunt us daily."

I took a long breath. It wasn't fair. Why should I have to run and hide? I thought about Vincent Gonzales and the news article. Did he die because of me? How many more people would get hurt? I took another breath.

"I need to see Triston before we leave," I said quietly.

"Kalib, we don't have time," Macelton argued.

"I need to warn him," I snapped. "Everybody knows he's my best friend. They'll take him and torture him until he tells them what he knows."

Damien threw a look at me. "Does he know anything?"

"Do you really think that matters?"

Macelton glared at me for what seemed like forever. "You have one hour," he finally said. "Damien, go with him. Meet me at the Old White Oak in the center of the woods at dusk. We've got a long journey ahead of us."

My thoughts reeled as I stepped out of Macelton's house onto the sun-soaked porch. I shook my head; nothing was the same anymore. I pulled my phone out from my pocket. With everything that was going on, I hadn't even thought to look at it. Twelve missed calls and fifteen texts, all from Triston. I hadn't even thought to tell him that I was alright last night. If he saw the news, he's probably freaking out. I unlocked my phone and sent Triston a text.

Kalib: *On my way. Will explain when I get there.*

15

I Went On My First Hunting Trip

"Kalib, you're alive!" Triston threw his arms around me once I had gotten safely inside his house. "I can't tell you how relieved I was to get your text. The news is calling you a terrorist. Why haven't you returned my calls?" Triston rattled questions off at rapid-fire. I'm not sure there was a breath between his questions to sneak in an answer if I wanted to. I had taken the long way to Triston's house. Besides wanting to stay out of sight and make sure I wasn't being followed, I needed time to clear my head and think about what I was going to say. The truth was I didn't know where to begin. So much had happened in the past twenty-four hours, and none of it seemed real. The explosion in the science lab seemed like forever ago.

When I had arrived at Triston's house, I asked Damien to wait outside. I wanted to explain things to Triston alone.

"After the explosion, it was total chaos," Triston explained, somehow still not taking a breath. "People were running and jumping over bleachers—it was a warzone. And by the time I got to your house, the cops were there, and they wouldn't let me in. I thought you were dead."

"Yeah, well, if it were up to them, I would be."

His eyes went wide. "What do you mean?"

"Those men in front of my house weren't cops," I explained. "They were Gray Suits, and *they* tried to kill me."

"They tried to kill you?!" Triston shrieked, "Are you alright? Never mind that. That's a stupid question. You're standing right here; of course you're alright. More importantly, how did you get out? Why did they try to kill you? How are you alive? I mean, I'm glad you're alive. It isn't that I'm not thrilled, but, like, how?" Triston rambled on in pure Triston fashion. The left side of my mouth curled into a nostalgic smirk as I thought about all the nights I had stayed up listening to his crazy ideas and conspiracy theories. Who would've thought I would find myself in the middle of one?

"Triston!" I waved my hand in the air. "I'll tell you everything, but you gotta breathe, man!"

Triston took several guided breaths, calming himself. He nodded when he was ready, and his red hair fell into his freckled face. I told him everything that happened to me since I had seen him at the football game, starting with the hellcat and ending with the knowledge dump Macelton had laid on me. When I finished, Triston bobbed his head up and down as he processed the new information.

"Great," he said. "So, am I completely filled in now?"

"Yeah, pretty much."

"Okay." He stood, walked to his closet, and began pulling out clothes.

"Okay?" I asked, unsure of what he was doing.

"Okay." He grabbed his book bag from the closet floor and began stuffing the clothes into it.

"What are you doing?"

"What does it look like I'm doing? I'm packing."

"Oh, Triston, I don't think you understand," I said. "I came here to say goodbye and to warn you—"

"Yeah, you see, I heard you say that," Triston said, still stuffing items into his bag. "But that's not going to work for me. We've done everything together since we were toddlers, so I'm not gonna let you start going solo now. If you wanna run off with strangers and get yourself killed, I'm gonna be right there with you."

"Triston, I can't let you do that."

"Well, then it's a good thing it's not your choice."

"Triston, this isn't a game," I argued, folding my arms over my chest. "This is really dangerous—"

"Do you know that saying, if your friend jumps off a bridge, would you do it too?"

"Yeah"

"Well, Kalib, I would jump off a bridge for you. And I have!" He narrowed his eyes. "I broke my collarbone remember? So, if you haven't gotten the picture by now, I don't know what else to tell you. I'm always going to have your back—I don't care how dangerous it is. If you're in danger, I'm in danger, because that's what we do. You got it?"

I was speechless. This was beyond two kids playing superheroes on the front porch. This wasn't make-believe and dress-up. This was real life, and if Triston came, he'd be in danger.

"Triston—" I started, but before I could finish, there was a knock at the front door. "Are you expecting anyone?"

Triston silently shook his head. Normally, a knock on the door wouldn't be scary, but considering the circumstances, we cautiously crept out of Triston's bedroom, careful not to make a sound. Crouched low, we made our way to the kitchen and peeked out of the window above the sink where we could get a clear view of the front steps.

Standing at the door were two men and a woman. They looked familiar, and the men were identical. Their greasy black hair was slicked straight back. They wore large black peacoats, and there was something strange about their eyes. Something about their pupils didn't quite seem human. The woman, on the other hand, was tall and slender. Her hair was platinum blonde, and her lips were the color of a ripe, red apple. Her eyes were hidden behind large sunglasses which covered most of her face. Even with her face obscured, I could tell that she was beautiful. I recognized her from the RavenTech building. She was the woman who had been arguing with Mr. Jones the other day, and the two gentlemen were her security guards. Why would they be here at Triston's house?

"I do not think anyone is at home, boss," the first man said in a thick Russian accent.

"Maybe you should ring doorbell," the second man suggested in an accent just as thick as his brother's.

"I do not need to ring doorbell, Friedrich," the first man snarled. "I knock on door. No one answers, so no one home."

"Maybe they do not hear, Dieter," Friedrich growled back. "Maybe if you ring doorbell, someone answer."

"Maybe if you stop being such a babaika!" Dieter retorted.

"I am not a babaika!" Friedrich jumped at Dieter, and the twins rolled down the stairs and into the yard in front of the house, snarling and growling at each other. These men definitely were not human.

"Boys," the woman said, a bite of irritation under her breath.

"When you go out for a hunt, does your prey come when you call or does it run?"

The brothers froze in a tangle of legs and arms on the front lawn. "They run?" one brother answered from the tangle.

"So why would this be any different?" the woman said, gesturing to the door. "You're wolves, for crying out loud! Use your noses!"

Triston's eyes grew so big he looked like a cartoon character. "Did she just say *wolves*?"

"I smell three inside!" one of the men shouted. "They are here."

"I told you they were here!" the other shouted as well.

The doorknob rattled. "It's locked."

"We've gotta get out of here before they—" The back door swung open, and Damien stood in the doorway as we scrambled to get up from our hiding spot behind the windowsill.

"Holy Mother of—," Triston shrieked. "Damien? What are you—are you trying to give me a heart attack?"

"We have to go," Damien ordered, "Like *now*."

The doorknob rattled a second time.

"For the record," Triston hissed, "I agree with the bully."

"Hurry up," Damien replied, pushing Triston and me out the door to the side porch just as the front door flew open. The door clicked shut behind us right as the wolves burst into the house.

"That was too close for comfort," Triston whimpered, climbing over the railing of the side porch.

"We're not in the clear just yet," Damien said quietly. "We have to get to the—" With a creak, a snap, and a crash, the porch railing gave out under Damien, sending him tumbling to the ground.

"What was that?" Vivienne demanded from inside. "Well, don't just stand there, sniff it out!" Two deep growls came from the other side of the door.

"Run!" Damien snapped. As we ran for the trees, something grabbed my leg, and I tumbled to the ground. My pant leg was caught on the splintered wood and rogue nails from the broken bits of the porch. I was able to untangle myself just as the porch door above me swung open. I looked up to see Damien and Triston disappear behind a tree as the two men burst through the door.

I quietly slid beneath the porch as the men investigated. I could see them through the slits between the wooden planks. The way they moved, scanning their perimeter in a crouched position, was like a dog raising its hackles, preparing to attack. Their teeth were sharp and canine-like, and their hands and feet were adorned with razor-sharp claws. They were werewolves. They didn't shapeshift into wolves or sprout fur on their body or anything like that, but somehow, I just knew.

I scooted further under the porch as the wolves examined the broken banister. They sniffed the air, growling low guttural growls. I shifted my weight trying to inch further into the shadows, but dry leaves cracked under my body. The wolves froze with their ears pricked up. They walked slowly until they were right above me, crouched down on all fours. Their claws tapped on the wood as they inched toward the edge of the porch. Wolf saliva spilled through the cracks of the wood and onto me below. *Gross!* They were salivating. They were hungry. Their lips curled over their teeth, revealing sharp fangs; their long claws peeked over the edge of the porch. They were going to find me.

Aahoooooo!!!!!

The howl came from the woods, and both wolves jerked their heads up toward the sound.

Aahoooooo!!!!!

The wolves growled menacingly. Baring their teeth, they darted into the trees. As soon as they had disappeared, I slid out from beneath the porch and dashed into the woods as well. I didn't know where Damien and Triston had run off to, but I needed to catch up to them. I ran as fast as I could, and suddenly, I was grabbed from behind and pushed up against a tree.

"Shhh." Damien hushed. He kept his forearm firmly on my chest and held a finger to his lips.

"Damien?" I whispered with relief. Then realizing he was alone, "Where's Triston?"

"I told him to stay put while I saved your sorry butt."

"You left him alone? They'll kill him!" I cried, as a howl cut through the woods behind us. "We have to get back to him before they do."

"Calm down," Damien snorted, "we'll save your little friend." He turned and ran through the trees. I tore through the woods behind him until we made it to a small clearing. Damien stopped running and looked around.

"What are you doing?" I whispered

"This is where I left him," he replied.

"Well, where is he?"

"I don't know. He was right here."

"Damien, I swear to god, if something happens to Triston …"

A snarl came from behind a nearby tree. We slipped out of the clearing and behind two trees opposite the approaching wolves. Dieter and Friedrich pushed their way into the clearing, sniffing the air.

"Come out, come out, wherever you are," Friedrich said in a deep voice.

"We know you are out here. We can smell you," Dieter added.

The wolves circled the clearing, nostrils flared. A soft snapping sound made me look up into the tree above me, and I spotted a mop of red hair straddling a branch. It was Triston.

"Well, hello," Friedrich licked his lips, alerted by the noise. "How kind of you to show up for dinner."

"Why do not you come down so that we can speak?" Dieter grinned.

"You know, I'm doing pretty good right where I'm at," Triston replied nervously. "The view from up here is amazing."

"We have to do something," I whispered to Damien.

Damien nodded and crept to the next tree, managing to avoid attracting the wolves' attention.

"What a shame," Friedrich smirked. "You would be a delicious dinner guest."

"I'm really not all that tasty," Triston said. "Too boney; not a lot of meat on me. Besides, most people think I'm salty."

The wolves growled. "We said, come down!" Dieter rammed the tree so hard with his shoulder, the entire tree shivered. Triston squeaked, hugging the branch as tight as he could.

"Come down!" Friedrich followed suit and rammed the tree a second time. If Friedrich and Dieter kept this up, the entire tree might fall over.

I had to do something. I'd never forgive myself if anything happened to him. I felt a slight tug in my stomach, and my heart pounded. I couldn't catch my breath. I was hyperventilating. *Now's not the time to lose control, Kalib! Think!*

No matter how hard I tried, I couldn't regain my composure. I was losing control. The wolves rammed into the tree again. Triston slipped and hung upside down on the branch for a terrifying moment before righting himself. If they kept this up, he was going to fall.

They rammed the tree again.

"What do you think you're doing, priv?" Damien quickly whispered.

I looked down at my hands. They were engulfed in flames!

"Cut that out," Damien hissed.

"I don't know how I'm doing it," I whispered back.

"Stop thinking about whatever you're thinking about," he replied. "Cut it out, or they're going to see you."

Luckily, Dieter and Friedrich remained focused on Triston. The fire spread from my hands to my arms. It burned so bright that flashes of white appeared in the lapping orange flames.

"Kalib, you've gotta stop this. You're gonna burn this place down," Damien said.

"I don't know what's happening." I shook my head. The flames continued to flash in my hands, I could feel the energy building up in side of me, just like it had done the night before with the Gray Suits. "I don't know how to control it."

Damien's eyes darted back and forth, looking for a solution. "Fine, priv. If you can't fight it, use it. When I give the word, let go of everything that you're trying to suppress. Every fear, every disappointment. Let it build up and then let it all out. but not until I give the word. You got it?"

I nodded. The flames continued to flicker now creeping from my arms to my entire body. But it wasn't warm. I wasn't burning. It felt … cold. In fact, I was shivering. I followed Damien's instruction, and thought about everything

I was afraid of. Losing Triston to these werewolves. My parents trying to kill me. The fact that everything that I had known was a lie. I could feel the anger, disappointment, and... energy. Yes, I could feel the energy building up in my stomach. Wrapping itself around my gut. And squeezing my insides into a knot. I wasn't going to be able to hold it any longer. I had to let it all out. I had to release it.

I glanced at Damien who had crept to the other side of the tree. His eyes met mine and he nodded giving me the cue to release, before he yelled for Triston to, "JUMP!"

Both wolves turned and stared blankly at Damien. But before they could register what was happening, I exploded. Damien and Triston dived for cover, just as every last bit of fire rushed from my body, towards the werewolves and scorched the woods within a hundred foot radius from where I was standing.

The next thing I knew, I was on my back. Staring up at Damien and Triston who were peering down at me. I groaned and coughed as I tried to get to my feet. I felt like I had been punched in the sternum and all the air had been knocked out of me.

"Good," Damien said, "You were only out for a few minutes this time. That's improvement."

"Have I mentioned lately how awesome you?" Triston praised. "Because you totally are!"

Damien peered at the fire which was quickly spreading in the woods, creating a barrier between us and the werewolves.

"C'mon," he said. "We better get out of here before anyone traces this fire back to us."

"Good idea," I replied, clambering to my feet weakly and nearly tumbling over. Damien and Triston, both grabbed an arm and the three of us fled the scene. We ran without stopping for what felt like miles. Once we'd reached the Old White Oak, we collapsed, panting on the ground.

"All I have to say," Triston looked at me as he wheezed between breaths, "is I told you so."

"Told me what?" My lungs screamed for air.

"I told you werewolves existed." Triston and I laughed at the irony. We were just chased by two twin Russian werewolf brothers, who I had set on fire. If you couldn't laugh at that, what could you laugh at?

"What took you so long?" a voice said from above. Macelton descended from his spot in the tree canopy where he had been levitating, watching us trying to catch our breath.

16

A Funny Thing Happened On The Way To...

"**A**m I tripping balls, or does anyone else see our history teacher floating in mid-air?"

"No, you see it correctly," I said, pulling myself up to a sitting position. "I'm still not used to it either."

"What happened?" Macelton said, a concerned look on his face. "Is everything alright? You were supposed to be here an hour ago."

"Vivienne and her wolves showed up at the house," Damien explained. Macelton sighed deeply, putting the bridge of his nose between his thumb and index finger. "I was afraid of this. Were you seen?"

"Yes," Damien answered. "But we took care of it."

"And by taking care of it … do you mean setting fire to the woods and drawing attention to where we are?"

"It was my fault," I admitted. "I started the fire. They had Triston cornered, and I—"

"Shut up priv," Damien snapped putting a hand up for effect. "I got this."

Then turning to Macelton he said, "I take full responsibility, Mac. It was my job to protect them. We ran as soon as we saw the wolves, but Kalib lost control. He doesn't know how to handle his abilities yet, so I told him to use his inadequacies to our advantage."

I glanced over at Damien. Why would he take the blame? The fire was my fault. I couldn't control myself. Macelton's eyes softened. "Well, it looks like you made the best of a bad situation," he sighed. "I'm glad you're safe."

I heard sirens in the distance, followed by more ominous howls that sent shivers down my spine. The werewolves were still looking for us.

"C'mon," Macelton said. "We need to keep moving. The smoke from the fire will cover our scent for now, and we need to get ahead while we have the advantage. Triston will have to come with us until the wolves are off our trail." He pushed a low-hanging branch to the side and motioned for us to follow.

"Who are those guys anyway?" I asked, ducking my head under the branch.

"That was Vivienne and her goons," Macelton sneered.

I picked up a small rock and threw it. "I've seen her before." I watched as the rock skipped along the path for a while before burying itself into a patch of leaves. "She was at RavenTech in Mr. Jones's office. Who is she? Is she a Gray Suit?"

"On the contrary," Macelton replied. "She's one of us. A Nephilim."

"If she's one of us, why is she tracking me?" I asked, not hiding my surprise. "Shouldn't she be on our side?"

"Vivienne is on no one's side but her own," Macelton said with a hint of bitterness in his voice. I wondered if there was history between the two. "She'll work with whomever she needs to in order to get what she wants, and then she'll double-cross them. If she *is* working with The Order, it is only because their plan will benefit her in some way."

"She said something about a payment back at RavenTech," I added. "I had assumed she was talking about a product that she hadn't received payment for, but now I'm not so sure."

"She meant the blood payment, priv," Damien called back from a few feet ahead of us.

"Blood payment?" I asked. "People keep saying that. Why is my blood so important?"

"The golden blood shall be paid at last on the night of his sixteenth sun," Macelton recited. "By letter, symbol, and liquid unlatched, the last-born Angel Warrior will forever be won."

"Okay … so … what does that mean?"

"They're ingredients," Macelton said.

"Ingredients to what?"

"To a resurrection," Damien answered. "By letter: The Book of Ambrosius. By symbol: the Enochian Stone. And by liquid: the blood of an Angel Warrior. And since you are the last existing Angel Warrior, they're looking for you."

"So that they could have my blood," I understood.

"That's what I am trying to prevent," Macelton said, pushing further into the trees,

"But you can't prevent the inevitable," Damien breathed. "You can't stop what is written. All you can do is alter the details and hope that the change works for you."

"Jamarion will lead us to the right path," Macelton said dismissively. I wondered how many times they'd argued about the prophecy. Something told me that Damien wasn't as optimistic as Macelton about the outcome of the future, but he opted to stay silent.

"What is the Enochian Stone?" I asked, changing the subject slightly. "Mr. Jones mentioned it at the meeting. He said he'd retrieved a fragment. Why is the stone so important?"

"It may not even be a stone!" Damien yelled over his shoulder. "Some people believe it was really a stolen fruit that crystalized when it was plucked from a forbidden tree in Pangaea. but I think that's just a myth."

"Myth or not, we can all agree that the fragmented stones came from the same original source," Macelton explained. "The Angel Warriors used the original Enochian Stone to lock the gates of the prison world."

"So, it was some kind of magical key," I concluded. "But why are there only fragments left?"

"After the gates were sealed, the Angel Warriors demolished the stone and scattered the pieces across the universe." Macelton pulled a branch out of the way and allowed me to pass by him.

"Why would they do that?" I asked.

This time it was Damien who answered. "Because no one should have unlimited power. Not even the Angel Warriors."

"Damien's right," Macelton agreed. "The Enochian Stone contained the oldest magic that was known to man. Anyone who got their hands on the stone in that form would undoubtedly have the power to rule the earth. That's why the Angel Warriors tried to destroy it?"

"Tried?" I repeated, "They failed?"

"Magic that powerful cannot easily be destroyed," Macelton admitted, "Despite the Angel Warriors' attempt to vanquish the stone, those fragments still contain magical properties within them. Your necklace and my ring are examples of that."

Macelton didn't say much after that. And I didn't press him

further. After the day I'd just had, I wasn't sure my brain could handle any more information. In addition to being forced to flee for my life, I had just discovered that the only family heirloom I owned was actually a lost fragment from an ancient magical stone.

I let out a deep breath. It was so unfair. My whole life had been defined by others before I even had a chance to consider it for myself, and now I was expected to be a part of this ancient war between demons and angels that I knew nothing about. But sure, everything was fine. Normal high school problems, right?

After a few miles, I saw Hunter flying overhead. The soft glow of the moonlight illuminated his feathers as he soared.

"How long will we be walking?" I asked Macelton; my legs were beginning to feel sore and tired.

"Until we get to Jamarion," he answered solemnly

"Well, where is Jamarion?"

"Ahead," he sighed before pushing back another branch and walking straight ahead. We must have walked for three or four hours that night. My legs were beginning to feel shaky and sore, and my eyes were getting heavy.

"We will camp here for the night," Macelton replied, pulling out a light blanket from his satchel.

"Oh, thank god," Triston cried. "I don't think I could have taken another step. Do we like, pitch a tent or something?"

"If you can pitch one with this?" Macelton said, tossing Triston the blanket.

"We're supposed to go to sleep right here on the ground?" Triston asked. "What if a snake comes and strangles us in our sleep?"

"Trust me." Macelton smiled. "With Vivienne and her wolves

out there tracking your scent, and the Gray Suits tracking Kalib's—"

"Don't forget the death demons," Damien added.

"Right," Macelton conceded with a smile. "Trust me, a snake bite is the least of your worries. I'll keep first watch. If there's a threat, be prepared to run."

Triston did not appear comforted, but he sat down quietly on a rock. Macelton gathered some branches and dry wood to fashion a campfire. He held his hand out and ignited it with a flame that jumped from his fingers. As usual, Damien didn't say much; he grabbed his blanket and moved to the far side of the fire. I kept an eye on him as he tore off a limb from a nearby bush plucking its leaves off one by one and throwing them into the fire. He had now saved my life three times. If you would have told me that a week earlier, I would have told you that you were on drugs.

"What's his deal?" I asked, "How'd he end up with you?"

Macelton looked at Damien and smiled. "Damien's a little rough around the edges."

"Yeah, I've noticed," I said, "I have the bruises to prove it."

"When I met him, he was a street kid," Macelton said, stirring the fire with a long branch. "He was about ten years old. I had come into town to check on you, and the next thing I knew, this kid had marched up to me and said, 'I know what you are; you're like me.'" Macelton smiled. Clearly, he had grown fond of Damien over the years. "He's always been perceptive. Perhaps too much for his own good. Even as a kid living on the streets, he fought demons on his own. So I let him stay with me for a while, until I could find a suitable foster home for him."

That little kid's room Triston and I stumbled into, must have been for Damien. I thought. *I wonder why Macelton hasn't changed it, after all these years?*

"I left town often and couldn't keep an eye on you," Macelton continued. "So I made Damien promise to look after you. And he's done a great job."

Damien Daslic had been looking out for *me*? At first, I didn't believe it, but then I thought about how Damien had taken the blame for me today, and even earlier when he saved me from the hellcat. How many other times had Damien protected me without me even knowing? I made a mental note to thank him, although I knew he would hate being acknowledged for it.

"Will you teach me how to fight?" I asked quietly.

"You're not ready to fight," Macelton responded.

"That's why I need to learn. Can you make me ready?" I threw a stick onto the fire and watched as the flames attacked the defenseless piece of wood. "My whole life has been one mystery after the next. Starting with Aedyn Andrews; I always wondered why he left. Now I find out that there's this whole other side of me that I never knew about. You and Damien won't be able to protect me forever. I've got to learn for myself."

Macelton sat silently for a moment before finally saying, "Kalib, close your eyes."

"What?"

"Just do it."

I stared at him for a moment. With a deep breath, I did as I was told.

"What do you hear?"

"I don't hear anything."

"Then, listen better."

I listened closely to the world around me. We were in the middle of the woods; I didn't know what I should be listening for. Directly in front of me was the fire pit. I heard the snapping and crackling of the fire as it devoured the wood. "I hear the fire."

"Listen past that," Macelton said. "What is beyond that?"

I listened more intently. What did Macelton expect me to hear? After what felt like forever, I heard a sound in the distance. I focused in on that sound, attempting to decipher what it was. "I hear an owl. It's ... hooting."

"What else do you hear?"

As I continued to listen, I heard other sounds around the owl. I heard the scurrying of raccoons as they fought over a bit of trash left behind by hikers. I heard other rodents going in and out of holes looking for food. I could even hear the steady marching of ants as they militantly went about their work. It was incredible.

"Go deeper," Macelton instructed. He couldn't be serious. How much further could I possibly hear?

But I could! Just beyond the woods, I heard the highway. I heard cars driving back and forth. I heard teens at the Big-Mart smashing bottles and crushing half smoked cigarettes under their heels. I couldn't believe it, but I could actually hear a conversation between two of them arguing over who gets to drink the last beer. "I can hear a conversation in the parking lot of the Big-Mart. What is that like ten miles away? How is that even possible?"

"Listen past that," Macelton prompted, more encouraging this time. "Listen further."

I didn't know how, but I attempted to block out that conversation and listen even further. I couldn't hear anything.

"Listen closer."

"How can I listen closer if I can't—"

"Shhh," he silenced me. That's when I heard it. A faint buzzing. No, not so faint. It was getting louder, like a bumblebee or the rumbling of an engine. Like static. The roaring of a river rapid. The passing of a train. The buzzing grew so loud it became unbearable. I brought both hands to my head and covered my ears until the noise faded.

"You heard it?"

"What was that?"

"It was life, Kalib, and life is full of energy. The world is full of it, just waiting to be harnessed. And if you listen closely, you can even hear it," Macelton explained. "Every part of the world has its place, and if you focus enough, you can learn to appreciate even the simplest molecule."

"What does this have to do with me learning how to fight?" I asked.

"There is a time and a place, Kalib," Macelton continued, "When I first told you to listen, could you hear everything at once or did you have to block something out so that you could hear the other things clearly?"

"I had to block other sounds out," I admitted.

"You see?" Macelton smiled. "Just as you sometimes have to deny sound, to receive sound, you must also separate yourself from a situation in order to see the situation clearly."

Macelton held his hands out in front of him. "There is a balance to everything. A yin and yang." He put his hands together. "Everything in the universe undulates between those two forces. The salmon undulates to keep his place in the stream, the tree sways back and forth to keep her center in the storm, and the baby finds its center before it can walk."

Macelton moved his hands back and forth until suddenly there was a ball of electricity in his hand. "You are like that baby, Kalib. This world is new, frightening, and exciting. But you must first understand how to become balanced within yourself before you can tap into the balance of the universe." Macelton sent the electricity from one hand to the other, creating an arc between his hands. "If we do not find balance, we will lose ourselves." He flicked his hand open and the electricity burst out of his hand, individual bolts spiraling in every direction. "Just as you lost yourself today in the flame."

Macelton closed his hand, and the electricity disappeared. "I know it seems that everything has been a lie, but in time, you will understand what it was all for. And you will use that pain. But before you can learn to fight, you must first learn to stop fighting."

Macelton's eyes twinkled as he registered my confusion. "Stop fighting your pain, Kalib. With patience, the opportune time to act will present itself. But until then, you must demonstrate patience."

It took a moment to process what Macelton was saying. I never realized I was fighting my pain, but I guess he was right. The truth was, I didn't want to think about everything I had lost. Before all of this, I had always tried not to think about my bio parents, or why they gave me away. That was a truth I just didn't want to face. I was afraid of what might happen if I allowed myself to feel it. Macelton was right, though; I could never fully embrace my power if I didn't first embrace my pain.

Macelton and I spoke late into the night about training and family and what it was like for him to grow up knowing his brother was out in the world somewhere. There was so much that I'd missed. It was unreal to learn the answers to questions that I didn't even realize I had been asking my entire life. Macelton told me about Pangaea and his travels through the Fortified cities. He told me about the green hills of Gaiv, the Nephilim city where I was born, and all the festivals we attended before our parents died. He told me the story of how our father met my mother in a faraway land during one of his expeditions as a soldier, and how they fell in love. I could have stayed up all night talking about our past, but eventually, I drifted away into sleep.

* * *

I was back on the green hills of Gaiv. An army of horned helmets marched toward my family and me from the valley below. This was the vision I'd had earlier ... or I guess it wasn't a vision at all, but a memory. One of my most repressed memories. The memory of the day my parents died. But this time it was different. There was someone else running with us. A red-haired woman that I didn't notice the first time I'd visited this memory. She looked familiar. Not in an 'I know this person' kind of way, but in a ... you know how you recognize someone in a dream, but when you wake up that next morning, you have no idea who that person is? Yeah, it was kinda like that. I knew this woman, but I couldn't figure out *how* I knew her.

"Take the child now." My mother turned to the woman, hurriedly pulling her out of view from the others. Then transferred a baby—me, I guess—into the woman's arms.

"Mom?" I asked, but she couldn't hear me.

"The ritual must be performed," she said. "There is no other

163

way."

"Are you sure?" The woman cradled me securely. "You could survive this. Maybe the ritual won't be necessary."

Tears welled in my mother's eyes. "You know as I do that the prophecy cannot be avoided," she replied. "I trust you will protect him, my friend. This is the only way." She kissed the baby version of me on the forehead, and hugged the red-haired woman, before grabbing a cloth and molding it to look like a baby in a bundle. Then she joined the rest of the family who was still racing toward the ocean.

Just as I was beginning to understand what was happening, the world began to dissolve around me.

No, I thought. *No, no, no, don't take me.*

But it was too late. I was no longer on the hill. I was standing in a room. This vision was much more recent than the previous one. The red-haired woman from the previous vision stood in front of a mirror. But now she was wearing a jean jacket, her red hair tied in a ponytail behind her back. For a second, I thought the woman was Ceanna McLain. Triston's mom. But I quickly put the thought out of my mind. I must have been mistaken. It couldn't have been.

"Hello?" I said. But she still couldn't hear me.

She was talking to someone. To herself? In the mirror? Suddenly, she jerked her head around and looked directly at me. Had she seen me?

"Hi. My name is Kalib," I began.

But if she'd heard me, she didn't show it. She returned to the mirror, but it was no longer her reflection looking back at her. A large hand reached out of the mirror and wrapped around the woman's throat

"Holy—" I shrieked.

The woman struggled in vain to get free. I tried to help her, but my hands passed right through her body. I wasn't really there. She kicked and struggled, and her eyes locked on mine as she struggled to take her final breath. Could she see me? She fell to the ground. I wanted to help, but I didn't know what to do. I rushed to her, but the world began to dissolve around me once more.

"No, I have to save her!" I shouted, but it was too late. The world shifted, and I was in a different place. I was back in the ruins of Hainesville. Just like before, a horned monster rampaged in the distance. Men and women marched in unison into a dark pit, blank expressions on their faces. And the book teetered on the edge, as translucent spirits ascended from of the widening hole. I ran toward it, but just as in the previous vision, I was too late. The book fell and disappeared into the darkness of the hole.

Then I saw Caliyah. That was new. She seemed different than the others. Weaving in and out of the crowd, a frightened expression on her face.

"I can't control it," she cried.

I tried to stop her from falling into the pit, but my hands passed right though her body like it had done earlier with the woman at the mirror.

"Caliyah!" I called, but if she could hear me, she made no sign. "Caliyah!" I chased after her, trying to think of anything I could do that might save her from the pit. She stepped off the edge of the gaping hole. I jumped toward the edge, fruitlessly reaching for her hand, and my fingers felt flesh! My hand grasped hers as she dangled from the pit. Her brown eyes locked onto mine. "Save me!" she cried. I saw myself reflected in the tears welling inside her terrified eyes. Then, those eyes changed. In an instant her pupils flashed with flickering flames. A devious grin crossed her face, and she began to laugh maniacally. It wasn't her voice; it was a low, guttural laugh. "Can't you see, Kalib?" The deep voice came from Caliyah's mouth. "We must give in to our true nature." In an instant, Caliyah's entire body was engulfed with flames. On instinct, I jerked my hand away, and she plummeted into the pit, laughing the whole way down.

"Nooooooo!" I shouted. But it was too late … I lost her.

17

I'm Sorry, What?

"What exactly did she say?" Macelton asked the next morning after I recounted my dream. Damien and Triston stayed quiet and listened, perched on a rock near the fire. No one said anything, but I could tell they were both unsettled.

"She said that, 'we must give in to our true nature,'" I repeated for the hundredth time. "And then she burst into flames and fell into the pit." I left out the part where I dropped her. I couldn't bring myself to admit that I'd let her go, even if it *were* only a dream.

Macelton steadied his eyes on a spot on the ground. "And the monster in the distance, you didn't recognize it at all?"

"No," I said. "And, whatever it was, it was destroying the city. Macelton, I've got a bad feeling about this. I think Caliyah's in trouble. I gotta go back."

A howl came from the woods causing Hunter, who was preening his feathers on a nearby tree branch, to lift his head and ruffle his feathers uneasily. Macelton raised an eyebrow, looking into the canopy of the trees as if calculating how far away it was. "We can't go back," he finally said. "You of all people can't. It's too dangerous." Macelton turned toward the campfire, removing the remains of the fire-roasted breakfast we had just completed.

"But if Caliyah's in trouble—" I started after him, but Damien stepped in front of me, gesturing with his hands for me to stop.

Another howl echoed in the distance. "We should get moving," Macelton said, kicking dirt onto the fire as the others began to break down the rest of the camp. "We have a long journey ahead of us."

"Where exactly are we going?" Triston asked.

Macelton didn't look up. "*We* are going to the river to seek information from an old friend," he answered, mixing the ashes of the now extinguished fire with a stick. "*You* are going to go back home. I'm sure your father is worried."

"Whoa, whoa, whoa, whoa, whoa." I swung around to face Macelton on the other side of the firepit. "You literally just said it was too dangerous to go home. It's okay for Triston to go home, but not me?"

"It is too dangerous for *you*." Macelton nodded. "That isn't the case for Triston. He'll be much safer at home."

"Safer?" I scoffed. "Vivienne and her hound dogs literally showed up on his doorstep yesterday. What's going to stop them from going back? And don't pretend you haven't been hearing those howls. I know that's them looking for us."

"And that's why he's safer away from you."

"Safer away from me?"

"Yes. You are who the wolves are tracking. Not Triston. The closer Triston is to you, the more dangerous it is for him," Macelton reasoned. "Based on their howls, I suspect they are several miles to the east. We are headed north. As long as

Triston goes south and stays downwind of their trail, he'll circumvent their pursuit altogether."

"But you don't know that," I argued. "You don't know that they won't follow him to get to me. Triston, has no powers, he's human. Which means if they find him, they'll kill him. I'm not letting my best friend get picked off, and eaten for dinner by werewolves. He's safer here where we can all protect him. So, if you send him away you might as well send me away too, because I'm not going anywhere without him."

"Kalib, this is not up for discussion!" Macelton snapped. "My priority is getting you to Jamarion, so that we can prevent the prophecy—"

"I don't care what *your* priority is!" I yelled, "My priority is making sure my best friend doesn't become werewolf chow! So either he stays with us or I go with him. We're a package deal, you got it!"

"Kalib I—"

A deafening screech erupted from the tree behind us. It was Hunter. He puffed up his feathers and flapped his humongous six-foot wingspan causing the entire tree to tremble. Leaves rushed to the ground in a furious flurry as the giant bird disrupted their peaceful slumber.

Macelton stopped midsentence and glared at the bird. His jaw tightened. Then returning his gaze to me he growled, "Fine! Then his blood is on your hands!" Another howl came from the distance. "We must leave. Now!" He whirled around and stormed away, pushing past a tree branch so hard that it snapped with an echoing crack. Hunter leaped off his branch and soared into the air, leaving us boys standing in awkward silence.

"What just happened?" I asked, glancing from Triston to

169

Damien. Damien rolled his eyes and disappeared behind the tree after Macelton.

"I didn't think I'd actually win." I admitted, fist bumping Triston and following the others into the trees.

We walked in the hot sun for another two hours. My clothes stuck to my body, and the Spanish moss irritated my skin. Even though we hadn't heard the howls since we'd left the camp, and Macelton was convinced, though I had no idea why, that the werewolves were headed in the wrong direction, I couldn't help but wonder how long it would be before they caught our scent again and were back on our trail. I didn't expect they were the type to give up easily.

In addition to my fears about canine-toothed wolfmen, I also couldn't get my mind off of the dream I had. Even though Macelton said it was nothing to worry about, I couldn't shake the feeling that I was missing something. It all seemed so real. I replayed the image of Caliyah bursting into flames and falling into that pit, repeatedly in my head. I couldn't help but feel that Caliyah was in some kind of danger? I didn't know why, but something told me that dream was some kind of warning. But a warning about what? What did it mean?

Meanwhile, Triston tried to make small talk with Damien. "So, you're a Nephilim now, huh? When did that happen?" As usual, Damien wasn't in the talking mood. He simply glared at Triston without saying a word. "Of course, that was a dumb question. You've always been a Nephilim. I just meant have you been working with Macelton for a while?" Damien pushed a branch out of his way. It swung back, nearly hitting Triston in the head. "Wait a minute, that's why you've been so mean to us, isn't it? Because you've been undercover for Macelton? You don't really hate us, do you? It's all been an act for Macelton, right?"

Damien gave Triston a death glare so intense I thought the Harbinger of Death had possessed him. "Or you just don't like us," Triston said. Damien pushed forward, walking alone between us and Macelton.

We finally stepped out of the woods near a dirty river, an old beat-up boathouse, and some abandoned motorboats on the riverbank.

"What are we doing here?" I asked.

"Shh." Macelton put his finger to his lips and walked toward the water. The river was dotted with large cattails that ran alongside the banks as the water zigzagged from the trees and into the ocean. Macelton kneeled, dipped his hand into the dirty water, and whispered something. Nothing happened.

At first, I thought Macelton was staring at his reflection, but then I noticed something in the water moving toward us. Suddenly, an arc of water shot into the air, pouring onto the ground like a fountain. The translucent shape of a man began to form right in front of us. Before long, the clear liquid began to solidify, first into a misty silver that sort of looked like ice, then as the color began to darken, the liquid shape hardened into an actual living and breathing being. He stood about six foot four, with a slim swimmer's body and skin that I swore was made of silk. He flashed his white teeth, which shone brightly in contrast to his smooth African skin. He stood in front of us with a grin on his face.

"Whoa," Triston said in awe.

"Jamarion!" Macelton said, greeting his old friend.

"Young Manaan," the man said. "It has been a very long time."

"That it has, my friend," Macelton agreed, extending his

hand to the man and pulling him into a firm embrace, "That it has."

I leaned over to Damien. "Manaan?" I whispered.

"His birth name," he replied.

"Jamarion, allow me to introduce you to my travel companions." Macelton backed away from Jamarion placing his hand on each of us as he spoke. "This is Damien. He has been a reliable ally and friend over the years, and a most helpful asset in protecting my brother."

"And let me guess," Jamarion said, "Yes, I can feel it. I can feel the power radiating off you." Jamarion walked over to Triston and put both hands around his shoulders. "This is the 'Utvalda, the Amhaina Roghnaigh, the Valgt En, the Chosen One."

Triston leaned away, glancing at me with *'help me'* written across his face. Macelton cleared his throat. "Um, Jamarion. That's Triston, Kalib's *human* friend."

Jamarion examined Triston suspiciously for a moment. "Yes, I see now that I was mistaken. I feel the power radiating from this young child right here. My judgment was skewed by his close proximity to his human friend. But now I see this child is indeed the one spoken of in the prophecy."

"Why do you talk like that?" I asked.

"Kalib, don't be rude!" Macelton said sharply.

"It is quite alright, my dear boy. I always seem odd whenever I come to the surface." Jamarion put a hand on my shoulder. His hand felt oddly like a rubber glove. "My duties remain on the ocean floor, so I have not seen the world above in many centuries, so my—what is the word—ah yes, vernacular, may not be up to date."

"Luckily, Jamarion's kind are masters of all languages. It will only take a day for him to adapt to modern ones. His kind can be away for centuries but assimilate to a new culture almost as quickly as one can be forgotten."

"Ocean floor?" I asked. "There are people on the ocean floor?"

"Oh, yes." Jamarion grinned, "Entire civilizations, kingdoms, and alliances."

"But how do people live on the ocean floor?" I asked, "Don't they drown?"

Jamarion threw his head back and laughed.

"No, child, they don't drown," he began. "Two percent of all living beings are born Water Dwellers—or Vandwyr, as we call them. But others teach themselves."

"You can teach yourself to breathe underwater?"

"Kalib, you can learn anything if you work hard enough to achieve it," Jamarion said. "Your father was a Water Dweller."

"He was?" I asked excitedly.

"Dylan El Ton." Jamarion smiled. "The Great Commander of the Sea. I fought many battles by his side. He was a great warrior."

I smiled, thinking about this. Dylan was a warrior? He fought underwater? Finally, something about my family I actually liked.

"Jamarion is what you would call a Selki," Macelton explained.

"A Selki?" I asked.

"Every so often, over the centuries, a new species—or adaptation rather—will be born from another species. Sort of like a sub-species. Over time, they become their own race and are able to breed and reproduce amongst themselves."

"So, what exactly are Selki's?"

173

"Let's just say we are the werewolves of the underworld." Jamarion smiled, flashing all of his white and very sharp canine teeth; they were just like the teeth of the men with Vivienne. "In fact, the werewolves are our cousins."

There was so much about the world that the *world* didn't even know.

Macelton started. "Unfortunately, Jamarion, our purpose for calling upon you today is not to simply introduce you to my family. As you may have already foreseen, today is Kalib's birthday."

I snapped my head toward Macelton. It *was* my birthday. I guess with all that had been going on, I had forgotten all about it. "Today, Kalib has reached the age of sixteen, and at sundown, the prophecy states—"

"Yes, yes," Jamarion interrupted. "I am well aware of the prophecy. I have seen it many times in my visions. 'For on this day, a great evil will rise, and the war that will end all worlds will begin.'"

"Patrick Jones, the high priest of The Order, has committed to raising Alatayi, whom he believes is the Goddess of Justice, from her prison in the depths of Xothog."

"I have seen this vision, many times." Jamarion dropped his gaze. His face looked strangely like a sad puppy. "It is not Alatayi who he wishes to raise. That is to say, Alatayi is not who she says she is. The threat is much greater than you realize."

"Jamarion, Kalib claims to have seen a Harbinger of Death," Macelton continued, "I fear Kalib may be marked by a Demon in Xothog."

Jamarion raised his head and stared into the distance. His eyes had changed from black to silver. A few moments later, he gasped, his eyes returned to their natural color, and a pitied expression crossed his face. "Your fear is correct." He nodded remorsefully. "Kalib has been marked by the very demon The Order is trying to release. I am afraid the prophecy is unavoidable—"

"No," Macelton interrupted, "I won't accept that. There has to be a way around it."

"Look, Mac," Damien interjected, "no one knows the true meaning of the prophecy. Maybe we shouldn't be trying to rescue Kalib. As much as I'd hate to admit it, maybe he's the one who is going to be rescuing *us*."

"By becoming a sacrifice?" Macelton fumed. "How is he going to save us, if he's dead?"

"The prophecy is unavoidable," Jamarion repeated, "despite your efforts, Kalib's blood *will* be spilled tonight before the moon reaches its zenith."

Macelton let out an exasperated groan, threw his hands into the air, and turned away from the group, shaking his head in disbelief. Jamarion had basically signed my death certificate. I suppose I should have been terrified, or determined, like Macelton, to not let that happen. And I felt both of those things. But the only words I could muster was, "Well … that sucks!"

I didn't know what else to say.

"The gates of Xothog will be opened tonight," Jamarion continued. "And the Spirits of the Cursed Ones will be released, wreaking havoc on the citizens of Hainesville and then the world."

"The Spirits of the Cursed Ones?" I asked. "What are they?" As if my impending sacrifice wasn't enough information for one day.

"They are the cursed souls of those who have pledged themselves to the one who calls herself Alatayi," Jamarion answered. "Thousands of souls tricked by Ogbunabali, the Demon of the Rift, and dragged to Xothog. If released, they will seek revenge on her behalf."

"That's why she calls herself the Goddess of Justice," I realized out loud, "It isn't justice for us at all, is it?"

"Nor is it justice for The Order, as they have been deceived to believe," Jamarion agreed. "The Cursed Ones will seek bodies to possess, and the members of The Order will be their first vessels."

"What happens to the people who get possessed?"

"They will become enslaved inside their own minds, unable to escape, and unable to fight against the cursed ones, who will slowly feed on their soul until there is nothing left."

"What happens when there's nothing left?"

Suddenly, no one in the know would meet my eye. "They die, priv," Damien finally said with an expression that told me he had witnessed this before.

"Wait." The realization hit me. "Alatayi? She's going to need a vessel, isn't she? What happens when a demon possesses a human? Is there a difference?"

Once again, those in the know suddenly became tongue-tied. Finally, Macelton answered, "Demons are powerful beings, Kalib. Unlike the Spirits of The Cursed, human souls can't handle the full essence of a demon. Especially, a high-ranking demon. As soon as the two come in contact, the human soul will be burned away … immediately."

My eyes widened. That's what my dream was about. I knew I was missing something. Caliyah was going to be possessed. It was bad enough that he wanted to sacrifice me, but Mr. Jones was also planning on offering up his daughter to be possessed by a demon! What kind of sick demented monster does that?

"We have to stop it from happening," I said urgently.

"The best way to prevent this is to keep you as far away from them as possible," Macelton replied.

"No, you don't understand," I argued, "My dream-—"

"Kalib, I need you to trust me," Macelton interrupted, trying to sound reassuring. "I need you to trust that I will always do what's best for you. I won't let anything happen to you."

"Yeah, but what about what's best for everyone else?" I stormed away. That's what Patrick Jones was planning: to infect everyone in Hainesville with the Spirits of the Cursed Ones. Including his own daughter. I had to stop it. I couldn't just let everyone die. There were so many people in the city that didn't deserve that, people I liked. And even the ones I didn't like, like Donald and Susan. They were undeniably the scum of the earth, but they didn't deserve to die. Maybe the dream was a warning. Maybe I was supposed to stop the resurrection from happening.

"Kalib," Triston called. He had followed me away from Macelton and the others, who were still engaged in a heated argument. "Are you alright?"

"Triston, I know why I've been having that dream," I said, pulling him to the dock on the other side of the raggedy boathouse.

"What are you talking about?"

Another aggravated noise came from the group on the riverbank. Macelton threw his hands into the air a second time and shouted something that I couldn't quite make out. They were going to be arguing about this for hours.

"I know why I've been having that dream," I whispered,

pulling Triston further out of sight into the boathouse. "It's Caliyah."

"What about Caliyah?"

"I think she's in danger." I paced back and forth. The inside of the boathouse was just as old and untouched as the outside. It was made completely out of wood, and a thick layer of dust coated the tables and the floors, giving the impression that no one had set foot inside for many years. "In my dream, there were men and women marching into the city, but Caliyah was different. She was weaving in and out of the crowd. I couldn't stop her, and then she burst into flames. Can't you see? This is exactly what they were talking about. Mr. Jones is planning on using the Gray Suits as vessels for the Cursed Ones. What if he's planning on doing the same with Caliyah?"

Triston stared at me blankly, the gears turning in his head. "You know, Duke University has published a few papers, proposing that some people have the ability to obtain information not gained from the physical world."

It was my turn to stare blankly.

"It's ESP!" Triston went on, "Maybe your dreams are like that. Like a sixth sense. Maybe Caliyah is trying to communicate with you through her dreams. Kalib, you could be right!"

"I can't let Caliyah get possessed, Triston."

"We have to tell Macelton."

"No! No, no. We *can't* tell Macelton."

"Why not?" Triston pulled back a dusty curtain, looking out the window to where the group was still arguing. "Macelton will come up with a plan—"

"Macelton only cares about one thing," I interrupted. "And that's saving me. You saw how he almost threw you to the wolves this morning. He was going to send you back home where Vivienne and the werewolves would have eaten you for breakfast. He doesn't care about saving Caliyah or the city. He only cares about getting me away so that the war doesn't begin."

"But Kalib, Macelton will—"

"Look, I'll let Macelton decide about the prophecy and what happens to me next," I interrupted, "But I can't leave knowing Caliyah's in trouble. I have to go back and get her. The river runs right through Hainesville. I'll take one of those old motorboats and be in Hainesville in a little over an hour—"

"But what if Macelton notices you're gone," Triston interrupted.

"He won't," I reassured, "they'll probably be stuck in that argument for at least an hour. That's enough time to get me to Hainesville. And by the time they figure out that I'm gone, Caliyah and I, will already be headed back."

"But what if he notices before then."

"Then stall," I said, urgently. "You can do that right?"

Triston didn't say anything. He stared at me with a terrified look on his face. I knew that he didn't like any part of my plan, but it was exactly the kind of plan he would have come up with. "You owe me," he finally said.

"You're the best, Triston," I said, climbing into one of the motorboats and unmooring it.

"If you die, I swear to god, I'm going to kill you," Triston said sternly.

"I won't die," I smiled. "I promise."

"Go save Caliyah then."

Triston started to push the motorboat out of the boathouse and onto the river. "Wait!" I said suddenly.

"What?"

"Let me have your phone."

"My phone? Why?"

"I'll text Caliyah when I get into the city. That way, I won't have to look for her. I'll be in and out."

"What's wrong with your phone?"

"I haven't charged it in two days. It's beyond dead."

Triston puffed his cheeks up and let out a deep breath. "Fine," he said, shoving his hand into his pocket and retrieving an old school Nokia flip phone. "Don't break my phone," he said, forcefully.

If this phone has survived this long, I don't think I could break it if I wanted to. I decided it was better not to mock Triston's taste in technology at this particular moment but filed it away for after the apocalypse. "Don't die. Don't kill your phone. Got it."

I sat forward in the motorboat, pulling it quietly out of the boathouse. Triston assisted by pushing the boat onto the water. I ducked down, careful not to choke the engine until I was sure I was a safe distance from Macelton and the rest of the group. As I sat up, several minutes later, I couldn't help but wonder how long it would be before Triston cracked under the pressure.

18

I'm Really Bad At Picking Up Girls

I took the motorboat down the Ogeechee River until it passed into Hainesville. When I was certain I was safe, I steered the boat onto the riverbank, hiding it among the bushes and trees there. I pulled out Triston's Nokia and began typing a message to Caliyah. How did anyone ever text on these things? It takes forever!

Anyway, I sent Caliyah a message telling her I needed to talk and that it was important. And waited. To my surprise, only a minute went by before she responded. Her brief message said:

Caliyah: *I'm at work, but I can slip away. Can you meet me at my place?*

She ended her message with a 'winky face' emoji. Now, I know I was in the middle of a crisis, but I have to admit, the thought of going to Caliyah Jones's house, filled my stomach with all sorts of butterflies. A mere month ago, I was just the guy with the locker next to hers. Now she was inviting me to her house to *talk*. If I didn't know her dad was a psychopathic killer trying to raise a demon goddess, I'd have been on cloud nine.

I carefully made my way to the Jones', sticking to the woods wherever possible. When I arrived, I looked both ways before jutting out of the trees and behind a bush on their front lawn. Caliyah said that she would be alone, but I couldn't be too cautious. I sent another text indicating that I'd arrived. Triston's phone buzzed a few seconds later with a text notification.

Caliyah: *Come inside. I'm waiting for you.*

I opened the front door and stepped into the marble foyer of the house. It was definitely a larger house than the house I'd grown up in.

"Hello?" I called. My voice echoed off the walls. Seconds later, another text notification buzzed on the phone.

Caliyah: *In my room. Come upstairs.*

My stomach fluttered slightly. *Pull yourself together,* I thought, shaking the dopey grin off my face. *You're here to rescue her.*

I climbed the stairs, cautiously looking over the banister at the row of doors on the second story. I assumed Caliyah's bedroom was the door that had 'Caliyah' painted on it in bright pink lettering. I pushed the door open, but when I stepped inside, all of the butterflies in my stomach clumped together and hardened into a giant stone that dropped itself right in the center of my gut. Caliyah's room had been torn to pieces. Her sheets had been thrown to floor and papers were strewn around the room. But there was no sign of Caliyah. *Oh my god,* I thought. *They got to her. They've kidnapped Caliyah.*

I rushed inside, carefully scanning the room for any sign of where they may have taken her. But before I could find any evidence, the door slammed shut. Something flew past my ear and landed in the corner behind me. It was a smoke bomb. *Where did that come from?* Immediately, the room began to fill with black smoke, and my eyes began to burn. The oxygen was forced out of my lungs and replaced by the toxic fumes. I had to get out of there.

I started toward the door, but that's when I noticed the dark figure standing between me and my exit. This was a trap.

"What do you want?" I asked, but the figure, whoever it was, didn't speak. I saw a blur out of the corner of my eye just as a foot slammed into my chest, sending me flying toward the wall on the other side of the room. I collapsed on all fours, coughing in pain. Before I had time to recover, I caught a glimpse of a gloved hand parting the smoke in route to my face. I rolled out of the way, dodging the fist by mere centimeters.

This guy meant business. I made a run for the door, but before I could reach it, a string of bullets flew past my head. I burst through the door and started down the stairs. I was not ready to fight. I hadn't been able to use my powers without exploding and passing out. And the only thing Macelton had taught me was to listen to the energy of the universe. That didn't feel very helpful.

There was a boom, and an object clattered on the stairs in front of me. In seconds, an explosion of bright light erupted from the object. It was a flash grenade. My vision went white; I couldn't see anything, but I heard a thud in front of me. The assassin had jumped over the banister. I knew it.

I had to do something. I promised Triston I wouldn't die. *Think, Kalib! Think.* I remembered Macelton's lesson about the yin and yang, and how he rubbed his hands together to form a ball of lightning. Imitating what I had seen, I rubbed my palms together, but instead of a ball of lightning. A jolt of electricity knocked me onto my back.

I groaned. I still had no control over my power. The assassin walked up the stairs and stood over me. For the first time I saw her face.

"Susan?" I crawled a few steps up the stairs.

Susan smiled. Her face was still blotchy and red from the boiling water I'd flung at her the previous night. In her hand was the phone that *she* had been texting me from. Caliyah's phone. I'd walked right into a trap. I felt so stupid.

"Oh, Kalib," Susan began with a condescending sneer. "You are so predictable. A few sweet words from a pretty girl, and you come running back. Foolish boy. And of course, all I had to do was throw a few clothes around a room, for you to take the bait and step inside, like a mouse in a trap. I thought I raised you better than that."

"Why are you doing this?"

"I told you not to take it personally, Kalib. It's only business." Susan pulled a handgun out from a holster on her hip and shot at me.

I rolled over quickly and ran up the stairs. Three more shots came from behind me. The first two buried themselves into the wall. The third grazed my arm as it followed the others' paths.

"Agh!" I groaned as pain shot through my arm. I needed more than luck to win this fight. I needed to think like Macelton, or Damien. I took a deep breath, and put both hands in front of me, sinking into a fighting position.

But Susan's confidence didn't fade. She walked slowly

toward me. "Now, now, Kalib. It's too late for that. I've already won." My arms began to feel heavy. My vision began to blur.

"What did you do to me?" I asked, "Y-you poisoned me?"

"Don't be so dramatic, Kalib, it's just a sedative." She reached into her pocket and retrieved a syringe. "Mr. Jones wants you alive." She plunged a needle into my neck, and my vision went to black.

* * *

My eyes fluttered open. *Where am I?* I thought as my consciousness slowly reinstated itself. *Ugh*, I moaned, massaging my temples to calm the battering ram pounding my skull. *This whole passing out and waking up in different places is getting old.* I attempted to sit up, but the room was spinning. I put both hands in front of me to stabilize myself before I face planted.

"Careful," a voice said, "Crotanium will give you vertigo. It has that effect on people."

"Crota-what?" It was difficult to see who was talking. My eyes were still heavy, and everything was blurry.

"Crotanium," he said. "It's the serum they give you before shoving you into this place."

I pressed my palm against a wall. Concrete. I guided myself into a sitting position. "Where am I?"

"You're at RavenTech. Well, technically, you're underneath RavenTech." The man spoke as if he'd had this conversation many times before. "The Order uses *this* floor to detain all of their 'experiments.'"

"Experiments?" I repeated, my voice sounding rough and shallow. "But, RavenTech isn't a testing facility. They only focus on schematics."

"Is that what they told you?" the man said plainly. The flickering fluorescents reinforced my nausea. I rubbed my eyes as the outlines and silhouettes of the objects in the room began to slowly come into focus. Soon, I was able to see clearly enough to tell that I was sitting on a concrete floor with three concrete walls. The final wall was floor to ceiling glass looking out into a row of rooms just like the one I was sitting in. There were no chairs or beds, simply thin blankets that offered no padding or comfort. One for me, and one for who I could only assume was my new roommate. This was a prison.

The memories came flooding back. It was Susan. She poisoned me and then ... "Let me out of here!" I screamed, "Let me out."

"There's no use in doing that, kid," the man said. "We've all done it. It's no use."

I took several deep breaths, trying to calm myself. I slid down the wall leaning my head against it in defeat. At least the cold concrete helped soothe the pounding in my head.

"Feeling better, Kalib?" the man asked. For the first time, I was able to see the large, dark-skinned, bald man sitting in the corner of the room. He had his back against the wall with one knee up, propping his resting arm. The man's arms were huge. His biceps alone were probably the size of my head. I wondered how the Gray Suits could have managed to restrain him.

"How did you know my name?"

"You told me," he said, with a laugh. "Like four hundred times already."

Really? Why didn't I remember that? I thought about my promise to Triston and how I snuck away to be some kind of hero for Caliyah. *What was I thinking?* I sighed. "Oh man,

Macelton is going to kill me."

"Yeah, you said that too."

"Oh, I-I did?" I scratched the back of my head. I didn't remember any of it.

"Yeah," he said. "It's alright. The serum normally makes us a little loopy. Trust me. In here, your ... Macelton fella is the least of your worries. I'm Sterling, by the way. In case you forgot."

"Nice to meet you, Sterling," I muttered.

"So, what's your story?" he asked, leaning his head back against the concrete wall.

"My story?"

"Yeah." He nodded. "How'd they get you? The Gray Suits don't bring you down here unless they think you're special. They normally just kill you. They seemed extra interested in you, though, when they brought you here."

"Oh, I-I don't know," I said, still trying to put all the pieces together. "Where is here, exactly?"

"I told you it's—"

"No, no, I know we're in some kind of prison underneath RavenTech, but why? What is this place for?"

For the first time since meeting him, Sterling's smiled faded from his face. "You don't want to know," he muttered.

The elevator doors at the end of the hall slid open, and a group of Gray Suits marched toward my cell.

"Well, well, well," Mr. Jones emerged from the crowd. "Look who decided to make a visit back home."

"Patrick." I gritted my teeth.

"What? Not Mr. Jones anymore?" he said with a smirk. "I suppose you're wondering where you are?" He examined the door, ensuring it was still locked.

"Let me out of here," I sneered.

"Shhh, I'm not going to hurt you. Not yet, anyway. I'm just here to talk. I'll leave the... maiming to the professionals."

Maiming? I thought. *This man is a lunatic.*

"Where is Caliyah?" I asked quietly.

"Caliyah?" Patrick laughed, "Is that what you're worried about? That's too sweet. A bounty on your head, and you're worried about my daughter. It's too bad you're going to die tonight, Kalib. The two of you would have really made an adorable couple. Though I must admit, it was a little too easy to get to you. An intercepted text message and voila, you're here in my cell."

I charged the door. "Let me out of here!" I shouted, electric sparks involuntarily crackled in my palms. As soon as I touched the glass barrier, it vibrated, rebounding the shock on me tenfold.

"Ah, ah, ah," Patrick tsked, "I wouldn't do that, Kalib. This cell was designed specifically for people with abilities such as yourself. As soon as this glass detects any kind of power, it defends itself. Let's call it smart glass. Try anything stupid, and it won't end well for you." The sly grin on his face told me that Patrick was enjoying every second of this.

One of the Gray Suits tapped a key card on the card reader, and the door slid open. The other men and women entered my cell with dangerous-looking metal rods extended towards Sterling. Sterling stumbled back, desperately avoiding the tips.

"What are you doing?" I asked as Patrick entered the cell.

"Well, as you must know by now, tonight you are going to make the blood payment," Patrick said, pulling out a small black box from his coat pocket. "But, before we take you out and perform the ritual, we're going to need to take precautions." He opened the box and pulled out a needle with a vial full of green liquid. "We wouldn't want you getting any ideas during the rising."

Two Gray Suits grabbed me by the arms and held me as Patrick jabbed the needle into my shoulder. "This," he said, "is Crotanium." He watched as the green liquid drained into my body. It hurt. It felt like fire spreading through my veins. "It will suppress your powers long enough for us to perform the ritual tonight. It's not quite as strong as the dose Susan gave you. We want you awake for the ritual." He took the needle out of my arm and cleaned his vial with a handkerchief, neatly placing it back in the box. "But it will make you a little drowsier than normal. Make yourself comfortable, young Angel Warrior, because tonight, the real fun begins." I watched as Patrick and the Gray Suits made their way down the hall and disappeared behind the elevator doors.

"Did he just call you an Angel Warrior?" Sterling finally said after a few moments of silence. "As in *the* Angel Warrior? From the prophecy?"

"You know about the prophecy?"

"Every person in Pangaea knows about the prophecy," Sterling said, his grin growing larger on his face, "I thought it was a myth."

"Well, I'm still not convinced it isn't," I replied, looking out the glass at the other cells. For the first time, I noticed the diversity of the other prisoners. They were old and young, big and small. Some looked human, while others didn't look human at all. "How long have you been here?" I asked, leaving the glass and moving to sit on the empty blanket on the floor.

"I lost count," he admitted.

"What are they doing here?"

Sterling clenched his jaw. "I told you, kid, you don't want to know."

"I'm bound to find out anyway, right?" I pressed, trying to sound confident.

He looked away, refusing to make eye contact. "They experiment on us," he said after a long pause. "They dissect us alive. Put needles and things in our bodies, sometimes while we're still conscious. They're working on something. I don't know what, but whatever it is, it'll help them kill more people like us. You see those elevator doors at the end of the hall?"

Sterling tilted his head toward the elevator. I followed his glance. "Those are one-way doors. You walk in, but you get carried out."

I shivered and tried not to think too hard about the inhumanity of it all.

"Have they experimented on you?"

Sterling bit his lower lip, focusing on a spot on the ground. "Yes," he said, nearly silently.

"I'm sorry." This was all so messed up.

"It was all worth it for a chance to meet the Angel Warrior." Sterling smiled and leaned his head against the cold concrete wall. "My parents used to tell me bedtime stories about you. I never thought I'd live to see the day."

"They tell bedtime stories about me?"

"All kinds of them," Sterling answered. "In Skaetha, where I'm from, they even had a holiday, honoring the day the Angel Warrior would rescue us from Xothogian rule."

I was shocked. I was still wrapping my head around being a Nephilim—not to mention some prophesied savior that was lost a thousand years ago. Some hero I turned out to be. The first time I attempted a rescue, I got caught. "How did you get here?" I asked. "You couldn't have been an easy catch. I mean, look at you, you're humongous."

"I came willingly," Sterling said plainly.

"You came *willingly?* That's crazy! Why would you choose to be in this place?"

Sterling smiled, dropping his head toward the ground. "I wanted to protect my family."

I instantly regretted asking.

"It was a long time ago. My family and I escaped Skaetha shortly after the Xothogians invaded. We knew it was forbidden to cross the border but . . . we had no other choice. The Xothogians are a ruthless nation. They destroy everything they come in contact with, and then rebuild it, putting their laws and customs in place." Sterling's smile didn't fade, but I could hear the hatred in his voice. "We made it for a while, my family and I. We assimilated into human culture. I got a job, and my kids went to school. I thought that we were really going to have a life here."

"So then what happened?" I asked. "How did The Order catch up to you?"

"They didn't." I could tell Sterling was lost in his memories. "The Xothogian's did. I had gotten a job at a bank. Things were going well, and then one day when I came home from work ..." He paused; this was clearly difficult for him to speak about. "My home was surrounded by Xothogian soldiers. I don't know how they found me. They had my wife and my kids bound. They told me—" His voice cracked. Sterling took a deep breath and regained his composure. "They told me if I didn't go with them, they would force my wife into servitude and send my son and daughter away to fight in the war. I

191

couldn't let them do that to my family. I'm a pacifist; I don't believe in war. I couldn't bear to see my children fight in one, especially on the side of the war nation. So, I surrendered. I went willingly without a fight. Even if I never see them again, at least I'll know they're safe." Sterling wiped a tear from his eye, shifting his weight uncomfortably. "I didn't expect them to bring me here, though. They're working together. The Xothogs and the humans. I don't know what either party gets out of the partnership, but with The Order's weapons, and the Xothogian's ruthless war strategies, whatever they're planning will be devastating to the planet and all the worlds inside of it."

I didn't know what to say. I wasn't sure there was anything I could say. The Order and the Xothogians had taken everything from this man: his wife, his children, and his values. Now he didn't know if he'd ever see them again. It was just wrong. I wanted to help. I needed to. I needed to believe there was hope.

"You're going to see your family again," I said confidently. "I'm going to get you out of here. I promise."

"Oh yeah?" Sterling smiled, though I wasn't sure how he had the strength to after the story he had just told. "You're going to rescue me, Angel Warrior? How are you going to do that?"

"I don't know," I said with a grin. "But I'm going to figure it out."

19

Happy Birthday Kalib, Now It's Time To Die!

I know, it seems unlikely that a sixteen-year-old runaway and a captured pacifist could come up with a plan elaborate enough to escape a high-security prison hidden beneath the world's largest technology company. But that was exactly what Sterling and I planned to do.

We spent the next hour formulating a plan to escape. Sterling had been there a lot longer than I had, so he filled me in on all the ins and outs of the prison. Every half hour, a pair of Gray Suits would come to take a prisoner from his or her cell. They'd take them to the elevator on the opposite side of the hall where, I assumed, they experimented on them. Normally, they'd come back broken and bruised, but alive. Sometimes they didn't come back at all.

"You're a big enough guy," I began. "Do you think you could handle one guard while I take the other?"

"I don't want to kill anybody," Sterling said cautiously, "I don't believe in violence."

"Okay," I said optimistically. "So … don't think of it as

violence. Think of it as … a game. Like football."

Sterling tilted his head to the side. "Football?"

"Seriously? They don't have football in Pangaea? What kind of world is that?" I muttered to myself. "Football is a game with a ball, and the main objective is to protect the runner while they make a run for the goal."

"Oh! Like Fleegtlieg!" Sterling said joyously.

I had no idea what Fleeglieg was, but I didn't have the time to question it. "Exactly! Just like Fleeg-lieg. Except instead of a runner, you have to protect *me*. We're going to trick the guards into coming in here, and all you have to do is keep the second guard away from me while I take care of the first. Can you do that?"

Sterling nodded. "But how are we going to get the guards in here?"

A devious smile crossed my face. "What do you know about Wrestle Mania?"

"What?"

"Never mind. Just say this …"

I told Sterling exactly what to say and do the next time those elevator doors slid open. It took a little convincing, considering Sterling's opposition to violence, but once I explained to him that it was only acting and assured him that he wouldn't actually be hurting me, he agreed to follow my plan.

The next time a pair of Gray Suits entered the prison, Sterling's award-winning performance began in true, cheesy Wrestle Mania fashion.

"You think you can come into Sterling's territory, and tell Sterling what to do?" Sterling shouted at me awkwardly. "Well, I got news for you, pipsqueak. This is Sterling's house, and what Sterling says goes."

Okay, you're probably thinking, *really Kalib? Did you have to tell Sterling to speak like Wrestle Mania?* But my ninth-grade drama teacher told me to commit, and that's exactly what I intended to do. Mrs. Taylor would be proud. Okay, now it's my turn to speak.

"I don't care who you are," I responded loudly. "Or where you come from. Whatever house I walk into belongs to me! You can just get your stuff and sit in the corner."

I pointed to the corner, glancing out the side of my eye to be sure the Gray Suits were still watching. They were. Then the fun began. Per my instructions, Sterling picked me up and held me over his head, shaking me like he was King Kong. The Gray Suits sprinted towards the cell, but before they could enter, Sterling swung me around the room and then 'threw' me against the window. It's a good thing Mrs. Taylor taught me how to fall in our stage combat section of drama class that semester. I hit the window and fell to the ground, motionless.

Okay, it did hurt a little. I'm not made of stone.

The Gray Suits rushed into the cell. As expected, one Gray Suit held his metal rod toward Sterling while the other rushed toward me.

"No, no, no, no—" The young guard stammered, "Get up!"

"Is he dead?" The other guard asked, still holding the metal rod toward Sterling.

"I don't know. He's not moving."

"Do something, Tom!" he shouted. "Mr. Jones will kill us if anything happens to the Angel Warrior!"

"What do you expect me to do, Steve?" the first guard, Tom, replied. "I'm not a medic."

"Do CPR or something?"

Tom set his metal rod beside me as he leaned forward to check my breathing. This was my cue ... I didn't have any intentions to kiss Tom that day. I quickly reached for the metal rod, grabbing it and immediately jabbing it into Tom's side. The guard convulsed as an electric shock flowed into his body.

"Now!" I yelled. On my command, Sterling tackled Steve, who had been too shocked by what was happening to Tom to keep an eye on Sterling. The guard flew into the glass window before he'd even had a chance to reach for his gun. I flipped the first guard up, still sending electric voltage through his body with his own weapon, and pushed him against the glass beside his companion, who was currently pinned beneath Sterling's massive forearms.

"You won't get far," Steve managed to say, still struggling against Sterling's grip. "The whole building is filled with our guards. You'll never make it past the first floor."

"We'll take our chances," I replied, examining the large window and remembering what Patrick had said about it being smart glass. I wondered how smart it really was. I touched the shocker part of the metal rod to the window. As I expected, the glass reverberated, inflicting an even larger shock on our two gray suited friends.

Tom and Steve both fell to the floor, unconscious. Sterling reached down and pulled the key card from the guard he was holding.

"Come on," he said, running into the hall. "Let's get out of here."

I followed Sterling into the hall, closing the door behind me and leaving the two unconscious guards locked inside our cell. Sterling and I made our way to the elevator. Punching the first-floor button as the doors slid closed. My heart was racing. I couldn't believe it. We had just escaped from a prison!

My jubilation soon transformed from excitement to alarm, however, when the elevator doors slid open and someone was standing in front of us.

"Kalib?" My heart skipped a beat. It was Caliyah. *Thank god!*

"Caliyah, y-you're here?" I said.

"Yeah, I worked all day today. What are you doing here? The newspaper said—"

I grabbed Caliyah's hand, scurrying out of the elevator and into the nearest broom closet. And just in case anyone is keeping track, that's three people inside one broom closet. You can imagine how cramped it was.

"Kalib, what's going on?" Caliyah finally asked. "Why are we in a closet? And who is this guy?"

"Hi …" he said awkwardly, still pressed up against the closet door. "I'm Sterling. Nice to meet you."

Caliyah looked him up and down. "Hi." Turning back to me, she said, "The news said you're a runaway."

"I'm not a runaway," I argued. "The news only said that because my parents tried to kill me."

"What?"

"Look, that's not what's important right now," I said quickly. "I came back here to find you. To warn you."

"Warn me about what?"

"This is going to sound crazy, but RavenTech isn't what it seems," I explained. "I know it's hard to believe because your dad runs this company, but it's true. They're kidnapping people and experimenting on them. There's a prison in the basement. Sterling and I just escaped it."

"You're right, Kalib. You do sound crazy."

"You gotta believe me, Caliyah," I pressed. "RavenTech is a cover for a secret society called The Order, and your dad is in charge of it. He's capturing supernaturals and experimenting on them. Sterling is one of them. Me too."

Caliyah peered at me compassionately. "Oh my god, Kalib. It all makes sense now."

"Really?" I was both shocked and relieved that she believed me.

"You really have lost your mind, haven't you?"

I reached for her, "Caliyah, please—" But she pulled away.

"Kalib, I don't know where you've been or if you're *on* something right now, but I think you need help. I'm going to go find my dad and see if he knows how to deal with this. It's going to be okay, alright?"

"No, your dad is the problem. He's who I'm trying to protect you from," I said, "I'm trying to stop him from—"

But it was too late. Caliyah had already squeezed past me and Sterling and started down the hall. "Caliyah, wait!" I followed her out of the closet, but despite my calling after her, she didn't turn back. Sterling looked at me sympathetically as she disappeared through a door on the other side of the hall. What was I going to do? If I didn't do something, Caliyah was going to be demon bait.

"There they are!" a voice echoed off the walls and down the hall. As if I didn't have enough to worry about already, a group of Gray Suits came clambering out of the elevator, our good friends, Tom and Steve, leading the charge.

"I'll take care of them," Sterling offered. "You go after your, girl."

"What are you going to do?" I asked, remembering that Sterling was a pacifist, "You're not going to fight, are you?"

"No," he said, igniting his two bright blue flames around his hands. I had never seen them that color. "I'm going to protect the runner. Now go."

Sterling smiled before turning toward the oncoming guards and sending a wall of blue flames in their direction down the hall. I turned and ran in the opposite direction. *Remember to ask him to teach me how to do that when this is all over,* I thought as I ran through the door on the opposite end of the hall.

Caliyah was headed to her dad's office. I needed to get to her before she got to Patrick. I ran to the east wing elevator and pressed the number fifteen button. My hands shook as I waited for the elevator to arrive on the top floor. What were the chances that Patrick wasn't in his office? If Caliyah was unsuccessful in locating her father, I'd be able to swoop in, try a different tactic or something, and get the two of us out, sacrifice- and goddess-free.

If only it were that easy. I didn't have a clue about what to say to get Caliyah to come with me, and something told me, *"Come with me if you want to live!"* wasn't going to work in this situation. And if you're thinking, *Dude, you're the freaking Angel Warrior! Why didn't you just show her your powers?* Well, I couldn't. Patrick gave me the serum, remember? So even if I could use my abilities, without them *literally* blowing up in my face, they still wouldn't work. And trust me. I wanted them to work.

The elevator dinged as I arrived on the Fifteenth floor. As the door slid open, I was met with twelve Order Guards, each with guns drawn and trained on me. "Hey guys," I said, "long time no see. I was just coming up to pay my dear old friend Mr. Jones a visit. Hey, you all should join me! Come on, let's go." I tried to make my way through the crowd of Gray

Suits. Someone jabbed a metal rod against my skin, sending an electric shock through my body. Another guard pushed me back into the elevator. The remaining guards followed me into the cramped space, taking hold of both of my arms and silently pressing the third-floor button.

Finally, the elevator dinged as we arrived on the third floor. Two of the Gray Suits shoved me out of the elevator into a crowded room. That was the first surprise. I wasn't expecting the room to already be prepared for me. The second surprise was that the room wasn't at all what I expected. When you hear Ritual of the Rising, you expect some ancient stone table with hundreds of cultists standing around, chanting, wearing cloaks, and holding candles. Instead, I was in a high-tech operating room, with an observation deck, and surgical equipment operated by robotic arms. The two men who had pushed me out of the elevator escorted me to a gurney at the center. I fought against them as they strapped me in, but each time I tried to use my power, my arms felt tired and heavy. Like I said, the Crotanium.

"Faith to The Order," a voice said from the back of the room: Patrick Jones.

As if on cue, every person in the room stood and responded in unison, "As she wills it." I caught a glimpse of a blonde-haired woman, pacing back and forth, in the crowd. It was Vivienne. I remembered, her argument with Patrick the first time I'd seen her. She said he had three days to make the payment. I knew now that payment was me. But what would Vivienne gain from Alatayi's rising? She wasn't human, so what was her angle?

Patrick cut through the sea of people to the gurney, and a smile spread across his face so wide that I could see all of his teeth.

"You've put up quite a fight today, Kalib," he said, arriving at the gurney. "Overpowering two of my guards, breaking out of the prison, and trying to save my daughter again. You are a real hero, aren't you?"

Patrick smiled again, then tilted his head to look at something on the other side of the operating room. I followed his eyes. For the first time since entering the room, I noticed a monitor on the wall above the observation deck. On the screen was Caliyah, pacing back and forth in Patrick's office. Two Order members waited on either side of the room, patronizing smiles plastered on their faces.

"But despite all of your attempts," Patrick continued, "you still ended up right where I wanted you. Do you know why? Because you can't change your destiny, Kalib, no matter how much you try. You're foolish if you think otherwise." As if on cue the two men, grabbed Caliyah, jabbing a needle into her neck and injecting her with Crotanium. Patrick grinned triumphantly before addressing the room once more, "As she wills it?" he shouted.

The Gray Suits responded in eerie unison, "to the cleansing!"

"Donald and Susan." Patrick called into the crowd. The crowd parted as my so-called parents approached. They looked different. They weren't the clean-cut politicians I had left in Hainesville three days earlier. These were the well-trained cultists who had been undercover for the past sixteen years. "Since you have already put in years of hard work leading up to this moment, why don't you do the honors of preparing the sacrifice for the ritual?" Patrick seemed to be relishing in the irony of my parents offering me up to Alatayi. Donald and Susan tightened my restraints and adjusted the gurney so that I was flat on my back.

"Brothers and sisters of The Order!" Patrick continued, "Alatayi is angry. She has been wrongly imprisoned by the Children of Michael. Now she seeks revenge on all who do not follow her. She seeks justice! Now is the time to raise our Goddess of Justice and be elevated to the sole inhabitants of Earth!"

"Earth for humans. For mankind," the Gray Suits responded.

"This Angel Warrior will be the one to open the gates of her prison," Patrick's voice boomed. "Ushering in a new world."

The Gray Suits cheered.

"Bring in the host!" Patrick ordered.

My eyes widened as the Gray Suits guided a drugged Caliyah into the operating room. The Crotanium had already taken its effect. Caliyah's head flopped to the side as they sat her in a large chair. It looked like something out of an old psych ward used to restrain difficult patients. My heart pounded. They bound her arms and feet. Patrick was really going to do it. He was going to offer his own flesh and blood to be a vessel for Alatayi. And I couldn't stop it. Despite everything I tried. I'd failed. I couldn't save her.

"The golden blood shall be shed at last on the night of his sixteenth sun." Patrick chanted, "By letter, symbol, and liquid unlatched, the last-born Angel Warrior will forever be won."

He pulled the red and black talisman, with the stone at the center of it, from the large breast pocket of his suit and placed on my chest. The talisman was heavy. I couldn't move. It was as if he'd dropped a millstone on my chest. He then reached again into his breast pocket and pulled out a well pen. "Now, brothers and sisters, let us demonstrate the impurity of our blood, made pure only by Alatayi."

202

I caught a glimpse of someone else in the crowd. He looked familiar. The other Gray Suits mimicked Patrick, grabbing their well pens from their breast pockets and holding them in the air. The man in the crowd stared at me with intense brown eyes. Was he trying to get my attention?

Patrick pressed the sharp tip of his pen into his hand and dragged it across his palm. The Gray Suits did the same, letting their blood fall to the ground. "Only the golden blood of the Angel Warrior can release Alatayi." Patrick opened the Book of Ambrosius and began to read:

"Le litir, agus samhla, agus an leaghan gun cháradh Thèid an Gaisgeach aingeal rugadh mu dheireadh a bhuannachadh gu bràth."

The Gray Suits began to chant:

Le litir, agus samhla, agus an leaghan gun cháradh.
Le litir, agus samhla, agus an leaghan gun cháradh.
Le litir, agus samhla, agus an leaghan gun cháradh.

My body felt warm. The blood in my veins began to boil. I could feel it changing beneath my skin. *What's happening?* Patrick took the same well pen he had used to cut himself and pressed it against my skin. I felt the sharp end of his pen pass through the flesh of my forearm. Blood spilled out of the incision, and it shimmered and glowed unnaturally. It was gold, just as Patrick had said it would be. Patrick brought the pen to my other arm, making another incision, then he pressed the pen against my chest. He was going to slice me wide open! This was gonna hurt. I closed my eyes, bracing myself, but the cut never came.

There was a loud boom, and purple smoke spread over the entire crowd. A hand removed the talisman. I took a deep breath as I felt the weight lift from my chest. I couldn't see through the thick fog, but I felt two hands begin to mop up the golden blood on my arms and then begin tugging at my restraints. I felt the relief of freedom as the restraint on my right hand popped open. As the purple smoke thinned, I saw the man who was helping me. It was the man I had seen in the crowd. The one who had looked familiar.

I expected someone to rush us and attack, but everyone around me was frozen in place, including Patrick Jones, who still had his pen pressed against my arm.

"What did you do?" I asked.

"No time to explain," the man said, cutting at the restraints around my ankles. "The stunning spell will only work until the smoke fades. We have to get out of here." With one last flourish, he cut off the final restraint. "Whatever you do, don't let that blood hit the ground." He ripped off the sleeves of his shirt. "Here, wrap your arms with these."

The purple smoke was fading quickly. I slid off the table and followed the man toward the door. Suddenly, the room was filled with a cacophony of confusion. We were too late. Gray Suits fumbled for their guns just as we made it to the door. Gun shots blared from the room as we raced down the hall, and in a flash, I felt someone grab my arm. Vivienne. She'd made it to me with unhuman speed. She dug her fingers into my arms, right where my incisions were. *Argh* I grimaced, tugging my arm away, but her long nails dug into my skin as she tore my makeshift bandage off my right arm. A drop of golden blood dripped from my arm and seemed to hang in the air for a moment before it splattered to the ground.

Oh crap.

20

O' Father Where Art Thou?

S tuff got weird fast. First, the ground began to rumble. I looked back at Vivienne, but she was gone. Vanished. Screams and gunshots came from the operating room down the hall. A translucent figure flew past me, cackling with laughter before disappearing through the wall on the other end of the hall. The doors of the prison world were opened, and the Spirits of the Cursed were being released. I turned down the hall to run and found I was alone. The man who had rescued me was gone.

More gunshots from the operating room shook me from my confused stupor. I had to get out of there before they came looking for me. I rounded the corner but only made it a few steps before running into someone. Before I could even process what was happening, the person covered my mouth, and we slid into a nearby observation room. He closed the door behind us and pressed his ear against it, listening as a mob of Gray Suits scurried past the door.

The room was dark, and moonlight cast strange shadows on the floor as it shone through the large window on the other side. The two of us stood in complete silence until the noise in the hall settled. "I'm going to let you go," the man whispered. "But you need to promise that you'll keep quiet, okay?"

I nodded. As soon as the man released me from his grip, I swirled around, hands extended until I could get a better look at him. It was the same man who had rescued me earlier. He must have come back when he realized I was no longer behind him. I took a step back, examining the man from head to toe. He was tall with broad shoulders and had curly brown hair like my own. He looked so familiar. "Who are you?" I asked.

"I don't blame you for not remembering me," the man said. "You were only a baby when I took you to the orphanage."

My mouth fell open. The man stepped into the moonlight so that I could see his face more clearly. I knew that face. I had a crumbled-up picture of it in my wallet. This was Aedyn Andrews, the man who—up until a few days ago—I thought was my father.

"Dad?" I whispered.

"Hi, Kalib." Aedyn tilted his head in a greeting.

"What are you …? How did you …? Why?" There were no words. It was like seeing a ghost, except this ghost was flesh and bone. A round of gunshots from outside interrupted our reunion and any subsequent explanation. Aedyn and I ran to the window. Gray Suits dotted the perimeter of the building, guns drawn and pointed at the sky. Thousands of cursed spirits darted back and forth, fleeing toward the city.

"They're going to possess everyone," I muttered.

"We don't have a lot of time." Aedyn ran to the door, cracking it open to peek outside. "We gotta get to the roof."

"The roof?" I asked. "Why not just go through the front door?"

"You saw the Gray Suits; they'll be all over the front door."

"I'd much rather deal with Gray Suits than the thousands of cursed spirits floating around."

"Don't worry about that," Aedyn said. "I've got that handled. C'mon."

Aedyn grabbed me by the arm, pulled me through the door, and together we ran down the hall.

"Wait!" I called, "What about Caliyah? We gotta go back and get her."

Aedyn looked at the door at the end of the hallway. "Right now, the safest place for her is in that chair. Alatayi won't be able to escape the prison until all the other spirits have.

"But—"

"We'll save your friend," he insisted, "I promise. But we've got to get you out of here first. Everything gets a lot worse if you get possessed."

Worse?

I followed Aedyn through the door at the end of the hall and hurried up the flight of stairs beyond. We heard the footsteps of Gray Suits descending the stairs above us. Aedyn grabbed my arm, yanked me through the fourth-floor door, and closed it behind us. We listened at the door as the last set of footsteps faded into the distance.

Click click.

"Put your hands up," a voice behind me ordered. We slowly raised our hands, turning cautiously to face a young man aiming a gun at us. He was younger than most of the Gray Suits, probably brand new to The Order. The barrel of his gun bounced as he shakily aimed it. "Don't move."

"Uh, what do we do?" I whispered nervously to Aedyn.

"Do what the man says," he said calmly.

"Drop your weapons!" the man yelled.

"I don't have any weapons." Aedyn opened his hands to expose his empty palms. "See? My hands are empty."

The man hesitated. That was all Aedyn needed. He balled his fists, then reopened them quickly, sending a flash of white flames spiraling toward the young guard. The man fell to the ground as Aedyn and I dodged through the door and up the stairs again.

"Is he dead?" I asked.

"I hope not," Aedyn answered.

I swallowed hard. Aedyn and I continued ascending the stairs, defending ourselves against every Order member that came down the staircase as we ran. Mostly we were able to immobilize them before they were even able to draw their guns. As we approached the seventh floor, the door burst open, and I ducked as a Gray Suit was suddenly thrown over my head and went tumbling down the stairs. Macelton burst through the door, sending another energy blast down after the guard.

"Macelton?" I said, both shocked and relieved to see him, "How did you—"

"Good," Macelton said, joining us in running up the stairs, "You found him. There's another squadron behind me."

"We have to get to the roof," Aedyn said, jumping over an unconscious guard.

"Wait, you're working together?" I asked.

"Yeah," Macelton said as we burst through the door onto the roof. The night swarmed with spirits and chaos. "After you foolishly ran off and got yourself captured, Aedyn was the one who told us where you were."

"I saw them take you from Patrick Jones' house." Aedyn

disarmed a guard as he spoke, pushing him down the stairs behind us into another group of Gray Suits. They tumbled like dominoes down the flight of stairs. "So, when Macelton and his team came back to Hainesville looking for you, I was able to tell them exactly where you were."

"But how did you know where they—"

"Kalib!" Macelton said, looking over the edge of the fifteen-story building. Gray Suits ran back and forth below, dodging demon spirits as they dove at individual cultists. I witnessed one spirit dive right into the back of a man, who then turned his gun on his colleagues and began shooting. "This really isn't the best time for twenty questions, if you know what I mean." Macelton swung around, stretched his arm past my face, and sent another blast of fire toward the door.

"Right." I nodded. "What do we do now?"

"Jump," Aedyn said.

"Jump?"

"Don't you know how to fly?" he asked.

"No!" I shrieked, "I don't!"

Another squadron of Gray Suits burst through the door with weapons drawn. "Well, you're about to learn fast," Aedyn said, shoving me off of the building and sending me spiraling toward the ground. I panicked. I didn't know what to do. Flailing as the concrete steps that led to the entrance rushed closer, Aedyn finally swooped down and caught me just inches above the ground. We shot back into the sky and flew toward the city.

"That was not cool!" I shouted, "Not cool at all!"

"Sorry, Kalib," Aedyn replied, though I noted the amusement in his voice.

Down below, I could see that the streets weren't much better than the skies. Some spirits had already chosen vessels to possess. Possessed Gray Suits and civilians alike marched the streets, capturing innocent people to offer up as bodysuits for their friends.

We landed in front of the MegaBite building, and Macelton looked both ways before reaching for the door. "The rest of the team is here."

"The team is in MegaBite?" I asked. "Were you planning to challenge the spirits to Call of Duty?"

"We needed a neutral meeting place." Macelton held the door open, gesturing for Aedyn and me to enter.

As soon as I'd entered, I was tackled by a flash of red hair. "Thank God, you're okay!" Triston's arms wrapped around my neck so tightly that I could hardly breathe. "What took you so long?" he said to Macelton, then turned back to me. "How dare you get caught in the first place! You promised you wouldn't get killed! Do you have any idea what you put me through?" Triston hugged me again. "I need to sit down."

"Well, priv, are you gonna tell us what we're dealing with or not?" Damien snapped in true Damien fashion. "Judging by the spirits rampaging through Hainesville, I'd say the gates of Xothog have been opened. But you're still alive, so what does that mean?"

I told the group everything that happened since being captured earlier that day: the fake texts from Caliyah, Susan's attack at the house, and the prison beneath RavenTech. Finally, I told them about the ritual and how Aedyn had saved me, but Vivienne got the last drop of blood.

"The door isn't completely open," Aedyn explained. "The spirits are only creeping in through a crack. Macelton and I will go back and get the book and then—"

211

"Hold up," I said, pumping the brakes. "You and Macelton? You're not going in there by yourself. There are Gray Suits and cursed souls everywhere. I'm going to help."

"That's dumb, priv," Damien sighed. "You're the one they're looking for. If they catch you, they'll get more of your blood, and then Alatayi rises."

"That's what I'm trying to prevent!" I said stubbornly. "Caliyah's still there. If we save her, then Alatayi won't have a vessel to possess."

"You're putting things in the wrong order," Macelton began, "It's safer if—"

"Aedyn, you promised!" I said, turning to Aedyn. "You promised we would go back and save her. I can't just leave her there."

Aedyn hesitated for a moment. I knew he was thinking about every possible thing that could go wrong. Eventually, he took a deep breath and turned to Macelton. "I did promise," he said with a sigh. "Besides, after we get the Book of Ambrosius back from Patrick Jones, Kalib is the only one who can reverse the spell."

"I am?" I said, shocked. Aedyn nodded. Great. No pressure at all.

"We can help!" a voice called from behind us. It was Jason Tahm. I'd forgotten we were in his family's shop. They'd been listening quietly from the counter. "It's my fault Patrick Jones got the third stone. That talisman was sitting here in our shop for a week, and we didn't know it. If you need someone to go into RavenTech, I can do it. Don't forget we're Zarofes. Stealth and blending in are our jam."

"That's kind of you, Jason," Macelton said, tilting his head. I think it was a "thank you?" "But the Spirits of the Cursed

Ones will be seeking people to offer to Alatayi, I need you and your family here to protect the city." Jason nodded and translated Macelton's words to Vietnamese for his parents, who in turn nodded in agreement. Jason, Brandon, and their parents all morphed into their true form, with black skin and multicolored hair. "We're ready to fight."

"Good," Macelton said.

"There's a back entrance to RavenTech that most people don't know about," Aedyn explained, "The loading dock. It's where they bring in all of the major shipments. We can enter the building easily through there, and hopefully, unnoticed."

"Damien, you come with Kalib, Aedyn, and me in case we need backup," Macelton ordered. "There's going to be a lot of spirits and Gray Suits running around. We're going to need your ability to think tactically. Triston, you and the Tahm's stay here. Hold down the fort and protect the city." Triston nodded proudly. "The Spirits of the Cursed Ones have an aversion to light, so use anything that produces light to combat them. Don't let them sneak up on you, and don't get possessed!"

21

Mind The Gap

Macelton, Damien, and I followed Aedyn through the city, back toward RavenTech. The streets were filled with chaos. Men and women screamed as cursed spirits cackled and chased them. Occasionally, Aedyn, Damien, or Macelton would shoot out a beam of light, warding the spirits away from us or an innocent person on the street, but we couldn't stop to help—we had to make it to RavenTech. When we finally arrived at the back entrance, two large metal grate doors barred the way.

"Do you have a code for this?" Macelton asked.

Aedyn raised an eyebrow, eying the small keypad next to the warehouse doors. "I stole an ID to get into the building the first time," he explained, "but I'm sure that by now they've flagged it."

Aedyn entered a code in the keypad. When he'd finished, the keypad buzzed and 'Access Denied' flashed across the screen in big red letters. "Any other ideas?" Aedyn asked.

Damien knocked on the grate, ascertaining its density and weight. "I have one," he said, squatting to slide his fingers beneath the metal.

"Damien, that's pure metal," I said. "It's gotta be at least two tons. There's no way you're going to lift that."

Damien smiled, gave a wink, took a deep breath, and lifted the grate over his head.

"Holy crap." I stared, frozen in awe. It suddenly dawned on me that I had never actually seen the full extent of Damien's capabilities. I mean sure, I'd seen him vanquish hellcats and shoot fireballs into my bedroom, but ... I guess I never pictured Damien lifting grates and throwing cars. Then again, I had learned a lot about Damien these last few days.

"Hey, Kalib," he grunted, "I know I make this look easy, but I'm still holding a four-thousand-pound piece of metal over my head." I blinked, realizing that both Aedyn and Macelton had already entered the building and hurried inside. Damien let the grate down, and it hit the ground with a dull, deep thud.

We were standing in a giant warehouse with rows of stacked boxes and thin pathways between them. The building was deserted. All the Gray Suits were outside defending themselves from cursed spirits, so there was no one inside.

"I'll go with Kalib to close the rift, and find the girl," Macelton began, dusting his hands and looking around. "Aedyn, you and Damien find Patrick Jones and get the book."

"Got it," Aedyn said, nudging Damien and starting down one of the narrow pathways in the warehouse. "Stay safe," he called over his shoulder before disappearing around a corner that I assumed led to the elevator.

"Now, where did they perform the ritual?" Macelton asked once they'd gone.

"We gotta go to the third floor," I answered. "That's where they have Caliyah." I scanned the warehouse. On the other side was another elevator. "Over there." I said quietly, climbing over boxes that had fallen into the narrow aisles and racing toward the metal doors.

Once inside, I punched the level three button and waited anxiously as the doors closed. I took a deep breath. The last time I had been inside an elevator, I was accosted by a group of Gray Suits.

I imagined that Caliyah would be guarded heavily. "We need a plan," Macelton whispered, as if reading my thoughts. "When we get to the third floor, you grab Caliyah. I'll take care of the rift, spirits and Gray Suits. Get in. Get her. Get out. Got it?"

"Got it." I nodded. I was determined to save Caliyah. The elevator doors dinged as they opened on the third floor, and Macelton and I rushed out, hands ready for battle. But to our surprise, the entire floor was deserted. The room was trashed, sure. Even the computers in the observation deck, where scientists and engineers safely reviewed their more lethal experiments, had been turned over and strewn across the floor. The Gray Suits must have trampled over tables and monitors in their attempt to get away from the cursed souls, but besides the flickering of broken computers on the floor and the translucent spirits that were still seeping through the crack in the rift above them, there was no other sign of life on this floor.

"This is where they did it?" Macelton scanned the room. I nodded silently as he cautiously entered, hands still extended. "Where is everybody?"

"Kalib!" a voice called weakly from the corner. It was Caliyah, still strapped in the chair. Her head hung down to her chest. I could tell that the Crotanium was beginning to wear off, but she was still pretty out of it.

"Caliyah!" I beelined toward the chair, pulling at her restraints.

"Kalib ... you're okay?" Caliyah tried to hold her head up, she was beginning to come too. "I... I... I saw you. You were tied up. What... What happened?"

"Everything's going to be okay," I said reassuringly. I looked around for something I could use to cut her free. I searched the floor and found one of the well pens the Gray Suits had used to cut my flesh. "Look, Caliyah, I know you think I'm a runaway. But that's not what happened. Your dad tried to—"

"How long has the rift been open?" Macelton interrupted.

"I ... I dunno.... Mr. Macelton?" Caliyah raised her eyebrows. "I'm confused. Why is our history teacher here?"

"Well, that's what I'm trying to tell you," I said hurriedly, cutting the last of her bonds. "Mr. Macelton saved me when your dad and my parents tried to—" As soon as she was free, Caliyah wrapped her arms around me and gave me the best hug I'd ever had in my life.

"Thank you," she said.

I instantly forgot what I was saying. "Oh, um, you're welcome." I blushed.

"I know how to close this!" Macelton said confidently, pulling my necklace from his pocket and handing it to me. "Kalib, point the stone towards the rift!"

"What?"

"Just do it," he said, grabbing a piece of paper and writing something down.

I wrapped my hand around my necklace, holding the stone in the air and pointing it at the rift. "Now say these words." He handed me the paper which now had strange words scribbled on it:

Gaeta un dlúth

"What does that mean?" I asked.

"Just do it."

I held the necklace toward the rift and read, "*Gaeta un dlúth.*"

I felt the *tug* in my stomach. The blue stone lit up, and just like that, the rift closed. The last spirit pushed his way out and disappeared through the wall.

"It's closed." I smiled, my eyes wide. "That's all it took?"

"The gate was only cracked." Macelton nodded. "But it's going to take a lot more than that, to put those spirts back where—"

Macelton suddenly stopped. He looked around the room urgently, as if expecting to see someone.

"What's wrong?" I asked.

"Something's not right," he said. "This was all too easy."

Then the operating room doors slammed shut. We snapped our heads toward the noise. "What the—" I said, rushing to the doors and tugging on them. They wouldn't budge.

"Kalib," a voice said from behind me. I swung around and noticed Patrick Jones, grinning at us, from the monitor above the observation deck. "How nice of you to come back. And to rescue my daughter no less. Very chivalrous, Kalib. You're winning points with me."

"Patrick," I sneered. I noticed a surveillance camera in the corner of the room, aimed directly at us. "Why don't you come out and face us instead of hiding behind a camera like a coward?"

"What would be the fun in that?" Patrick laughed.

"Dad?" Caliyah looked up at the surveillance camera and then back at the screen.

"Hi, darling," Patrick said. "I'm sorry you didn't get to become the goddess you were supposed to be. The mean men foiled my plans. For now."

"Why are you doing this?" She rushed to the camera, looking straight into the lens.

"Because it's what we're destined for," Patrick said, sounding more and more like a maniac. "You are destined for greatness, sweetheart."

"This isn't greatness, Daddy! This is wrong!" Caliyah shouted.

"You'll understand when you're older, baby girl. I just need you to do me a favor right now, okay, darling? Stay away from the hellcats, would you? I don't want you to get hurt."

"The what?" I said, spinning around just in time to see two hellcats pulling themselves out from separate shadows on the ground.

"What are those?" Caliyah asked, her voice quivered as she cautiously retreated from the hellcat until her back pressed against the large window of the observation deck. The two demon cats licked their paws, and examined us hungrily. Their bony spiked tails swaying back and forth behind them.

"Hellcats," I whispered, joining Caliyah against the window.

"I thought you said there was only one, last time," Macelton asked.

"There was," I answered. "Apparently, they're multiplying."

"Great!" Macelton replied, looking around desperately for a way out.

With a snarl the hellcats crouched down, preparing to lunge, but before they managed to tear us to shreds, Macelton snapped his fingers sending a... well, what I could only describe as a sonic boom, in every direction around us. The

THE LAST ANGEL WARRIOR

glass behind us shattered, and the hellcats flew back and disintegrated into the wall on the other side of the room, leaving two cat-shaped, burns behind them.

"What was that?" I shrieked excitedly.

"Energy manipulation," Macelton responded, stepping through the now shattered glass of the observation deck. "I'll teach it to you one day."

Sweet.Finally. I thought.

"The hellcats won't be gone for long," Macelton warned. It might have just been me, but he looked a little more tired than he had a few seconds earlier. "I don't know how long it will be before Patrick Jones is able to summon them again. You have to get out of here."

"What about Patrick?" I asked. "We've got to stop him."

"You and Caliyah get to safety," Macelton ordered. "And I'll take care of Patrick Jones."

Macelton ran down the hall and disappeared around the corner. I took Caliyah by the hand and started rushing toward the elevator.

"Wait. Wait. Wait." Caliyah pulled her hand from mine. She was trying to take it all in. "What is happening?"

"That's what I've been trying to tell you," I said looking back at the hall that Macelton had just run down. There wasn't a lot of time. That energy manipulation trick that Macelton had just performed, seemed to take a lot out of him. If the hellcats *did* return, Macelton wouldn't be able to take them by himself. "Basically, your dad tried to sacrifice me so that you can become one with a goddess," I blurted.

"Wait, what?"

"Also, I was never a runaway." Before I could control myself, the words just poured out of my mouth. "My parents were working with your dad, to capture and sacrifice *me*, so that *you* could be possessed by a fake Goddess. Mr. Macelton and Damien rescued me and told me that I'm the last Angel Warrior. That's why they need my blood. We ran away, but then I found out that your dad was planning to use you as Alatayi's vessel, so I came back to warn you ... And got caught. But then I got rescued by my biological father ... I think ... I'm still figuring that out. But you were still here so I convinced everyone to come back and save you. And now we're here ... Oh yeah, and Macelton's my brother."

Caliyah stared at me blankly. I hadn't intended on unloading all of that on her at one time. Nice going, Kalib. There was no way in Xothog she was going to believe, anything that I had just told her. It all sounded crazy. After a lifetime of silence Caliyah blinked, took a deep breath and said, "Okay."

"Okay?" Before I got my hopes up, I had to ask, "You believe me?"

"I don't know what to believe," she said with a laugh.

"It's crazy. I know." I put both my hands on her shoulder and peered into her beautiful chestnut colored eyes. "I'll explain everything to you after this is all done. But right now, I have to go help Macelton. I need you to get out of the building, okay? Take the elevator to the front door. And go. As far as you can. I'll find you after."

Caliyah nodded and stepped into the elevator. I was relieved that she might actually believe me this time. I watched as the metal doors closed, before turning down the hall and racing after Macelton.

I didn't know where he'd gone. But I wanted to get to him before the—I heard a hiss followed by a loud booming sound. Too late. The hellcats must have already rematerialized and found Macelton. I rounded the corner to find the two hellcats closing in on him at the end of the hall. Fangs bared, and the spiked ends of their tails pointed at him like scorpions. He shot a fire ball but it was weaker than normal. The hellcats simply pawed at the embers, baring their fangs once more and crouching down in preparation to pounce. He stumbled back against the wall.

He was weak. The trick he had performed in the operation room had definitely drained him and in his current state he was no match for a hellcat. And these hellcats were poised to attack him and drag his soul to hell. I realized that I needed to protect him but I didn't know how. Suddenly, I felt that *tug* in my stomach and a burst of white light exploded from me and rushed down the hall, momentarily vanquishing both hellcats and searing a hole in the wall behind Macelton, who quickly jumped out of the way.

"Oops," I said, once the light had faded, revealing the deep sore in the wall.

"We've really gotta teach you portion control," Macelton said, shaking his head and pulling a piece of metal from the newly remodeled wall.

"Are you okay?" I asked. "You seem—"

"I'm fine," Macelton interrupted, holding the piece of metal like a sword. "I miscalculated the force of my previous attack, and it took a lot out of me. I just need time to recuperate."

A circular shadow appeared on the floor before us, and the sound of hissing cats could be heard from the distance, as if they were running toward us.

"C'mon," he said urgently. "I'd rather not become cat food today."

We ran down the hall, toward the stairwell door, just as the hellcats emerged from the shadow on the ground. We burst through the door and began to ascend the stairs.

"Peek-a-boo. I see you." Patrick laughed from the monitor above our heads. "There's nowhere to hide. I see your every move."

True to his word, just as we had made it to the fifth-floor landing, a hellcat appeared in front of us out of nowhere. Its razor-sharp claws slashed just inches away from my face.

"This way," Macelton yelled, pulling me through the fifth-floor door. "There's a staircase on the other side."

We ran down a hall that stretched the length of the fifth floor, passing by several unmarked doors. We made it halfway, before the stairwell door on the opposite end exploded open. And the other hellcat came bounding through.

"How did it get in front of us?" I asked.

"Shadow Travel," Macelton whispered.

"What the heck is that?" I whimpered.

We were surrounded. One hellcat in front of us and one behind. And as if that wasn't enough, both hellcats burst into flames, as if to say *yeah punks, we're terrifying.*

"Aren't my little kitty cats just lovely," Patrick cooed from another monitor. "Most people use *hellhounds* to drag the souls of their victims to the prison world. They're more compliant. But personally, I prefer hellcats, they're more … vicious." The hellcats crouched low once again, their bodies engulfed in flame. Their teeth bared, ready to sink into our flesh and complete their hellish mission.

Before I could formulate a plan, however, a thick foam came shooting down the hall, covering both the hellcats and extinguishing their flames. The cats, now soaked in white froth, hissed and growled as they retreated back into the shadows.

22

He Kills At Night

I was shocked. Caliyah stood in front of us, holding a fire extinguisher, still aiming its black hose at me and Macelton.

"You're not supposed to be here!" I exclaimed.

"Why, because I'm a woman, I'm supposed to just sit around and let you save me like some damsel in distress?" She crossed her arms and scanned me up and down. "I just saved your butt. A thank you would suffice."

"No—I just meant— because you—" I stammered, looking at Macelton, who simply raised his eyebrows. I let out a defeated breath and muttered, "Thank you."

"Just shut up and follow me," she said, moving toward the large metal breaker box that hung on the wall in the stairwell. "I think I know where my dad is."

"You do?" I asked.

Caliyah nodded, opening the large box and examining the switches. Before long, Caliyah picked up the fire extinguisher and used it to smash the breaker box. Sparks and smoke billowed from the panel. The lights above our heads flickered, before all together shutting off. "Whoa, what are you doing?" I asked, shocked at Caliyah's sudden destructive impulse.

Just as the emergency lights turned on, Caliyah began ascending the stairs, beckoning us to follow. "My dad isn't in his office," she continued. "He wouldn't be so obvious. Besides I recognized the background in the video. The only place he can broadcast and watch our every move is the—"

"Seventh floor security and surveillance room," I gathered.

"He's been watching us, this whole time," Caliyah said angrily, rounding the seventh-floor landing and stealthily exiting through the stairwell door. "I can't believe he planned to have me possessed by a goddess," she whispered, but I could tell she was fuming. "I could kill him."

Caliyah stopped at a door labeled Security and Surveillance. The three of us looked at each other, gathered our nerve, and together we rushed into the room. Patrick spun around in a high-backed leather chair, a crazy smile painted on his face. "Whoopsie," he laughed. "Looks like you found me."

Before I knew it, Macelton had Patrick restrained, using the piece of metal that he had ripped from the wall earlier as a blade, and pressed it firmly against his throat.

Immediately, the two hellcats emerged from the shadows on the other side of the room, baring their teeth, ready to defend their master.

Macelton tightened his grip on the blade. "Call off your pets."

"Call them off?" he laughed. "But that would ruin all my fun."

"Do it!" Macelton, hair wild and falling over his face, drew the blade up against the skin of Patrick Jones' throat, drawing a few drops of deep red blood. "Or you die."

Patrick considered this for a moment, then called to them, "It's okay. Daddy's alright. Sleepy time." The hellcats purred before curling up in the doorway, licking their paws and melting into the shadows.

With unfaltering force, Macelton threw Patrick against the wall of monitors on the other side of the room. The monitors cracked and sparked as Patrick's body slammed against them and he fell to the ground like a rag doll.

"Now, here's what you're going to do," Macelton demanded, "You're going to hand over the talisman and the Book of Ambrosius." Macelton jabbed him with the blade. Patrick reached into his pocket and pulled out the talisman that he'd placed on my chest during the ritual. Macelton took it. "Now the book."

"It's in the desk." Patrick motioned toward the desk in the corner of the room. Macelton nodded toward me to check.

"Top right drawer," Patrick added. It was there, just as he said. I grabbed the book and stepped as far away from Patrick as I could.

"How could you daddy?" Caliyah said, fighting back tears. "What you're doing … all of this … it's just wrong."

"But darling, I did it for you," the leathery smile on Patrick's face, never faded. "You were born to be one with the goddess. You were born to usher in the new world order. It would have been an honor."

"An honor?" Caliyah asked incredulously. "To be possessed?"

"I was doing it for the greater good," Patrick reasoned.

"You don't get to decide what happens to my body," she said sternly. "No goddess will be possessing me. Not today, not ever."

"You lost, Patrick." I said, "Now that she knows the truth,

she'll never let Alatayi in. It's over."

A dark gleam crossed over Patrick's eyes. "You're right, Kalib." He said, flashing his teeth. "As long as she knows the truth, she will never let Alatayi in." Patrick snapped his fingers and Caliyah went slack, tumbling to the ground.

"Caliyah!" I ran to her, turning her over to see her face, she was unconscious. "What did you do?"

"They're so much easier to control when they don't remember," he sneered. "You boys are so predictable. Since the day you met, you've played into my plan every step of the way. The secrecy. The distrust. Breaking into houses. Everything leading up to this very moment. Except for your escape from the ritual. *That* I didn't plan on. Kudos for that."

"Who are you working for?" Macelton demanded, letting a few sparks of flame loose from his fingertips to emphasize his point.

"Who am I working for?" A mischievous look played across Patrick's face. "Why, I'm working for The Order, of course."

"You're not working for The Order." Macelton moved the blade in closer once again. "And you don't care about their cause. If you did, you wouldn't have offered them up as vessels. You've been deceiving them all along, feeding them lies about a fake goddess who will build a world for humans."

"Very perceptive, Manaan," Patrick answered. It wasn't lost on me that he'd used his real name. "Perhaps I misjudged you."

"Who are you?" Macelton jabbed Patrick with his blade again. Patrick's lips curled upward into a devious grin.

"He kills at night," he whispered.

"What is that supposed to mean?"

Patrick Jones adjusted himself, sitting up with a smug look on his face. "We've met before, you know," he said, eyes focused on the ground. "That's how I knew to come to Hainesville. I knew exactly where to find the Angel Warrior. I don't blame you for not remembering. It was a long time ago, while you were still voyaging the seas, claiming to be a Sea God. But the God of the Sea couldn't save his crew from the Harbinger of Death."

I looked to Macelton for some confirmation, but his face remained steely and emotionless.

"You were too obsessed with finding your brother," Patrick went on. "The one who had disappeared all those years ago. The one that would return on the eve of war. The prophesied one. I should thank you for tipping me off that I might save my mistress. Of course, I still devoured your crew, dragged them to the prison world, and left you with one single warning."

"He kills at night," Macelton repeated. "Ogbunabali. It's you. The Demon of the Rift."

"Right again." Patrick gave a theatrical bow. "Pleasure to finally speak openly. Now, let's get down to business. I have a job to perform, and I still have, mmm—" Patrick looked at his watch, "—an hour left to perform it. Give me the Angel Warrior, and I'll let you leave here alive, with your soul intact."

"I'll rip you to pieces if you come anywhere near my brother," Macelton snarled through gritted teeth.

"You can kill me," he said deviously, "but I'll just keep coming back. The rising is inevitable. Now that the Angel Warrior's blood has been spilled, the gates to the prison world have been weakened. Who's to say that the doors won't be opened with just a little push? You cannot stop the reaping."

"What are you talking about?" Macelton asked.

"Oh, come on, Manny—" The smile on Patrick's face was psychotic. "Mannan. You've tried to prevent this, but no matter what you did, I always won. You searched for centuries, looking for your brother. I found him first. You thought that keeping him close to you would protect him from the prophecy, but I still won his trust and turned him against you. You thought that you could keep the sacred items away from me, but I manipulated the Angel Warrior to retrieve them for me."

A pit formed in my stomach. Patrick had been using me all along. I had gone to him for advice about Macelton. He goaded me into breaking into Macelton's house. He *knew* I would find the book. I played right into his hands.

"And despite all the obstacles, I was still able to get Kalib here to perform the ritual." Patrick chuckled. "The inevitability of it all is exhilarating. My masters will rise, and all of Pangaea will bow to them."

"You're working for the Big Three?" Macelton said. "What do they want with Kalib?"

"That's a stupid question, Manny. What do we all want with, Kalib? The blood of the Angel Warrior to loosen the bonds of our saviors."

"Saviors?" Macelton repeated. "You think they want to save you? The Big Three were tyrants. They sought to destroy Pangaea."

"They sought to unite Pangaea. A new Pangaea." The side of Patrick's mouth twitched. "But Michael didn't want that. Michael wanted to separate the realms so that he could rule them all himself."

"You speak as if you were there."

"I was there," Patrick said, suddenly deadly serious. "I served as an advisor to Beelzebub. I led her troops. I served her gloriously until she and her brothers were wrongly imprisoned."

She? I thought. *Beelzebub is a woman?*

"Is that who Alatayi really is?" Macelton pressed, "The third of the Big Three—Beelzebub?"

"Those *Mudwellers* would have never agreed to the resurrection if they knew she was Beelzebub," Patrick sneered. "I needed a Goddess of Justice."

"But she isn't a Goddess of Justice, is she?" Macelton questioned.

"She *will* bring justice," Patrick countered. "When she rises again, she'll bring judgment on all who oppose the Xothogian Order."

"And that's what you want?" Macelton asked, though it seemed pretty obvious to me. "For Pangaea to be remade in the image of Xothog?" Macelton gestured toward the Book of Ambrosius with his eyes. He was stalling. He wanted me to do something with the book, while he held Patrick Jones' attention.

"Xothog is the only world worth living in."

I quietly flipped through the yellowed pages. I didn't even know what language it was written in. How was I supposed to find what Macelton needed?

"Who sent the *Harbinger* after Kalib?"

Harbinger. He put emphasis on the word. He wanted me to find a spell for a Harbinger. I turned through the pages quickly, looking for anything that might mean Harbinger, but I didn't know what I was looking at. What language was this? Latin? Greek?

"Manaan, you already know the truth," Patrick said coldly. "I *am* the Harbinger of Death."

A phrase appeared at the top of a particular page: *Seek, and you will find. Find, and you will seek,* written in English. It was the same sentence I'd seen in the vision at Macelton's house.

Sudden understanding dawned on me. I stopped looking for a spell and placed my finger at the center of the page. The words *tuar báis* lit up. *The only way to find what I seek is to stop seeking.* With a cackle, Patrick dissolved into smoke, and in a flash, he was in front of me, his hands reaching toward my throat. I shouted the words, *tuar báis,* and a beam of light burst from the book, sending Patrick flying back into the monitors.

When he stood, he was no longer the well-dressed business-man he'd been just a second earlier. Instead, a familiar cloaked shadow figure with red eyes and yellow teeth stood out in contrast to his gray skin. The unforgettable smell of rotten eggs and burned hamburger meat filled the room. It was the shadow that had attacked me on the street a week earlier.

"Clever use of the spellbook, Kalib," the Harbinger laughed, "Too bad it won't do you any good." Before I knew it, the Harbinger was inches away from me, and his talon-like fingers swiped at my hands, sending the book flying toward the wall. Another brilliant flash of light emitted from behind me, and the Harbinger was sent back across the room.

Macelton ran to my side, his hands at the ready, "Light," he whispered, "Harbingers are creatures of the shadows. They don't like light."

If only I knew how to produce light. But there was no *tug* and I didn't know how to summon it. I'd only had one short lesson with Macelton and the little that I'd achieved, I had done by accident. I made a run for the book. Instantly, the Harbinger flickered in front of me driving me back toward Macelton. He swirled around, shooting another blast of light at the Harbinger, but the cloaked figure was too fast. He dissolved into smoke, then reanimated on the other side of the room.

"Your brother won't be able to protect you forever, Kalib," the Harbinger said, blinking from space to space around the room. Macelton and I turned in tandem. "You're going to have to fight me, eventually." The Harbinger appeared in the corner right in front of Macelton who shot an energy beam. But just as quickly as he had appeared the Harbinger evaporated, and the beam exploded into the wall behind him. We looked around the room but the Harbinger was gone.

"Do you think your brother and a spellbook are enough to keep me from draining the rest of your blood?" His disembodied voice echoed through the room.

No. I didn't. I knew that I would have to join the fight, in order to stop him. But nothing was working.

"You still haven't seen the full extent of my abilities," the voice taunted. A shriveled hand grasped my ankle and pulled me down through my own shadow. I landed on the floor with a thud. I looked around and realized, I had landed on the same floor I had just fallen through.

How did he do that?

With a series of flashes, the Harbinger traversed the room, managing quick jabs at Macelton through his shadow portals. Macelton swung around, anticipating his next flash, and shot an energy beam at the Harbinger. Patrick fell to his knees, back in human form.

"Give it up, Patrick," Macelton said. "I'll never let you have Kalib. It's over."

A defiant smile crossed Mr. Jones' face, "That's where you're wrong." His voice boomed deeper than before. "It's only just begun."

The room grew darker. And all the shadows in the room were pulled to one place— towards Patrick Jones. And now, Patrick's own shadow seemed to grow, stretching up the wall and peering down at Macelton and me. Then I realized, Patrick was no longer standing in front of the shadow. He had *become* the shadow. His giant shadow hand opened and stretched toward me from the wall. But before it reached me, Macelton pushed me out of the way, and the shadow hand torpedoed through the wall behind us, as if it were solid. *He's controlling the density of his shadow,* I thought. *How is that even possible?*

Macelton swung around and willed another blast of white energy at the giant shadow. But Patrick was no longer there.

"Oh, that's cute Manaan. You think you can actually keep me away from Kalib." The phantom voice disoriented me; my eyes bounced around the room. I knew his attack was eminent, but I didn't know from where it would come. "Well that's over."

The shadow beneath me suddenly became solid, and rapidly sprung upward under my feet like a mountain, and I held onto its peak. The shadow mountain crashed through the ceiling above me, and then continued to smash through the ceilings of every floor above that.

Do you have any idea how it feels to be smashed through *eight floors* of concrete? I'll give you a hint. Not good!

The shadow mountain stopped once I'd made it through the roof of the RavenTech building. I gasped for air, half expecting to cough up blood, judging by the amount of pain I was in. Patrick shot into the air, and before I knew it, he was flying right in front of me. His long ethereal cloaks billowed into smoky wings.

"Give up now, Kalib," Patrick said, landing on the solidified shadow mountain. His wings melted back into his misty cloak. "It's already been written. You will complete the ritual and Beelzebub will rise again."

"I'll never help you raise her!" I shouted.

"Of course, you will. It just a question of *motivation*." Patrick snapped his fingers and I heard a commotion from below. I looked down through the giant hole in the roof just in time to see that Patrick had awakened his hellcats.

"Macelton!" I shouted, just as the hellcats pounced on him. I had to get to him. I needed to help. But before I could act, Patrick grabbed me by the throat and launched us both into the sky, his long nails dug into my neck as we ascended.

"It didn't have to be this way, Kalib. You could have come willingly, and no one else would have gotten hurt. But now everyone you love is in danger. Look around." He jerked my body around, forcing me to look at the ground below. Aedyn and Damien were rushing from the RavenTech building, a large group following behind them. It was the prisoners. Aedyn and Damien must have stumbled upon the prison beneath RavenTech while they were looking for the book. For a moment, I was relieved that the prisoners were escaping. But as soon as Aedyn, Damien, and the prisoners made it into the open they were swarmed by an army of possessed Gray Suits who picked off several of the prisoners, overpowered them, and offered them to be possessed by the Cursed Ones.

"All their efforts are in vain," Patrick sneered, as my friends struggled to fight the translucent spirits. "In just a few moments, the Spirits of the Cursed will take control of the city, ushering in the Xothogian Order. Everyone you love will be forced into servitude for Beelzebub. And it's all because of you."

As I watched, possessed prisoners joined possessed civilians, terrorizing all who opposed them. Aedyn manipulated energy with his hands, futilely attempting to ward off cursed spirits as they came near. Damien slashed his fire-engulfed sword back and forth, but was unable to impede the crowd of demon possessed prisoners closing in on him. Macelton, still engaged in an intense brawl with the hellcats, narrowly escaped a strike from the tail of one beast, while the other was poised to attack. This was the end. We were going to lose.

The truth of Patrick's words hit me. The truth that I had been avoiding my entire life. It *was* all my fault. None of this would be happening if it wasn't for me.If it wasn't for who I am. The city wouldn't be in danger. My friends wouldn't be on the verge of death. Caliyah would never have been offered to Beelzebub. My adopted parents wouldn't have hated me. My real parents wouldn't have been killed. Everything bad that has happened in my life was because of who I am. The pain of that realization shook me. And for the first time, I not only felt hopeless but truly and undeniably alone.

I looked helplessly at the battle beneath me. And to my amazement I saw Triston. He must have seen the chaos at RavenTech from the city and came to help. He wasn't hiding. He wasn't afraid. He stood in the midst of the battle, staring at me. Our eyes met.

He nodded as if to say, *you can do this.* Even though Triston didn't have any powers of his own, he was risking his life because he believed in me. Ever since we were toddlers Triston had seen something in me that I couldn't see. He *believed* in me. And then suddenly I was hit with a new set of realizations; my parents risked their lives because *they* believed in who I am, Donald and Susan were afraid of me, Caliyah trusted me, my friends were fighting with me, and my brother spent his entire life searching for me, because *they* believed in who I am. Was this the balance Macelton was talking about in the woods? The yin to my yang? Suddenly the pain that had been holding me back all these years transformed into the fuel that gave me purpose.

I put my hand to my chest and I could feel the energy flowing through my body. I could hear it all around me. It was the *tug.* Every time I'd tried to use my power before, it always ended with disastrous results. The shockwave. The fire ring. Even the small things that I had tried had either backfired or nearly hurt someone. But this time was different. A warm tingling ran through my veins, igniting every molecule inside of me. Just like before, I could feel the energy building up inside of me. Pure power, radiating on my skin, waiting to be controlled. *I can never fully embrace my power, until I first embrace my pain.* Suddenly, I felt the release. An explosion of energy erupted from me and rushed out in every direction. Surging over the RavenTech grounds and incasing the entire building in a dome of magnificent white light.

Trapped inside my dome of light, Patrick Jones and his minions of darkness, shrieked. The Spirits of the Cursed Ones abandoned their host bodies in search of a shadow in which they could hide. The two hellcats exploded into smoke. And Patrick, trapped in my dome, had no shadows to manipulate. For the first time, I could feel the balance of my power. I knew if I leaned too far into any one emotion, I would lose control of the energy. In order to harness it, I had to keep a level head. I clenched my fist and called the light back toward me, careful not to extinguish its power.

"You're right Patrick," I said triumphantly. "It is because of me. I'm the Angel Warrior."

With both fists, I focused the light energy at Patrick, hitting him with every ounce of light I had just recalled. Soon, another blast of white energy connected with Patrick. It was Aedyn. And then another. Damien. Before long, all of the prisoners joined in, and finally, a bright red beam connected with Patrick. Macelton. Together we held Patrick Jones in place as he juddered, attempting to break free from the blasts.

"You fools!" he screamed. "You cannot stop Beelzebub. Her prison has already been weakened. She will reign supreme."

"Kalib!" Macelton shouted. Sweat beaded on his brow. He had lifted into the air, still holding Patrick in his blast. "Use the book." He tossed me the spellbook. He must have grabbed it once the hellcats had been defeated. "You have the power to send these spirits back to Xothog."

It made sense. The Angel Warriors had created the prison. Only an Angel Warrior could send the spirits back. I opened the spellbook and turned to the first page. "Seek, and you will find. Find, and you will seek," I muttered. A spell appeared on the page in front of me, this time in English. I read it out loud:

By the binding of blood and magick
Conquer life by the purest of race
Send the plague of the underworld to its doom
Death will be powerless by blood's pure moon

The stone in my necklace began to glow. It floated in the air in front of me. The symbols carved on the blue stone lit up, and a beam of white light extended from the stone, wrapping itself around Patrick.

"What's this?" Patrick shrieked. "What are you doing?"

"The stone!" I shouted to the others. "Point your beams at the stone!"

My friends, along with the freed prisoners, shifted their beams of power to my necklace. Another passage appeared on the page below the first, and I shouted the words as they appeared:

> Break the stone and lock the key
> Close the door and trapped they'll be
> To be free just pay the toll
> For only he can free their souls

The large yellow rift re-appeared in the air in front of me. And like an infected sore, it tore open. The Spirits of the Cursed Ones squealed as they were sucked back inside. Patrick's skin began to crack and crumble like half solidified lava.

"No!" he shouted his body began disintegrating and flying into the rift. "I can't go to the prison world!" Several spirits hung on to Patrick, pulling him toward the rift with them. "The Cursed Ones. They'll torture me." Patrick resisted the clawing of the spirits, as he fought to stay in the physical world. "Xothog will rise again," he said, suddenly giving a devious grin. "See you next lifetime, Angel Warrior." A surge of energy emanated from the stone and Patrick Jones exploded, closing the rift and bringing the entire building down with me on top of it.

23

Good News, Bad News

Everything was black. I was falling. No, I was floating. A deep laugh echoed around me. "It isn't over, Kalib," a voice said. "Our destinies are intertwined. You can't stop the rising."

"Kalib!"

Macelton's voice was far away. "Kalib, wake up!" He shook me, and I realized I was lying atop the rubble of the fallen building. I blinked. Bleary-eyed, Macelton's face was the first thing to come into focus. I coughed. "I'm awake," I managed to say, trying to find my bearings. "I'm alright."

"Are you sure? Macelton asked, examining my body for wounds. "Are you hurt?"

"Happy to know you care," I said with a weak laugh.

"You just surfed a fifteen-story building as it crumbled to the ground, so as your older brother, I'm allowed to be concerned," Macelton replied. "You *are* alright, though?"

"Yeah, I'm fine." I nodded. "But I'd be better if you'd let me sit up."

"Oh." Macelton hadn't realized he was holding me down.

He jumped to his feet, allowing me to sit up.

"Are *you* okay?" I asked, referencing the large gash across Maceltons torso. "It looks like those hellcats did a number on you."

"I'm fine," he insisted, "Just a few cuts and bruises."

I looked around the rubble. There were no cursed souls in sight. There were, however, dozens of confused civilians speckled throughout the crowd, wondering how they had gotten to the now-demolished RavenTech building. Richard Marsden, my former manager from the diner, ran from person to person, demanding an explanation. Sarah Withers, extended her prosthetic arm, to escort a confused Mr. and Mrs. Abernathy back to their homes. She was completely unaware that her parents were Gray Suits who had fled the scene.

"What about Patrick?" I asked. "What will happen to him?"

"Well, I think he was sent to the prison world with Beelzebub and the souls that he dragged there," Macelton answered. "I don't think he'll be bothering us for a while."

"You are the most awesomest guy I have ever met!" someone shouted. "That monster was like *'roar,'* and then Kalib was like *'Agh,'* and then the whole building went BOOM!" It was Triston, frantically rushing over to me with Damien at his side. "Hey, everybody, that's my best friend! I'm with the hero!"

"I'm no hero, Triston." The sudden realization hit me like a freight train. What little pride I felt about defeating Patrick Jones and winning the battle, turned to shame and guilt. Caliyah. She was inside of the building when it fell.

"Oh no!!!" I said, urgently turning over large chunks of cement to find my friend.

"What happened?" Triston asked with a confused look on

his face. "Woah. Kalib? What are you doing?"

Triston grabbed my shoulder and forced me to look at him. "Caliyah. She was in the building when it fell. Patrick somehow put her to sleep and that was the last time I—"

"Do you mean *that* Caliyah?" Triston stretched a finger toward someone on the other side of the rubble. It *was* Caliyah. Covered from head to toe in dust.

How is she alive? I thought.

Caliyah was on the seventh floor when the building collapsed. There was no way she could have survived. I quickly shook the thought out of my head. I was relieved to see her. But my relief was short lived.

"Has anyone seen my dad?" she cried pushing over large slabs of concrete. "He's the CEO of this company. He was in the building when the bomb went off."

Bomb? What was she talking about? "Caliyah," I said, placing my hand on her shoulder. "What's going on? Are you—"

"Kalib! Thank God you made it out," She interrupted. "Do you know what happened? Did a bomb go off or something?"

"You don't remember?"

"Remember what? Do you know who did this?"

I searched her face. Was she serious? "Your dad," I said. She had to be joking. "You know this was all your dad. He was—and then I had to…"

"My dad?" She disputed, "Kalib, that doesn't make any sense. My dad would never—"

"Caliyah, you were there," I insisted, "Your dad tried to kill me, and then possess you. Remember? He sent the hellcats."

"Hellcats? Kill you? Kalib you're talking crazy." Caliyah reached out to console me, offering a sympathetic frown. But her frown was quickly replaced by a look of fear. She stepped back. Her memory was returning. "You're talking crazy ... just like you were when you locked me in that closet earlier. You said my dad was the problem, and he needed to be stopped." She cupped her hand over her mouth, "Oh my God. Kalib, did you do this?"

Was that all she remembered? What about the ritual? What about the hellcats? Then I recalled what Patrick said after he'd snapped his fingers and put her to sleep. He said, *they're so much easier to control when they don't remember.* Patrick had erased her memory. The last thing she remembered was thinking that I was crazy. That was before the ritual. Before I rescued her. Before she'd found out about her dad. "Caliyah," I said cautiously, stepping toward her. "I didn't do what you think I did."

"Then what exactly did you do?"

What could I say? I was paralyzed.

"I don't know how to answer that," I admitted.

"Then answer this," she demanded. "Did you hurt my dad?"

I paused. I couldn't tell her the truth. I took her hand, but words failed me. I opened and closed my mouth. Nothing came out.

Caliyah snatched her hand away. "Get away from me, Kalib," she said. Tears welled in her eyes. "I never want to see you again." She pushed past me, rushing into the crowd.

I started to follow, but a hand grabbed my shoulder. It was Macelton, "Don't," he said, "Trust me, it will only make things worse. If her father *has* been controlling her memories, it will take a lot of time and a skilled empath to unravel the lies."

I watched as Caliyah pushed her way through the crowd and disappeared into the distance. In one night, I had been kidnapped, fought a demon, claimed my birthright as an Angel

Warrior, and lost the only girl I'd ever loved. Or ... at least could have loved one day, if given the chance. Happy Birthday to me, I guess.

* * *

It wasn't long before the fire department, news reporters, and of course, Triston's dad, Sheriff McLain, arrived on the scene. Like Caliyah, people reported a hostage situation at RavenTech. To my relief, no one accused me of being the bomber. I did, however, detect a hint of suspicion remaining from Triston's dad and the other police officers concerning the explosion in the chemistry lab. I may have been counted among the survivors at the RavenTech explosion, but as far as the police were concerned, I was still a person of interest at the school.

That night, we all went back to Macelton's house. Except Triston, who was instructed by his father to go straight home. I'm sure he had a lot of explaining to do concerning his unexplained absence the night before. I didn't really have a home to go back to. When your parents have tried to kill you—twice—the house you grew up in stops feeling like home. Macelton extended the offer for Damien and me to stay at his place. For some reason Damien declined. He made up a story about, needing to be back at the group home, but I had a feeling that wasn't the real reason.

Macelton made up the guestroom for me. I guess he was still saving Damien's room in the hope that he'd come back to stay someday. I couldn't even think about sleeping. I snuck out of the house and slipped away to one of my favorite places in town: the pier on the Ogeechee River. I sat on the dock, thinking about the events of the night, while my feet hung into the water. I wondered how many times Patrick had erased Caliyah's memory in the past. I wondered if she'd ever remember the truth. If she'd ever trust me again. I also wondered what happened to Sterling. I didn't see him among the freed prisoners. The last time I saw him, he was running toward the Gray Suits to protect *me*. What happened after that? Had he escaped? Or was he still in the building when it fell? Guilt racked my body. I thought about the promise I had made to him. That I'd make sure he saw his family again. If something *did* happened to him, it was my fault.

Eventually, the sun slowly peaked over the horizon. "Mind if I sit here?" Aedyn kneeled beside me.

I shrugged. "I don't mind."

Aedyn dipped his feet into the water next to mine, and I stared at our reflection in the river. We looked alike. Apart from his eyes, which were chestnut brown, his curly hair and mocha skin resembled my own. I was surprised by the welling of emotion, building inside of me, I hadn't realized it before, but seeing someone who looked like me was … important.

"I have something for you," he said, holding out his hand. Dangling from his grip was my necklace. I thought I had lost it in the explosion. "It's a little beat up, but I managed to grab it from the rubble."

"I thought this thing was done for," I admitted. I ran my finger over the blue stone and the engraved hieroglyphs, then I noticed a crack down the center of the stone.

"The spell drained the stone of its power," Aedyn explained. "The explosion on the rooftop was basically the last of its magic."

"So, it's just a normal necklace now?"

"I'm sure there's still a little more magic inside." Aedyn winked. After a moment of silence, Aedyn took a deep breath and placed his hands on his knees. "I guess we have a lot to talk about."

I raised an eyebrow. That was the understatement of the century. For years I'd wondered what happened to him, and now he was sitting beside me like he'd never left at all.

"I'm not your father, Kalib," Aedyn said quietly.

Of course, I knew that Aedyn wasn't my real father. Macelton had already told me the story about my birth parents sending me forward in time to hide me from the demons. But it still stung. Seeing him after years of wondering why he disappeared allowed my childhood fantasies to come flooding back.

"Who are you then?" I asked quietly.

Aedyn leaned back and rubbed his hands on his thighs. His eyes were round and familiar; it was difficult for me to believe that he could be anything other than my father. "I am a man who has only ever wanted the best for you."

"That doesn't make sense," I said. I couldn't imagine life would have been any worse with him than with the Donovan's. "If you wanted the best for me, then why did you leave? I was only a baby, and you abandoned me at some orphanage."

Aedyn opened his mouth and then closed it, searching for the right words, but the *right* words never came. He dropped his head so that he was eye level with me. "Kalib, I know that it might be difficult to believe, but I left because it *was* what was best for you." He looked over his shoulder, though I'm not sure for what. "I know it may not seem like it, but everything that has happened, up to and including this very moment, needed to happen."

Aedyn spoke in hushed tones as if telling a secret. "I don't understand—" I began.

"You will, " Aedyn said quickly. "Very soon. You will understand exactly what I'm talking about." He kicked his feet back and forth, creating little dimples in the water. "Your friends and family have all based their lives on the assumption that you are the prophesied one, the last Angel Warrior, the Savior of Worlds, the Finisher of Wars."

"Well, aren't I?" I asked.

"Technically," Aedyn answered, "you are capable of becoming all of those things, but I know that *that* is not what you become."

"I don't understand." I tilted my head.

Aedyn looked down at the water, choosing each word delicately. "Kalib, you don't save the world." He lifted his gaze and stared directly into my eyes. "You end it."

24

We Need An Epilogue!

Triston stood on what was left of the RavenTech building. How did he get there? He looked around. He had just washed up and gone to bed. Now he was standing on the rubble of what used to be RavenTech? He heard footsteps and quickly hid behind a concrete slab.

A man walked into the center of the rubble, looking around as if waiting for someone. Triston recognized him. Mayor Donovan? The news had said he was dead. The mayor nervously waited, fiddling with something in his hand.

Before long, Triston heard footsteps coming from the opposite direction. It sounded like there were a lot of people. An army of werewolves emerged from the trees. The soldiers wore armor resembling that of medieval knights. Donovan walked across the clearing to greet them as a tall blonde-haired woman emerged from the sea of soldiers and approached. Donovan knelt and bowed reverently.

Triston recognized her too. He'd seen her once before. This was Vivienne, the woman who had come to his house looking for him. Why would the thought-to-be-dead mayor be meeting with Vivienne?

"Did you bring the item?" Vivienne asked.

Donovan stood, presenting an object. "The halfling ring, from the pockets of the Angel Warrior."

"Well done, Donald." Vivienne stroked Donald's cheek. "You will be rewarded greatly."

"It is an honor to serve you, mistress," Donald said. "But mistress, will the ritual work now that the Angel Warrior's birthday has passed? Didn't Ogbunabali fail?"

"Ogbunabali is a fool," Vivienne sneered, walking toward the center of the rubble. "What he failed to realize is there is always another way. Ogbunabali tried to raise a Xothogian army. That would have taken hours. All I need is one from the prison world."

Vivienne held something up in the air. Triston strained is eyes to make it out. It was a cloth. "I have here the blood-stained bandages the Angel Warrior used to stop his golden blood from spilling to the ground." She laid the cloth down on the rubble and then held up the ring. "One fragment of the Enochian stone to unlock the gate."

Vivienne placed the ring on top of the cloth, then held up a piece of paper. "And the spell, ripped from the Book of Ambrosius, to unlatch the bonds of the forsaken."

"Béalzabúl, Le litir, agus samhla, agus an leaghan gun cháradh
Fosgail slabhraidhean aice thoir air aice. "

As she spoke, the dried blood on the cloth returned to liquid form, and rolled off the cloth into the ground. Suddenly, the blood began to glow. Triston couldn't believe his eyes. The blood was gold. A rift opened on the ground and stretched a mile into the air. Triston held his breath, but nothing came out of the rift. "Bring me the vessel," Vivienne ordered. A scream came from the crowd, and two soldiers emerged with a young black-haired woman who couldn't have been older than twenty. Triston recognized these wolves. Friedrich and Dieter. The two wolves who had chased him in the woods. The young woman's hands were bound. She begged and pleaded as the werewolves dragged her to Vivienne.

"Loosen her bonds," Vivienne ordered. Dieter extended a sharp claw and sliced through her bonds.

"Le litir, agus samhla, agus an leaghan gun cháradh."

With those words, Vivienne pushed the woman into the rift. The woman screamed as she fell, and the army cheered. The rift began to glow golden like Kalib's blood. With a flash, the rift was gone. The woman who fell stood in its place. She was no longer a scared civilian begging for her life. She was different. Confident, regal, and somehow more beautiful.

"Welcome home, Beelzebub," Vivienne said.

The woman smiled. She looked around, gazing at each soldier, but said nothing. She took a deep breath, her first in two thousand years. She looked toward the slab of concrete where Triston was hiding.

"There is a spy in our midst," she replied, her voice was elegant but cold. Triston's heart pounded. Was she talking about him? "Ooh, he is a powerful one. He will be a useful ally." Triston blinked, and the woman was standing beside him.

"Ahhh!" Triston jerked up in bed, drenched in sweat. His heart pounded as he struggled to catch his breath. *What was that?*

He dragged his fingers through his red hair and swung his feet out from under the covers. His toes stung as his feet touched the cold floor, but he pushed himself out of bed and stumbled toward the bathroom.

"It was just a dream," he said, looking at himself in the mirror. He turned the faucet on and bent down to splash water onto his face.

What would Beelzebub want with me anyway? he thought, returning his gaze to the mirror. But it was no longer his reflection that stared back at him.

"Hello, Triston," the figure in the mirror said. "We've got a lot to discuss."

Triston screamed, stumbling back. It was the same woman he'd seen in his dream: Beelzebub.

"Oh, now, Triston, don't be jumpy," she said. "That's no way to greet your family."

About the Author

John W. Wells III was kicked out of the third grade because he had an overactive imagination. Okay maybe not kicked out— but he was sent home for telling other students, that he had super powers. So what better profession could he have chosen other than story telling? John prides himself for being an actor, playwright, and author of the debut novel The Last Angel Warrior. To learn more about John and his books visit www.johnwellsiii.com or www.thekalibandrewschronicles.com

You can connect with me on:

- https://www.thekalibandrewschronicles.com
- https://twitter.com/jwaymanwells
- https://www.facebook.com/TheKalibAndrewsChronicles
- https://www.instagram.com/j.waymanwells
- https://www.johnwellsiii.com

Subscribe to my newsletter:

- https://www.johnwellsiii.com

Made in the USA
Columbia, SC
16 October 2020

22986965R00159